(Manual type barcode

 **Support**

CW01267294

H005211720

Schools Library Service

A *Young Person's* GUIDE TO THE GOTHIC

A *Young Person's*
GUIDE TO THE GOTHIC

RICHARD BAYNE

ILLUSTRATED BY
RICHARD SALA

IndieBooks

HAMPSHIRE SCHOOLS LIBRARY SERVICE	
H005211720	
Askews & Holts	09-Feb-2016
133.4	£16.00

A Young Person's Guide to the Gothic

By Richard Bayne
Illustrated by Richard Sala

ISBN: 978-1-908041-06-7

Published by IndieBooks Ltd
4 Staple Inn, London, WC1V 7QH

www.indiebooks.co.uk

This edition © IndieBooks 2014

The Red Room, The Cone and the extract from The Island of Doctor Moreau are reproduced with the kind permission of A P Watt at United Agents on behalf of The Literary Executors of the Estate of H G Wells.

The extract from The Wendigo is reproduced by kind permission of A P Watt at United Agents on behalf of Susan Reeves-Jones.

Set in Myriad Pro and Century Schoolbook

Printed by TJ International, Padstow, Cornwall

HOW THIS BOOK WORKS

You'll see that this book is divided into five sections – scary **Settings**, spooky **Scenery**, devilish **Plot Devices**, creepy **Characters** and monstrous **Antagonists**. These are the main elements that combine to make the best Gothic stories and for each one there are examples in short chapters: in Settings you have the **Castle**, the **Abbey**, some **Ruins**, the **Haunted House** and the **Forest**. All of these have a brief introduction, explaining a bit about why they've been chosen. I've named some modern books, authors and films that use each one (you'll know plenty more) and then you'll find a short extract or two from the "classic" Gothic books and stories. Every now and then there is a complete short story, or longer extract from a story.

To help you explore the cobwebby passageways of the book, the first time one of the main sections or example chapters is mentioned on a page, it is highlighted in **bold**. So if you are reading about the **Abbey** and wonder what the **Inquisition** was all about, then you'll know it has its own chapter and you can go there to find out more. It's like links on a website, except you have to actually turn the pages instead of tapping your finger.

Where only an extract from a "short" story appears, it's mainly because the particular story is actually quite long, and I wanted to make room for more of the best bits. I have to confess that occasionally I've done it to make them easier to read. With writing styles changing over the years, and the way we enjoy reading changing too, some of the earlier authors really do seem to use a lot of words. There are tales by American author Edgar Allan Poe – many people would say the most famous writer of Gothic "short" stories – that I still haven't finished reading: they are rather long for my taste. But if you're grabbed by any of those extracts and shortened stories (and I'm sure you will be), then you'll find the complete texts on our website:

www.indiebooks.co.uk/gothic.

CONTENTS

THE INTRODUCTION	9
ONE: SETTINGS	21
Including CASTLES, ABBEYS, RUINS, HAUNTED HOUSES and FORESTS	
TWO: SCENERY	57
Where we explore TOWERS, DUNGEONS, HAUNTED ROOMS, GRAVEYARDS, MARSHES and the WEATHER	
THREE: PLOT DEVICES	103
In which we meet CURSES & PROPHECY, the SCEPTIC, IMPRISONMENT, ANIMATED ART and LIGHTS GOING OUT	
FOUR: CHARACTERS	147
Introducing the HERO and HEROINE, the VILLAINESS and VILLAIN, and that Gothic curiosity the ANTIHERO	
FIVE: ANTAGONISTS	205
Who are MOSTLY MONSTERS and include VAMPIRES, CONSTRUCTS, MUMMIES, WEREWOLVES and also THE INQUISITION	
AFTERWORD	255

THE COMPLETE STORIES

THE OUTSIDER	25
THE ROOM OF THE EVIL THOUGHT	69
THERE WAS A MAN DWELT BY A CHURCHYARD	78
THE VOICE IN THE NIGHT	88
THE CASK OF AMONTILLADO	117
THE RED ROOM	136
THE YELLOW WALLPAPER	160
THE CONE	191
THE DANCING PARTNER	220
THE GRAY WOLF	237
TORTURE BY HOPE	249

THE INTRODUCTION

Not many people, when looking for a good read, start with the introduction. You've probably already dipped into this book, choosing the chapters and stories with the best titles, or maybe, like me with story collections, you just picked the shortest first. If you really are starting at the beginning, good for you, but do feel free to break off at any point to visit a **Haunted Room** or confront a **Werewolf**. And if you do chose to read your way through the book in sequence, but later find a particular chapter or story is boring, skipping on to the next one is entirely acceptable: we can't all like the same stories equally.

So, if you have tried out a tale or two, you will have a pretty good idea of what the book is all about, but the rest of this introduction gives the stories some background.

What I have done is pick out a few of the best (perhaps that should be "my favourite") stories and bits of books from the earlier years of a tradition known as the Gothic. It's a tradition that is still alive (undead) and kicking vigorously today: just try counting the recent books, films and TV series starring vampires, werewolves, zombies and the supernatural.

So what is the Gothic? Critics have written fat books all about it, but often fall back on making lists. The basic list says the Gothic is a style of fiction focused on gloom, mystery and the grotesque. (My dictionary defines "grotesque" as "strangely or fantastically distorted; bizarre", deriving from the Italian word for cave. Use your own dictionary if you want to check "bizarre".) Then there are longer lists, of things we expect to find in a piece of Gothic writing or film-making. The chapter titles and sub-headings of this book make up my list, or at least part of it: I only had room for a certain number of stories. One of the things I hope this collection will do is encourage you to go looking for books and stories by other writers, or more stories by the same writers, which could help you build an even longer version of your own list.

And if you think falling back on lists is a cop-out, here is what I think: a good Gothic work, whether book, film or other piece of art - will absolutely literally send a shiver down your spine.

Scary

We enjoy being scared. Some people get their kicks from jumping off things with bungee rope tied round their legs, others by watching horror films from behind the sofa. These experiences are exciting, they make us feel alive, and so we go looking for safe ways to enjoy being scared. One way is to read a book, or a short story, where terrifying events are described. These events affect characters we sympathise with. We imagine the horrors, and enjoy the shiver or shudder that is like an echo of what the real experience would be like. Deep down, though, we know we are sitting safe in our favourite chair.

The first person to write a book specifically designed to press his readers' horror buttons was Horace Walpole. *The Castle of Otranto* was published in 1764 and set the pattern for a whole bunch of imitators. Most of the things on our list crop up in his Gothic masterpiece. Helpfully, Walpole himself told us that his book "…was an attempt to blend the two kinds of romance, the ancient and the modern. In the former, all was imagination and improbability: in the latter, nature is always intended to be, and sometimes has been, copied with success." He wanted, he was saying, to combine "ancient" stories and their myths and magic with a "modern" (for him!) style of story-telling that was real and true to life. He wanted his characters to "…think, speak, and act, as it might be supposed mere men and women would do in extraordinary positions…". He wanted to scare and entertain us, by describing weird and creepy events as realistically as possible.

And this is exactly what the Gothic is still doing today. Whether it's Harry Potter at Hogwarts, Lyra in *His Dark Materials* or Bella in *Twilight*, these books and stories try to explore how people with the same sorts of thoughts, feelings and emotions as you and me would react to the extraordinary or supernatural.

So why did he do it?

The idea of the novel as we understand it – a long story told in prose, rather than in poetry or at the theatre – was still relatively new, as was the word itself (which actually means "new", if you think about it). There had been a move away from what Walpole called the "ancient" kind of "romance" – which for readers of his time meant grand and historic tales of a hero's adventures, along the lines of King Arthur and his Knights. The fashion instead was for what he was calling "modern" story-telling, where the focus was on realism. *Robinson Crusoe* (1719) and *Moll Flanders* (1721), both by Daniel Dafoe, are the sort of books he meant, stories about characters living in the "real" world of his present or recent past.

This change in how people were writing books took place alongside a change in the way people were thinking in general. There was a move away from what were seen as the superstitions of the past, towards a world-view based on analytical thinking and science. This movement, which has become known as the Enlightenment, is linked with the discoveries of scientists like Isaac Newton and the ideas of philosophers like John Locke and Voltaire. The technical progress that followed played a big part in the Industrial Revolution, which most historians reckon began around 1750, when machines and factories began to take over from people making and doing things by hand.

So the Enlightenment – with its realistic novels – dominated thinking for most of the 18th Century. But there were still people who didn't want everything to be explained away, who began to feel the emphasis on realism had gone too far. They worried that if everything were limited to pure science and reason, people would miss out on spiritual and emotional happiness. They wanted to get away from the growing towns and the machines, to stay in touch with the wonder of the unexplained and the marvels of nature's extremes. They became known as the "Romantics".

Meet the Romantics

The Romantics were especially interested in feeling strong emotions, which they believed could come from an aesthetic experience – from appreciating art and beauty. The names we most associate with Romanticism are poets like Wordsworth, Coleridge, Keats and Shelley, but the movement influenced all art and literature, and novelists like Walter Scott and later the Brontë sisters very much played their part. The Gothic really took off alongside Romanticism; you could say it was at one extreme of the Romantic scene. If the Romantics were Rock music, the Gothic would be Heavy Metal. And with the Romantics interested in the relationship between art and strong emotion, the Gothic writers decided to experiment with the strong emotion of fear.

Walpole, with *The Castle of Otranto*, actually got a head start on the Romantics. He was complaining that in the realistic novels of his time, "…the great resources of fancy have been dammed up, by a strict adherence to common life…" By "fancy", he meant imagination, and he was saying that all the benefits of using imagination to tell a story were being lost, because writers were too hung up on sticking to real, ordinary life. His answer was to include the magical, supernatural and extraordinary parts of older stories, but still use a realistic and matter-of-fact style of writing to create his new recipe for a novel.

He then invited other writers to follow his lead, and make a better job of it.

The first person to take up the challenge was Clara Reeve. In 1777 she published a novel best known as *The Old English Baron*, and she openly acknowledged her debt to Walpole. "This Story is the literary offspring of The Castle of Otranto, written upon the same plan, with a design to unite the most attractive and interesting circumstances of the ancient Romance and modern Novel…" But she went on to claim that Walpole's book went too far with its supernatural events. She objected to such extreme wonders as "…a sword so large as to require an hundred men to lift it; a helmet that by its own weight forces a passage through a court-yard into an arched vault, big enough for a man to go through; a picture that walks out of its frame; a skeleton ghost in a hermit's cowl." Her own novel toned down the ghostly stuff: to some spooky moans and groans and a walking suit of blood-spattered armour. She believed readers would be more likely to pay attention to the moral of her story if she didn't go too far over the boundary between real and unreal. And she was very keen on the importance of a story having a moral. Her book was originally called *The Champion of Virtue* (would you have read it with that title?) and aimed to show that evil people always come to grief in the end.

Terror and Horror

The next high-profile Gothic author was Ann Radcliffe. She wrote a series of extremely successful novels (Walpole only wrote the one), and while Walpole gets the credit for the first Gothic novel, Radcliffe is reckoned to be the true founder of the genre. Her first book was published in 1789 and four more followed through the 1790s, making her the star writer of this new type of story. Radcliffe is famous for her skill with exciting descriptions of setting and landscape and, like Reeve before her, she was careful to make sure her Hero and Heroine were rewarded for good behaviour.

Radcliffe had thought very carefully about the effect she was trying to achieve with her writing. She came to the conclusion that frightening events could be handled in two different ways, to get two different types of reaction, which she called "Terror" and "Horror". "Terror and Horror are so far opposite, that the first expands the soul and awakens the faculties to a high degree of life; the other contracts, freezes and nearly annihilates them... and where lies the great difference between horror and terror, but in uncertainty and obscurity, that accompany the first, respecting the dreaded evil?"

Radcliffe believed that "terror" was exciting and stimulating in a good way, opening up the mind and "soul". It was a reaction to uncertainty, to knowing there is something scary out there, but not knowing what. In her books she uses hints and suspense, keeping the reader in doubt and so "respectful" of the dangers just around the corner. "Horror", on the other hand, she thought was deadening and destructive, closing the mind down instead of opening it up, and was a reaction to something clearly and openly described. Jumping briefly to the present, we can see that Stephen King, usually called a horror writer but in fact today's most successful Gothic author, agrees with Radcliffe's definitions: "I recognize terror as the finest emotion and so I will try to terrorize the reader. But if I find that I cannot terrify, I will try to horrify, and if I find that I cannot horrify, I'll go for the gross-out. I'm not proud."

Evil Deeds

Radcliffe believed her contemporary, Matthew Lewis, whose book *The Monk* was published in 1796, made far too much use of horror: to the point of gross-out (read the extract in our **Dungeon** chapter!). But his more gruesome and explicit approach was certainly popular. He argued that his clear and detailed descriptions of his **Villain** and **Villainess'** evil deeds were more satisfying for the reader. According to him, too much doubt and uncertainty, of the sort Radcliffe preferred, in fact weakened the effect of the story.

You might like to think, as you read these stories and others, whether you agree more with Radcliffe or Lewis.

Anyway, critics of the time attacked Lewis. Famously the poet Coleridge, although he gave Lewis credit for his "rich, powerful and fervid" imagination, also said he had "a low and vulgar taste". He wrote: "…the Monk is a romance , which if a parent saw in the hands of a son or daughter, he might reasonably turn pale". This sort of review can always be relied on to produce plenty of readers! (Coleridge uses the word "romance", where we might expect "novel". The change to the new label for a long story told in prose was not yet complete. The word for "novel" in many other European languages is still "romance": *roman* in French, *romanzo* in Italian, and so on.)

So the 1790s saw the first real flowering of the Gothic, when Radcliffe and Lewis were publishing their novels and inspiring many others to do the same. Jane Austen's *Northanger Abbey* came out at the same time. She had started it nearly twenty years earlier and on one level it is a "spoof" of a Gothic novel, as written by Ann Radcliffe (the title is a clue). Her **Heroine**, seventeen year old Catherine Morland, is a great fan of Radcliffe's *The Mysteries of Udolpho,* and on being given a list of other Gothic novels she might like to read asks eagerly: "but are they all horrid, are you sure they are all horrid?" If you think about it, a parody can only work if everyone is familiar with what is being spoofed, so Jane Austen's book is more evidence of how popular the Gothic novel had become.

This first burst of Gothic creativity peaked in 1800, but continued into the 19th Century, and was not limited to English novels. French and particularly German writers were also part of the picture. Books were translated into and out of the various languages, with ideas and inspiration exchanged and borrowed, as the fashion for terror and horror spread across Europe. The theatre was important too, with many successful Gothic plays adapted from novels, or written specially. Matthew "Monk" Lewis wrote several, including *The Castle Spectre*, which was so popular it also transferred to New York. The critics gave him a hard time again, this time because he put a ghost (the Spectre of the title) in an active role. In the play the **Villain** Osmond is on the attack: "Drawing his sword, he rushes upon Reginald, who is disarmed, and beaten upon his knees; when at the moment that Osmond lifts his arm to stab him, Evelina's Ghost throws herself between them: Osmond starts back, and drops his sword." So the ghost is actually a goodie, but that wasn't what the critics minded. They were prepared to let Shakespeare have ghosts in his plays – in *Macbeth* and *Hamlet* for instance – because his audiences, two centuries years earlier, would still have believed in ghosts. But now (1797) everyone knew better, so it was ridiculous to put a spectre on the stage – they thought.

Shakespeare's ghosts are a useful reminder that these new Gothic novels were not the first stories to use spooky events to frighten and amaze an audience. Ghosts and monsters crop up in legends and tales all the way back to the Romans and Greeks. The collection of stories often called the *Arabian Nights* includes at least one haunted house and loads of ghouls. Aladdin's Djinn (or Genie) and Ali Baba's "Open Sesame" are just the best-known examples of magical messing about. No-one knows exactly when the stories were written, but some go back to the 10th Century and earlier. The first English translation came out in 1706, long before Walpole thought up his recipe for a Gothic novel. The difference, as we have seen, is that Walpole was the first to write a whole book based purely on the idea of what everyone was calling "terror".

Sublime

And there was some hard thinking being done about this concept of enjoying terror. The people looking beyond the pure science and reason of the Enlightenment, who were beginning to come up with the ideas that turned into the Romantic Movement, talked about the "Sublime". Don't let the every-day use of this word ("Darling, how sublime!") put you off. They were using its philosophical meaning, which is unmeasurable greatness. The Sublime is something so extreme, so big, so great, that we cannot calculate or measure it. We can only experience it emotionally. Philosopher Edmund Burke, in 1757, put it like this: "The passion caused by the great and sublime in nature… is Astonishment; and astonishment is that state of the soul, in which all its motions are suspended, with some degree of horror." These thinkers were trying to work out the relationship between terror (and/or horror – Radcliffe's separation of the two came a little later) and the enjoyment we get from scaring ourselves.

Poet and critic Anna Laetitia Aikin wrote an essay, published in 1773, about exactly this subject. She started by saying that "…the apparent delight with which we dwell upon objects of pure terror … is a paradox of the heart…" and talked about "…the greediness with which the tales of ghosts and goblins, of murders, earthquakes, fires, shipwrecks, and all the most terrible disasters attending human life, are devoured…" She pointed out that tragedies are always popular, and often include, and are more powerful because of, supernatural events: Shakespeare's ghosts again. She decided that we enjoy these things because they are extreme, or Sublime, as the philosophers would say. "Passion and fancy cooperating elevate the soul to its highest pitch; and the pain of terror is lost in amazement. Hence the more wild, fanciful, and extraordinary are the circumstances of a scene of horror, the more pleasure we receive from it." Published with her essay was a short piece by her brother, which was supposed to help make her point. In a couple of pages John Aikin managed to pack in most of our Gothic list, with his **Hero** Sir Bertrand facing a series of increasingly amazing, extraordinary and terrifying events. He then abandoned the action in the middle , just as the **Heroine** is about to…

Some people believe the Aikins did almost as much as *The Castle of Otranto* to kick-start the Gothic. Stuff that until then was only good enough for fairy tales – or for plays written long enough ago for their original audience still to believe in ghosts – could, it turned out, be included in full-length, serious novels. In fact, by using this material, writers could do more, could have a bigger impact, than if they stuck with being true to nature like the "realistic" novelists.

In 1795, nineteen Gothic novels were published. It might not sound like very many, but when you realise that only fifty novels of any type were published that year, it becomes clear that the terror writers were a massive part of the literary scene. The Gothic continued, into the first decades of the 19th Century, to have a big "market share" of the growing number of novels published, but the fashion never again dominated like it did in the 1790s.

Teenage Rebels

We've already begun to look at why the time was right, in the second half of the 18th Century, for this new type of book to appear and then become so popular. We've touched on the way the Enlightenment, with its scientific focus on reasoning and measuring, helped push the Romantics towards emotion, terror and the sublime. It's almost as if the Romantics were teenage rebels, looking for excitement, wanting to break the boring, grown-up rules set by the Enlightenment. But there was, of course, more going on. Historical events played an important part. I'm talking, in particular, about the French Revolution.

The ordinary people of France were, to put it mildly, fed up with how they were being governed. They were being bossed about by an absolutist King, by the aristocracy, and by the Church - no democracy there! In 1789 they rose up against their oppressors. Their aim was to set up a system based on "liberty, equality and brotherhood". This revolution led to a period of great disturbance, change and above all, uncertainty.

Some people make a direct link between what they see as the horrors and terrors of the French Revolution – riots, rebellion, mass execution by guillotine – and the new fashion for horror and terror in literature. Others point out that the Gothic was already well established by the time the Revolution kicked off. They have a more complicated, but more interesting view of the connection. It's all about the uncertainty.

Uncertainty did not just follow the French Revolution, but also preceded and helped create it. The Enlightenment had brought changes: scientific advances, the beginnings of industry, and, hugely importantly, questions about old systems of government and authority. Why, if we're going to be rational and scientific about things, should one person (the King), or a small group of people (the aristocracy), have more right than everybody else to decide what the rules should be, just because of who their parents are? These changes, these questions, all added up to an overall atmosphere of uncertainty. What's going to happen next? Who is actually in charge? What information can I trust? And when we are uncertain, we tend to worry.

Now think about how a Gothic novel works. It takes what worries us, what we are frightened of, exaggerates it, and puts it in a book. We get to enjoy the fear, because, apparently, that's how the sublime works, but we also get to control it, because it's in a book, not happening for real. The shrinks would say we use the Gothic novel to "work through" our worries, to deal with them. (Fairy tales – which when you think about it often have some pretty nasty things going on, mostly involving children about to be eaten – work in the same way.)

This is why these first Gothic novels are almost always about a battle between someone who stands for the old ways, and a **Hero** representing the new. The **Villain** is an aristocrat, who is determined to preserve his fading power by forcing himself on a virtuous young woman; or he is a wicked priest, trying to protect his reputation by locking up anyone who challenges the Church. These authors were writing about changes going on around them, and trying to deal with the worries those changes created.

As the 19th Century continued, the Gothic stopped being quite so fashionable - that is, after all, how fashion works. Maybe things got a little less uncertain too. Mary Shelley's *Frankenstein* was published in 1818 and many people think it marked the end of this first great flowering of the Gothic. (Its full title is *Frankenstein, or, the Modern*

Prometheus. We'll just call it *Frankenstein*: everyone else does.) But just because the Gothic was no longer the leading trend, the literature of terror was certainly not going away. More and more writers explored what it offered, different types of Gothic developed, in America particularly, and items from our Gothic list were used by "mainstream" authors. Sir Walter Scott with his persecuted **Heroines**, the Brontës using **Weather** for **Scenery**, and who – once they've read it – can forget the **Graveyard Setting** at the beginning of Charles Dickens' *Great Expectations*?

Then, towards the end of the 19th Century and into the early 20th, there came another burst of Gothic writing. These new Gothic writers were especially keen on stories where the human body is changed in gruesome and horrible ways. There is the transformation in Robert Louis Stevenson's *Dr Jekyll and Mr Hyde* (1886), the hideous portrait in Oscar Wilde's *The Picture of Dorian Gray* (1890/1), strange creatures on H. G. Wells' *The Island of Dr Moreau* (1896), the Count changing from human into dog, wolf, bat and… wait for it… fog in Bram Stoker's *Dracula* (1897), not to mention Gaston Leroux's *The Phantom of the Opera* (1910), with a face of rotting flesh. And in the same way that the first explosion of Gothic activity was all about uncertainty, this second burst was again a reaction to people's worries in times of change.

The Horror of Science

It was Darwin's fault. Not revolution this time, but evolution. It turned out that we, human beings, were not in fact the perfect creatures we had always believed, modelled by God on God. We were instead a mess of bits and bobs, begged and borrowed from other, older animals. We were descended from "a hairy, tailed quadruped", and further back "from some amphibian-like creature" according to Darwin's *The Descent of Man* (1871). These new Gothic novels were trying to deal with the scary fact that we are animals. And that animals change over time, evolving. The books looked at the worries and fears running through society at that time.

Jump forward again; what have we been worried about in modern times? What new and unknown threats have emerged? How about HIV/

A Young Person's Guide to the Gothic

AIDS, a terrifying disease carried in the blood? Is that why **Vampires** have been so popular in recent decades? And all those films, books and computer games about a future apocalypse, full of cyborgs and monstrous aliens? Might they have something to do with the fact that we are worried about weapons of mass destruction, nuclear bombs and bio-engineered plagues? Or is it that we are all feeling increasingly cut off and alienated? We walk through our modern cities with our headphones on, surrounded by people we don't know, people who seem increasingly strange to us, people who might almost be **Zombies**.

The patterns are clear.

The times when we – a society - are most worried have proved to be the times when Gothic stories are most popular. Readers and writers encourage each other to explore the fears of their own era. But the Gothic is timeless too: as we will see reading through our list, it uses certain ideas and arrangements over and over. Some fears are eternal and keep recurring: **The Lights Go Out** in the first Gothic novel and do so again and again, right through to the first episode of *American Horror Story*.

The bottom line is that the Gothic from any period entertains us, while also helping us, at a deeper level, to face our demons.

One: SETTINGS

For Walpole, writer of the first Gothic novel, and those who followed soon after him, the word "Gothic" was simply a label for a distant historical period. It meant more or less the same as "Medieval" does to us, with a hint of the barbarian on top. Gothic was useful code for everything to do with ruins and castles, knights and princesses, fables and superstitions. It did not yet mean "weird and spooky stuff". But these authors wanted to scare their readers. To do so they needed to scare their **Characters**. They set their adventures in a time when people believed in magic and ghosts, because that way they felt justified in using magic and ghosts to terrorise their **Heroes** and **Heroines**. So for them it was the **Setting** that was Gothic (in other words Medieval), not the spookiness. Over time though, because of all these stories about ghosts in a Gothic Setting, Gothic meaning "Medieval", became Gothic, meaning "spooky stuff in a Medieval setting" (and, eventually, just "dark, spooky stuff").

There is nothing more Medieval than a **Castle**, which means there is nothing more Gothic than a Castle. If you've read the introduction, you'll know that the first Gothic authors were interested in conflicts between old types of authority, where kings and the aristocracy ruled just because of being born in charge, and the new, where virtue and noble behaviour were more important than having the right parents. This was another reason to choose Medieval Settings, because of course the aristocracy of that time lived in Castles.

Then of course the sheer size of a Castle can be used to create complexity and confusion, with plenty of room for things to remain secret and hidden.

Finally, Castles are (almost) always at least beginning to fall down, and so can symbolise the way the **Villain's** morals are on a downward spiral.

As the Gothic develops over time, so do the **Settings**. The **Castles** become **Haunted Houses**, or their close cousins abandoned prisons and derelict hospitals. But what remains constant is the sense of something old or past, where the unknown can easily lurk in dark corridors, murky cellars and creaky attics.

And of course Settings are not limited to buildings. **Forests** can offer much of what a Castle does in terms of darkness, getting lost and having nasty things jump out at you from behind.

In this chapter, therefore, you'll find some of the classic Settings for a Gothic tale, showing how the first Gothic writers, and some of those who followed, set about creating the all-important environment for their spooky goings on.

THE CASTLE

If you have seen the Harry Potter films, you don't need to use your imagination to conjure up what a Castle should look like. Hogwarts is the ultimate Gothic Castle, complete with all the traditional features of high towers and tall walls, secret rooms and underground tunnels. After becoming accustomed to the magnificent sets and special effects on the screen, it is perhaps a little surprising to find how simply the famous school for witches and wizards is first described in *Harry Potter and the Philosopher's Stone*.

> The narrow path had opened suddenly onto the edge of a great black lake. Perched atop a high mountain on the other side, its windows sparkling in the starry sky, was a vast castle with many turrets and towers.

It's fairly simple stuff, and if we go back to the first Gothic novel, we find the Castle in *The Castle of Otranto* is in fact hardly described at all. Walpole's story unfolds in and around chambers, halls, turrets, ramparts, battlements, vaults, postern gates and, of course, a secret passage, but there is very little physical description of the building or its location. In his preface to the book Walpole actually says, with dodgy grammar, "There is no bombast, no similes, flowers, digressions, or unnecessary descriptions." Perhaps he was being deliberately vague, so readers could imagine their own idea of a **Castle** more easily.

Ann Radcliffe, the first author to write a successful series of Gothic novels, takes a more descriptive approach. Her best known book, *The Mysteries of Udolpho* (published in 1794), provides a marvellous example of how the Gothic Castle should be introduced. For Radcliffe, it's all about atmosphere.

"There," said Montoni, speaking for the first time in several hours, "is Udolpho."

Emily gazed with melancholy awe upon the castle, which she understood to be Montoni's; for, though it was now lighted up by the setting sun, the gothic greatness of its features, and its mouldering walls of dark grey stone, rendered it a gloomy and sublime object. As she gazed, the light died away on its walls, leaving a melancholy purple tint, which spread deeper and deeper, as the thin vapour crept up the mountain, while the battlements above were still tipped with splendour. From those, too, the rays soon faded, and the whole edifice was invested with the solemn duskiness of evening. Silent, lonely, and sublime, it seemed to stand the sovereign of the scene, and to frown defiance on all, who dared to invade its solitary reign. As the twilight deepened, its features became more awful in obscurity, and Emily continued to gaze, till its clustering towers were alone seen, rising over the tops of the woods, beneath whose thick shade the carriages soon after began to ascend.

The extent and darkness of these tall woods awakened terrific images in her mind, and she almost expected to see banditti start up from under the trees. At length, the carriages emerged upon a heathy rock, and, soon after, reached the castle gates, where the deep tone of the portal bell, which was struck upon to give notice of their arrival, increased the fearful emotions, that had assailed Emily. While they waited till the servant within should come to open the gates, she anxiously surveyed the edifice: but the gloom, that overspread it, allowed her to distinguish little more than a part of its outline, with the massy walls of the ramparts, and to know that it was vast, ancient and dreary. From the parts she saw, she judged of the heavy strength and extent of the whole. The gateway before her, leading into the courts, was of gigantic size, and was defended by two round towers, crowned by overhanging turrets, embattled, where, instead of banners, now waved long grass and wild plants, that had taken root among the mouldering stones, and which seemed to sigh, as the breeze rolled past, over the desolation around them. The towers were united by a curtain, pierced and embattled also, below which appeared the pointed arch of a huge portcullis, surmounting the gates: from these, the walls of the ramparts extended to other towers, overlooking the precipice, whose shattered outline, appearing on a gleam, that lingered in the west, told of the ravages of war. Beyond these all was lost in the obscurity of evening.

You will have guessed that we get our English word "bandit" from *banditti*, a plural Italian word, meaning a group of outlaws. As dangerous occupants of wild landscapes, banditti made frequent appearances in the early Gothic novels; to the extent that they have earned themselves an honourable mention in the **Plot Devices** chapter. You may also have noticed that Radcliffe manages to use the word "melancholy" twice in six lines, not to mention "gloomy", "lonely", "awful", "solemn", and so on. Hopefully you are beginning to get the picture.

THE OUTSIDER
H. P. LOVECRAFT

First published in 1921, this story provides a splendid example of a Gothic **Castle** Setting. Lovecraft combined elements of horror, fantasy and science fiction to create his own unique genre some label "weird fiction"; he certainly made plentiful use of traditional Gothic devices, to the extent that it is tempting to call him the originator of "modern" Gothic. If you like his intense style, you would enjoy meeting his fish monster in *Dagon* and discovering the truth about *The Dunwich Horror*.

Unhappy is he to whom the memories of childhood bring only fear and sadness. Wretched is he who looks back upon lone hours in vast and dismal chambers with brown hangings and maddening rows of antique books, or upon awed watches in twilight groves of grotesque, gigantic, and vine-encumbered trees that silently wave twisted branches far aloft. Such a lot the gods gave to me - to me, the dazed, the disappointed; the barren, the broken. And yet I am strangely content and cling desperately to those sere memories, when my mind momentarily threatens to reach beyond to the other.

I know not where I was born, save that the castle was infinitely old and infinitely horrible, full of dark passages and having high ceilings where the eye could find only cobwebs and shadows. The stones in the crumbling corridors seemed always hideously damp, and there was an accursed smell everywhere, as of the piled-up corpses of dead generations. It was never light, so that I used sometimes to light candles and gaze steadily at them for relief, nor was there any sun outdoors, since the terrible trees grew high above the topmost accessible tower.

was one black tower which reached above the trees into known outer sky, but that was partly ruined and could not be ascended save by a well-nigh impossible climb up the sheer wall, stone by stone.

I must have lived years in this place, but I cannot measure the time. Beings must have cared for my needs, yet I cannot recall any person except myself, or anything alive but the noiseless rats and bats and spiders. I think that whoever nursed me must have been shockingly aged, since my first conception of a living person was that of somebody mockingly like myself, yet distorted, shrivelled, and decaying like the castle. To me there was nothing grotesque in the bones and skeletons that strewed some of the stone crypts deep down among the foundations. I fantastically associated these things with everyday events, and thought them more natural than the coloured pictures of living beings which I found in many of the mouldy books. From such books I learned all that I know. No teacher urged or guided me, and I do not recall hearing any human voice in all those years – not even my own; for although I had read of speech, I had never thought to try to speak aloud. My aspect was a matter equally unthought of, for there were no mirrors in the castle, and I merely regarded myself by instinct as akin to the youthful figures I saw drawn and painted in the books. I felt conscious of youth because I remembered so little.

Outside, across the putrid moat and under the dark mute trees, I would often lie and dream for hours about what I read in the books; and would longingly picture myself amidst gay crowds in the sunny world beyond the endless forests. Once I tried to escape from the forest, but as I went farther from the castle the shade grew denser and the air more filled with brooding fear; so that I ran frantically back lest I lose my way in a labyrinth of nighted silence.

So through endless twilights I dreamed and waited, though I knew not what I waited for. Then in the shadowy solitude my longing for light grew so frantic that I could rest no more, and I lifted entreating hands to the single black ruined tower that reached above the forest into the unknown outer sky. And at last I resolved to scale that tower, fall though I might; since it were better to glimpse the sky and perish, than to live without ever beholding day.

In the dank twilight I climbed the worn and aged stone stairs till I reached the level where they ceased, and thereafter clung perilously to small footholds leading upward. Ghastly and terrible was that dead, stairless cylinder of rock; black, ruined, and deserted, and sinister with startled bats whose wings made no noise. But more ghastly and terrible still was the slowness of my progress; for climb as I might, the darkness overhead grew no thinner, and a new chill as of haunted and venerable mould assailed me. I shivered as I wondered why I did not reach the light, and would have looked down had I dared. I fancied that night had come suddenly upon me, and vainly groped with one free hand for a window embrasure, that I might peer out and above, and try to judge the height I had once attained.

All at once, after an infinity of awesome, sightless, crawling up that concave and desperate precipice, I felt my head touch a solid thing, and I knew I must have gained the roof, or at least some kind of floor. In the darkness I raised my free hand and tested the barrier, finding it stone and immovable. Then came a deadly circuit of the tower, clinging to whatever holds the slimy wall could give; till finally my testing hand found the barrier yielding, and I turned upward again, pushing the slab or door with my head as I used both hands in my fearful ascent. There was no light revealed above, and as my hands went higher I knew that my climb was for the nonce ended; since the slab was the trapdoor of an aperture leading to a level stone surface of greater circumference than the lower tower, no doubt the floor of some lofty and capacious observation chamber. I crawled through carefully, and tried to prevent the heavy slab from falling back into place, but failed in the latter attempt. As I lay exhausted on the stone floor I heard the eerie echoes of its fall, hoped when necessary to pry it up again.

Believing I was now at prodigious height, far above the accursed branches of the wood, I dragged myself up from the floor and fumbled about for windows, that I might look for the first time upon the sky, and the moon and stars of which I had read. But on every hand I was disappointed; since all that I found were vast shelves of marble, bearing odious oblong boxes of disturbing size. More and more I reflected, and wondered what hoary secrets might abide in this high apartment so many aeons cut off from the castle below. Then unexpectedly my hands came upon a doorway, where hung a portal of stone, rough with strange chiselling. Trying it, I found it locked; but with a supreme burst of strength I overcame all obstacles and dragged it open inward. As I did so there came to me the purest ecstasy I have ever known; for shining tranquilly through an ornate grating of iron, and down a short stone passageway of steps that ascended from the newly found doorway, was the radiant full moon, which I had never before seen save in dreams and in vague visions I dared not call memories.

Fancying now that I had attained the very pinnacle of the castle, I commenced to rush up the few steps beyond the door; but the sudden veiling of the moon by a cloud caused me to stumble, and I felt my way more slowly in the dark. It was still very dark when I reached the grating – which I tried carefully and found unlocked, but which I did not open for fear of falling from the amazing height to which I had climbed. Then the moon came out.

Most demoniacal of all shocks is that of the abysmally unexpected and grotesquely unbelievable. Nothing I had before undergone could compare in terror with what I now saw; with the bizarre marvels that sight implied. The sight itself was as simple as it was stupefying, for it was merely this: instead of a dizzying prospect of treetops seen from a lofty eminence, there stretched around me on the level through the grating nothing less than the solid ground, decked and diversified by marble slabs and columns, and overshadowed by an ancient stone church, whose ruined spire gleamed spectrally in the moonlight.

A Young Person's Guide to the Gothic

Half unconscious, I opened the grating and staggered out upon the white gravel path that stretched away in two directions. My mind, stunned and chaotic as it was, still held the frantic craving for light; and not even the fantastic wonder which had happened could stay my course. I neither knew nor cared whether my experience was insanity, dreaming, or magic; but was determined to gaze on brilliance and gaiety at any cost. I knew not who I was or what I was, or what my surroundings might be; though as I continued to stumble along I became conscious of a kind of fearsome latent memory that made my progress not wholly fortuitous. I passed under an arch out of that region of slabs and columns, and wandered through the open country; sometimes following the visible road, but sometimes leaving it curiously to tread across meadows where only occasional ruins bespoke the ancient presence of a forgotten road. Once I swam across a swift river where crumbling, mossy masonry told of a bridge long vanished.

Over two hours must have passed before I reached what seemed to be my goal, a venerable ivied castle in a thickly wooded park, maddeningly familiar, yet full of perplexing strangeness to me. I saw that the moat was filled in, and that some of the well-known towers were demolished, whilst new wings existed to confuse the beholder. But what I observed with chief interest and delight were the open windows – gorgeously ablaze with light and sending forth sound of the gayest revelry. Advancing to one of these I looked in and saw an oddly dressed company indeed; making merry, and speaking brightly to one another. I had never, seemingly, heard human speech before and could guess only vaguely what was said. Some of the faces seemed to hold expressions that brought up incredibly remote recollections, others were utterly alien.

I now stepped through the low window into the brilliantly lighted room, stepping as I did so from my single bright moment of hope to my blackest convulsion of despair and realization. The nightmare was quick to come, for as I entered, there occurred immediately one of the most terrifying demonstrations I had ever conceived. Scarcely had I crossed the sill when there descended upon the whole company a sudden and unheralded fear of hideous intensity, distorting every face and evoking the most horrible screams from nearly every throat. Flight was universal, and in the clamour and panic several fell in a swoon and were dragged away by their madly fleeing companions. Many covered their eyes with their hands, and plunged blindly and awkwardly in their race to escape, overturning furniture and stumbling against the walls before they managed to reach one of the many doors.

The cries were shocking; and as I stood in the brilliant apartment alone and dazed, listening to their vanishing echoes, I trembled at the thought of what might be lurking near me unseen. At a casual inspection the room seemed deserted, but when I moved towards one of the alcoves I thought I detected a presence there – a hint of motion beyond the golden-arched doorway leading to another and somewhat similar room. As I approached the arch I began to perceive the presence more clearly; and then, with the first and last sound I ever uttered – a ghastly ululation that revolted me almost as poignantly as its noxious cause – I beheld in full, frightful vividness the inconceivable, indescribable, and unmentionable monstrosity which had by its simple appearance changed a merry company to a herd of delirious fugitives.

I cannot even hint what it was like, for it was a compound of all that is unclean, uncanny, unwelcome, abnormal, and detestable. It was the ghoulish shade of decay, antiquity, and dissolution; the putrid, dripping eidolon of unwholesome revelation, the awful baring of that which the merciful earth should always hide. God knows it was not of this world – or no longer of this world – yet to my horror I saw in its eaten-away and bone-revealing outlines a leering, abhorrent travesty on the human shape; and in its mouldy, disintegrating apparel an unspeakable quality that chilled me even more.

I was almost paralysed, but not too much so to make a feeble effort towards flight; a backward stumble which failed to break the spell in which the nameless, voiceless monster held me. My eyes bewitched by the glassy orbs which stared loathsomely into them, refused to close; though they were mercifully blurred, and showed the terrible object but indistinctly after the first shock. I tried to raise my hand to shut out the sight, yet so stunned were my nerves that my arm could not fully obey my will. The attempt, however, was enough to disturb my balance; so that I had to stagger forward several steps to avoid falling. As I did so I became suddenly and agonizingly aware of the nearness of the carrion thing, whose hideous hollow breathing I half fancied I could hear. Nearly mad, I found myself yet able to throw out a hand to ward off the foetid apparition which pressed so close; when in one cataclysmic second of cosmic nightmarishness and hellish accident my fingers touched the rotting outstretched paw of the monster beneath the golden arch.

I did not shriek, but all the fiendish ghouls that ride the nightwind shrieked for me as in that same second there crashed down upon my mind a single fleeting avalanche of soul-annihilating memory. I knew in that second all that had been; I remembered beyond the frightful castle and the trees, and recognized the altered edifice in which I now stood; I recognized, most terrible of all, the unholy abomination that stood leering before me as I withdrew my sullied fingers from its own.

But in the cosmos there is balm as well as bitterness, and that balm is nepenthe. In the supreme horror of that second I forgot what had horrified me, and the burst of black memory vanished in a chaos of echoing images. In a dream I fled from that haunted and accursed pile, and ran swiftly and silently in the moonlight. When I returned to the churchyard place of marble and went down the steps I found the stone trap-door immovable; but I was not sorry, for I had hated the antique castle and the trees. Now I ride with the mocking and friendly ghouls on the night-wind, and play by day amongst the catacombs of Nephren-Ka in the sealed and unknown valley of Hadoth by the Nile. I know that light is not for me, save that of the moon over the rock tombs of Neb, nor any gaiety save the unnamed feasts of Nitokris beneath the Great Pyramid; yet in my new wildness and freedom I almost welcome the bitterness of alienage.

For although nepenthe has calmed me, I know always that I am an outsider; a stranger in this century and among those who are still men. This I have known ever since I stretched out my fingers to the abomination within that great gilded frame; stretched out my fingers and touched a cold and unyielding surface of polished glass.

THE ABBEY

For the early Gothic writers, the **Abbey** (or Monastery, or Convent) shared many features with the **Castle**. It was a big, old building with plenty of room for the sort of secret passages and underground chambers through which Gothic **Villains** like to pursue their sinister activities and hunt down their victims, but there were added bonuses too. The Abbey was of course linked to religion and religious figures – priests, monks and nuns – which gave authors an opportunity to look at confrontations between God and the Devil, good and evil. Many writers of the period were also hostile to Catholicism, for reasons tied up with recent history and Enlightenment thinking. They believed the older form of Christian religion had become authoritarian and corrupt, in contrast to the more "democratic" values of Protestantism. A novel set in an Abbey provided plenty of opportunities to make figures of Catholic authority look bad.

The Monk, one of the earliest and most famous Gothic tales, was published 1796. Its author Matthew Lewis was not yet twenty when he wrote the three volumes of his only novel – in just ten weeks! Much of the book is set in and around an Abbey in Madrid, where the monk of the title makes a pact with the Devil. We will be coming back to it frequently in later sections, but as with Walpole's *Castle of Otranto*, there are in fact few physical descriptions of the buildings.

The Ruins of the Abbey of Fitz-Martin is a story from 1801, right at the crest of the first wave of Gothic writing, and was penned by that well-known writer Anonymous. It features a favourite Gothic character, the nun who is persecuted because she has slept with a man or, in this particular case, failed to keep her "vows of vestal celibacy", which is a polite way of saying the same thing. There is a similar plot strand in *The Monk*. The **Abbey** of the title is a "gloomy, remote, and even terrific habitation" and a "terrific and ruinous a place"; in 1801 terrific meant much the same as terrifying. Here is how Sir Thomas (and his servant Owen), visiting the Abbey after it has been abandoned for over a century, first encounter it.

… a violent flash of lightning ended his doubts; as it glanced in an instant on the walls of the abbey, and displayed its tottering turrets and broken casements. It showed also, at no great distance, a small postern, whose weak state seemed to promise greater success; and they determined to try it if they could not here find a more willing admission. The postern was extremely old, and seemed only held by the bolt of the lock, which soon gave way to the attack of the travellers; and crossing beneath a heavy Gothic arch, they found themselves within the area of the first court. …. Owen summoned up a sort of desperate courage, and declared his intention of attending his master: and lighting a torch, he followed his calm and undaunted conductor, who now advanced with caution through the wide area of a second court, which, being covered with crumbling fragments of the ruins, rendered his advances difficult, and even dangerous. At length he reached a flight of steps, that seemed to lead to the grand portal of entrance. Sir Thomas, however, determined to ascend; and Owen, though tottering beneath his own weight with terrors, dared not interpose his resistance: his trembling hand held the light to the great folding doors, and Sir Thomas, after some efforts, burst them open, and entered what appeared an immense hall, terminating in vistas of huge pillars, whose lofty heads, like the roof they supported, were impervious to the faint rays of the torch, and enveloped in an awful and misty gloom, beyond expression impressive and solemn, and creating astonishing sensations in the startled beholder.

The tale has a complicated story-within-a-story structure (another favourite Gothic trick), with Sir Thomas' young daughter finding documents that tell how, many years before, the evil Baron Vortimer first seduced, then abandoned a woman, Anna. She became a nun, but after her pregnancy was revealed, she was imprisoned in the **Abbey** and left to starve to death. The climax of the tale comes with the nun returning from the dead to avenge herself (and God) on her persecutor.

> The vengeance of heaven hung heavily over the conscience of the wicked Baron...
> The sullen bell had tolled the hour of midnight ere he could compose his mind to repose. On this night, however, unusual restlessness pervaded his frame; nor could he for some time close in forgetfulness his eye-lids. At length a kind of unwilling stupor lulled for a moment his tortured spirits, and he slept. Not long did the balmy deity await him: troubled groans of anguish sounded through the apartment, and piercing shrieks rung bitterly in his ears. Starting in horror, he wildly raised himself, half bent, on his couch, and drew aside his curtains. The chamber was in total darkness, and every taper seemed suddenly to have been extinguished. At that moment the heavy bell of the abbey clock struck one. A freezing awe stole over the senses of the Baron: he in vain attempted to call his attendants; for speech was denied him; and a suspense of trembling horror had chilled his soul. His blood ran cold to its native source; his hair stood erect, and his countenance was distorted; for, as his eyes turned wildly, he beheld, standing close to the side of his bed, the pale figure of a female form, thinly clothed in the habiliments of a nun, and bearing in one hand a taper, whilst the other arm supported the ghastly form of a dead infant reclining on her breast. The countenance of the figure was

pale, wan, and horrible to behold; for from its motionless eyes no spark of life proceeded; but they were fixed in unmoving terrific expression on the appalled Baron. At length a hollow-sounding voice pronounced through the closed lips of the spectre, "O false, false Vortimer! accursed and rejected of thy Maker! knowest thou not the shadowy form that stands before thee? knowest thou not thy wretched bride? seest thou not the murdered infant thou hast destroyed?"

I couldn't resist including that impressive climax to the tale, even if it only includes a single direct reference to the **Abbey**. I also wanted to compare it with a story written just over a hundred years later, during the second great surge of Gothic writing. *Thurnley Abbey* was published in 1908 and also set (no prizes for guessing) in an ancient Abbey. Perceval Landon, the author, was mostly a journalist, who spent his adult life travelling the world as a War or Special Correspondent, but this is his best known work. Staying with his friend Broughton, the narrator, like the evil Baron above, has gone to bed. But he can't sleep, and decides to read instead.

… I switched on the bedside lamp. The sudden glory dazzled me for a moment. I felt under my pillow for my book with half-shut eyes. Then, growing used to the light, I happened to look down to the foot of my bed.
I can never tell you really what happened then. Nothing I could ever confess in the most abject words could even faintly picture to you what I felt. I know that my heart stopped dead, and my throat shut automatically. In one instinctive movement I crouched back up against the head-boards of the bed, staring at the horror. The movement set my heart going again, and the sweat dripped from every pore. I am not a particularly religious man, but I had always believed that God would never allow any supernatural appearance to present itself to man in such a guise and in such circumstances that harm, either bodily or mental, could result to him. I can only tell you that at the moment both my life and my reason rocked unsteadily on

their seats.

Leaning over the foot of my bed, looking at me, was a figure swathed in a rotten and tattered veiling. This shroud passed over the head, but left both eyes and the right side of the face bare. It then followed the line of the arm down to where the hand grasped the bed-end. The face was not entirely that of a skull, though the eyes and the flesh of the face were totally gone. There was a thin, dry skin drawn tightly over the features, and there was some skin left on the hand. One wisp of hair crossed the forehead. It was perfectly still. I looked at it, and it looked at me, and my brains turned dry and hot in my head. I had still got the switch of the electric lamp in my hand, and I played idly with it; only I dared not turn the light out again. I shut my eyes, only to open them in a hideous terror the same second. The thing had not moved. My heart was thumping, and the sweat cooled me as it evaporated. Another cinder tinkled in the grate, and a panel creaked in the wall.

My reason failed me. For twenty minutes, or twenty seconds, I was able to think of nothing else but this awful figure, till there came, hurtling through the empty channels of my senses, the remembrances that Broughton and his friends had discussed me furtively at dinner. The dim possibility of its being a hoax stole gratefully into my unhappy mind, and once there, one's pluck came creeping back along a thousand tiny veins. My first sensation was one of blind unreasoning thankfulness that my brain was going to stand the trial. I am not a timid man, but the best of us needs some human handle to steady him in time of extremity, and in this faint but growing hope that after all it might be only a brutal hoax, I found the fulcrum that I needed. At last I moved.

How I managed to do it I cannot tell you, but with one spring towards the foot of the bed I got within arm's-length and struck out one fearful blow with my fist at the thing. It crumbled under it, and my hand was cut to the bone. With a sickening revulsion after my terror, I dropped half-fainting across the end of the bed. So it was merely a foul trick after all. No doubt the trick had been played many a time before: no doubt Broughton and his friends had had some large bet among themselves as to what I should do when I discovered the gruesome thing. From my state of abject terror I found myself transported into an insensate anger. I shouted curses upon Broughton. I dived rather than climbed over the bed-end of the sofa. I tore at the robed skeleton — how well the whole thing had been carried out, I thought — I broke the skull against the floor, and stamped upon its dry bones. I flung the head away under the bed, and rent the brittle bones of the trunk in pieces. I snapped the thin thigh-bones across my knee, and flung them in different directions. The shin-bones I set up against a stool and broke with my heel. I raged like a Berserker against the loathly thing, and stripped the ribs from the backbone and slung the breastbone against the cupboard. My fury increased as the work of destruction went on. I tore the frail rotten veil into twenty pieces, and the dust went up over everything, over the clean blotting-paper and the silver inkstand. At last my work was done. There was but a raffle of broken bones and strips of parchment and crumbling wool. Then, picking up a piece of the skull--it was the cheek and temple bone of the right side, I remember--I opened the door and went down the passage to Broughton's dressing-room. I remember still how my sweat-dripping pyjamas clung to me as I walked.

You might think that was that, but if you seek out the complete story, you'll find it takes another, rather unpleasant twist.

SOME RUINS

There is only one location with more potential for spooky goings on than a **Castle**, and that is a Ruined Castle. A **Ruin** is the result of long decay over time, or violent events in the past, both of which provide excellent material for the sorts of events the Gothic writers are interested in. Ann Radcliffe, in her 1791 novel *The Romance of the Forest*, has La Motte, one of the protagonists, who is lost in the **Forest** with his family, explore a **Ruin** where he hopes to find refuge. As well as describing the Ruins in splendidly gloomy terms, the author uses her character's reaction to them to emphasise the impression of mystery.

> He approached, and perceived the Gothic remains of an abbey: it stood on a kind of rude lawn, overshadowed by high and spreading trees, which seemed coeval with the building, and diffused a romantic gloom around. The greater part of the pile appeared to be sinking into ruins, and that, which had withstood the ravages of time, showed the remaining features of the fabric more awful in decay. The lofty battlements, thickly enwreathed with ivy, were half demolished, and become the residence of birds of prey. Huge fragments of the eastern tower, which was almost demolished, lay scattered amid the high grass, that waved slowly to the breeze. "The thistle shook its lonely head; the moss whistled to the wind." A Gothic gate, richly ornamented with fret-work, which opened into the main body of the edifice, but which was now obstructed with brushwood, remained entire. Above the vast and magnificent portal of this gate arose a window of the same order, whose pointed arches still exhibited fragments of stained glass, once the pride of monkish devotion. La Motte, thinking it possible it might yet shelter some human being, advanced to the gate and lifted a massy knocker. The hollow sounds rung through the emptiness of the place. After waiting a few minutes, he forced back the gate, which was heavy with iron work, and creaked harshly on its hinges.
>
> He entered what appeared to have been the chapel of the abbey, where the hymn of devotion had once been raised, and the tear of penitence had once been shed; sounds, which could now only be recalled by imagination — tears of penitence, which had been long since fixed in fate. La Motte paused a moment, for he felt a sensation of sublimity rising into terror

— a suspension of mingled astonishment and awe! He surveyed the vastness of the place, and as he contemplated its ruins, fancy bore him back to past ages. "And these walls," said he, "where once superstition lurked, and austerity anticipated an earthly purgatory, now tremble over the mortal remains of the beings who reared them!"

The deepening gloom now reminded La Motte that he had no time to lose, but curiosity prompted him to explore farther, and he obeyed the impulse. — As he walked over the broken pavement, the sound of his steps ran in echoes through the place, and seemed like the mysterious accents of the dead, reproving the sacrilegious mortal who thus dared to disturb their precincts.

From this chapel he passed into the nave of the great church, of which one window, more perfect than the rest, opened upon a long vista of the forest, through which was seen the rich colouring of evening, melting by imperceptible gradations into the solemn grey of upper air. Dark hills, whose outline appeared distinct upon the vivid glow of the horizon, closed the perspective. Several of the pillars, which had once supported the roof, remained the proud effigies of sinking greatness, and seemed to nod at every murmur of the blast over the fragments of those that had fallen a little before them. La Motte sighed. The comparison between himself and the gradation of decay, which these columns exhibited, was but too obvious and affecting. "A few years," said he, "and I shall become like the mortals on whose relics I now gaze, and, like them too, I may be the subject of meditation to a succeeding generation, which shall totter but a little while over the object they contemplate, e'er they also sink into the dust."

It's not exactly action-packed, but the point is the ominous description, and the message that a **Ruined** building carries, of human weakness and mortality.

In this next piece the Ruin has another message. As well as providing a spooky setting (of course), it gives the author an opportunity to express, through his **Antihero**, an opinion on what he sees as the corruption and decay of the Catholic Church. It also, appropriately, contains a first appearance in this book of the **Inquisition**, which crops up so often in the Gothic that I've given it its own segment later on. The Inquisition's role was to seek out and combat heresy: beliefs that go against the teachings of the Church. In Medieval times it was very powerful. In its Gothic form, the Inquisition comes across a bit like the Taliban, doing a lot of torturing and executing in the name of God. In this case it is investigating potential misbehaviour by the former inhabitants of the monastery.

The extract comes from Charles Maturin's *Melmoth the Wanderer*, published in 1820. The title character has sold his soul to the devil in exchange for 150 extra years of life. He wanders the world searching for someone to take on the pact in his place. This is one of latest novels of what is considered the first flowering of Gothic literature. The author is well aware of his debt to his predecessors and in his introduction defends himself against accusations that the story is too like a "Radcliffe-Romance"; then, on the second page, with his tongue in his cheek, he compares a pair of his characters to figures from Lewis' *The Monk*.

Maturin may be poking a little fun at the genre, therefore, but he enters fully into the Gothic spirit. Melmoth's life is told in a spectacularly complex series of stories within stories. In this passage he has persuaded the **Heroine** Isidora to elope with him.

"There is," said he, "a ruined monastery near—you may have observed it from your window."

"No! I never saw it. Why is it in ruins?"

"I know not—there were wild stories told. It was said the Superior, or Prior, or—I know not what—had looked into certain books, the perusal of which was not altogether sanctioned by the rules of his order—books of magic they called them. There was much noise about it, I remember, and some talk of the Inquisition,—but the end of the business was, the Prior disappeared, some said into the prisons of the Inquisition, some said into safer custody—(though how that could be, I cannot well conceive)—and the brethren were drafted into other communities, and the building became deserted. There were some offers made for it by the communities of other religious houses, but the evil, through vague and wild reports, that had gone forth about it, deterred them, on inquiry, from inhabiting it,—and gradually the building fell to ruin. It still retains all that can sanctify it in the eyes of the faithful. There are crucifixes and tomb-stones, and here and there a cross set up where there has been murder…"

At these words, Melmoth felt the slender arm that hung on his withdrawn,—and he perceived that his victim, between shuddering and struggling, had shrunk from his hold.

"But there," he added, "even amid those ruins, there dwells a holy hermit,—one who has taken up his residence near the spot,—he will unite us in his oratory, according to the rites of your church."

Melmoth succeeds in persuading Isidora to continue.

In silent horror she proceeded, till Melmoth, pointing to a dusky and indefinite mass of what, in the gloom of night, bore, according to the eye or the fancy, the shape of a rock, a tuft of trees, or a massive and unlighted building, whispered,

"There is the ruin, and near it stands the hermitage,—one moment more of effort,—of renewed strength and courage, and we are there."

Urged by these words, and still more by an undefinable wish to put an end to this shadowy journey,—these mysterious fears,—even at the risk of finding them worse than verified at its termination, Isidora exerted all her remaining strength, and, supported by Melmoth, began to ascend the sloping ground on which the monastery had once stood. There had been a path, but it was now all obstructed by stones, and rugged with the knotted and interlaced roots of the neglected trees that had once formed its shelter and its grace.

As they approached, in spite of the darkness of the night, the ruin began to assume a distinct and characteristic appearance, and Isidora's heart beat less fearfully, when she could ascertain, from the remains of the tower and spire, the vast Eastern window, and the crosses still visible on every ruined pinnacle and pediment, like religion triumphant amid grief and decay, that this had been a building destined for sacred purposes. A narrow path, that seemed to wind round the edifice, conducted them to a front which overlooked an extensive cemetery, at the extremity of which Melmoth pointed out to her an indistinct object, which he said was the hermitage, and to which he would hasten to entreat the hermit, who was also a priest, to unite them.

"May I not accompany you?" said Isidora, glancing round on the graves that were to be her companions in solitude.

"It is against his vow," said Melmoth, "to admit a female into his presence, except when obliged by the course of his duties."

So saying he hasted away, and Isidora, sinking on a grave for rest, wrapt her veil around her, as if its folds could exclude even thought. In a few moments, gasping for air, she withdrew it; but as her eye encountered only tomb-stones and crosses, and that dark and sepulchral vegetation that loves to shoot its roots, and trail its unlovely verdure amid the joints of grave-stones, she closed it again, and sat shuddering and alone. Suddenly a faint sound, like the murmur of a breeze, reached her,–she looked up, but the wind had sunk, and the night was perfectly calm. The same sound recurring, as of a breeze sweeping past, made her turn her eyes in the direction from which it came, and, at some distance from her, she thought she beheld a human figure moving slowly along on the verge of the inclosure of the burial-ground. Though it did not seem approaching her, (but rather moving in a low circuit on the verge of her view), conceiving it must be Melmoth, she rose in expectation of his advancing to her, and, at this moment, the figure, turning and half-pausing, seemed to extend its arm towards her, and wave it once or twice, but whether with a motion or purpose of warning or repelling her, it was impossible to discover,–it then renewed its dim and silent progress, and the next moment the ruins hid it from her view. She had no time to muse on this singular appearance, for Melmoth was now at her side urging her to proceed. There was a chapel, he told her, attached to the ruins, but not like them in decay, where sacred ceremonies were still performed, and where the priest had promised to join them in a few moments.

"He is there before us," said Isidora, adverting to the figure she had seen; "I think I saw him."

"Saw whom?" said Melmoth, starting, and standing immoveable till his question was answered.

"I saw a figure," said Isidora, trembling, "I thought I saw a figure moving towards the ruin."

"You are mistaken," said Melmoth; but a moment after he added, "We ought to have been there before him."

And he hurried on with Isidora. Suddenly slackening his speed, he demanded, in a choked and indistinct voice, if she had ever heard any music precede his visits to her,–any sounds in the air.

"Never," was the answer.

"You are sure?"

"Perfectly sure."

At this moment they were ascending the fractured and rugged steps that led to the entrance of the chapel, now they passed under the dark and ivied porch,–now they entered the chapel, which, even in darkness, appeared to the eyes of Isidora ruinous and deserted.

"He has not yet arrived," said Melmoth, in a disturbed voice; "Wait there a moment."

And Isidora, enfeebled by terror beyond the power of resistance, or even entreaty, saw him depart without an effort to detain him. She felt as if the effort would be hopeless. Left thus alone, she glanced her eyes around, and a faint and watery moon-beam breaking at that moment through the heavy clouds, threw its light on the objects around her. There was a window, but the stained glass of its compartments, broken and discoloured, held rare and precarious place between the fluted shafts of stone. Ivy and moss darkened the fragments of glass, and clung round the clustered pillars. Beneath were the remains of an altar and crucifix, but they seemed like the rude work of the first hands that had ever been employed on such subjects. There was also a marble vessel, that seemed designed to contain holy water, but it was empty,–and there was a stone bench, on which Isidora sunk down in weariness, but without hope of rest.

She remains for a time contemplating the moon, until...

At that moment the moon, that had so faintly lit the chapel, sunk behind a cloud, and every thing was enveloped in darkness so profound, that Isidora did not recognize the figure of Melmoth till her hand was clasped in his, and his voice whispered,

"He is here – ready to unite us."

The long-protracted terrors of this bridal left her not a breath to utter a word withal, and she leaned on the arm that she felt, not in confidence, but for support. The place, the hour, the objects, all were hid in darkness. She heard a faint rustling as of the approach of another person,–she tried to catch certain words, but she knew not what they were,–she attempted also to speak, but she knew not what she said. All was mist and darkness with her,–she knew not what was muttered,–she felt not that the hand of Melmoth grasped hers,–but she felt that the hand that united them, and clasped their palms within his own, was as cold as that of death.

The Gothic expert will no doubt already have guessed what is only revealed to Isidora several chapters later, as she is being questioned by a priest of Inquisition.

"My examination!" repeated Isidora with surprise, but evidently without terror, "on what subject am I then to be examined?"

"On that of your inconceivable union with a being devoted

and accursed."

His voice was choked with horror, and he added,

"Daughter, are you then indeed the wife of–of–that being, whose name makes the flesh creep, and the hair stand on end?"

"I am."

"Who were the witnesses of your marriage, and what hand dared to bind yours with that unholy and unnatural bond?"

"There were no witnesses–we were wedded in darkness. I saw no form, but I thought I heard words uttered–I know I felt a hand place mine in Melmoth's–its touch was as cold as that of the dead."

"Oh complicated and mysterious horror!" said the priest, turning pale, and crossing himself with marks of unfeigned terror; he bowed his head on his arm for some time, and remained silent from unutterable emotion.

"Father," said Isidora at length, "you knew the hermit who lived amid the ruins of the monastery near our house,–he was a priest also,–he was a holy man, it was he who united us!"

Her voice trembled.

"Wretched victim!" groaned the priest, without raising his head, "you know not what you utter–that holy man is known to have died the very night preceding that of your dreadful union."

THE HAUNTED HOUSE

Haunted Houses have appeared in literature as far back as Roman times: Pliny the Younger, writing in the First Century A.D., tells the story of a house frequented by a chain-rattling ghost of the classic variety. The tradition is of an old house, often partly abandoned, sometimes completely, where an unexplained presence is felt or experienced. The story told will generally, but not always, reveal why, or by whom the building is haunted.

A Young Person's Guide to the Gothic

The first Gothic writers, as the earlier segments show, tend to want their **Settings** to be bigger and grander than a simple "house". There is plenty of haunting going on, but generally of **Castles** and **Abbeys**. An early example of an actual Haunted House in a Gothic novel is American author Nathaniel Hawthorne's *The House of the Seven Gables*, published in 1851. The book begins with a very brief introductory description.

> Halfway down a by-street of one of our New England towns stands a rusty wooden house, with seven acutely peaked gables, facing towards various points of the compass, and a huge, clustered chimney in the midst.

The house, we learn, was actually built on the site of an earlier one, whose owner was hanged for witchcraft. From the scaffold he cursed the man who took the land and went on to build a new house on the exact spot. The new house…

> …would include the home of the dead and buried wizard, and would thus afford the ghost of the latter a kind of privilege to haunt its new apartments.

Hawthorne soon provides a more detailed description of the new house, as it appeared when the building work was only just complete.

> There it rose, a little withdrawn from the line of the street, but in pride, not modesty. Its whole visible exterior was ornamented with quaint figures, conceived in the grotesqueness of a Gothic fancy, and drawn or stamped in the glittering plaster, composed of lime, pebbles, and bits of glass, with which the woodwork of the walls was overspread. On every side the seven gables pointed sharply towards the sky, and presented the aspect of a whole sisterhood of edifices, breathing through the spiracles of one great chimney. The many lattices, with their small, diamond-shaped panes, admitted the sunlight into hall and chamber, while, nevertheless, the second story,

projecting far over the base, and itself retiring beneath the third, threw a shadowy and thoughtful gloom into the lower rooms. Carved globes of wood were affixed under the jutting stories. Little spiral rods of iron beautified each of the seven peaks. On the triangular portion of the gable, that fronted next the street, was a dial, put up that very morning, and on which the sun was still marking the passage of the first bright hour in a history that was not destined to be all so bright.

The Addams Family would have been happy to move straight in, but it's the interior of the building that is important in this next extract. Its author, Edward Bulwer-Lytton, was a busy man, a politician as well as a prolific writer in many genres. We have him to thank for the notorious line "It was a dark and stormy night…" (the first words of his 1830 novel *Paul Clifford* which are now regarded as a cliché of bad, over-dramatic writing) as well as the even more famous phrase "the pen is mightier than the sword" (which comes in a play he wrote about Cardinal Richelieu). This story, *The Haunters and the Haunted*, was published in 1859 and begins by introducing the familiar Gothic character of the brave and curious investigator who hears about a haunted house and decides to spend the night there…

I communicated my name and my business frankly. I said I heard the house was considered to be haunted, that I had a strong desire to examine a house with so equivocal a reputation; that I should be greatly obliged if he would allow me to hire it, though only for a night. I was willing to pay for that privilege whatever he might be inclined to ask.

"Sir," said Mr. J——, with great courtesy, "the house is at your service, for as short or as long a time as you please. Rent is out of the question,—the obligation will be on my side should you be able to discover the cause of the strange phenomena which at present deprive it of all value. I cannot let it, for I cannot even get a servant to keep it in order or answer the door. Unluckily the house is haunted, if I may use that expression, not only by night, but by day; though at night the disturbances are of a more unpleasant and sometimes of a more alarming character. The poor old woman who died in it three weeks ago was a pauper whom I took out of a workhouse; for in her childhood she had been known to some of my family, and had once been in such good circumstances that she had rented that house of my uncle. She was a woman of superior education and strong mind, and was the only person I could ever induce to remain in the house. Indeed, since her death, which was sudden, and the coroner's inquest, which gave it a notoriety in the neighbourhood, I have so despaired of finding any person to take charge of the house, much more a tenant, that I would willingly let it rent free for a year to anyone who would pay its rates and taxes."

"How long is it since the house acquired this sinister character?"

"That I can scarcely tell you, but very many years since. The old woman I spoke of, said it was haunted when she rented it between thirty and forty years ago.

"Have you never had a curiosity yourself to pass a night in that house?"

"Yes. I passed not a night, but three hours in broad daylight alone in that house. My curiosity is not satisfied, but it is quenched. I have no desire to renew the experiment. You cannot complain, you see, sir, that I am not sufficiently candid; and unless your interest be exceedingly eager and your nerves unusually strong, I honestly add, that I advise you NOT to pass a night in that house.

"My interest *is* exceedingly keen," said I; "and though only a coward will boast of his nerves in situations wholly unfamiliar to him, yet my nerves have been seasoned in such variety of danger that I have the right to rely on them,—even in a haunted house."

Mr. J—— said very little more; he took the keys of the house out of his bureau, gave them to me,—and, thanking him cordially for his frankness, and his urbane concession to my wish, I carried off my prize.

A Young Person's Guide to the Gothic

The narrator sends his servant (F——) ahead to prepare the house for them to spend the night, then joins him later.

I reached the house, knocked, and my servant opened with a cheerful smile.

We did not stay long in the drawing-rooms,—in fact, they felt so damp and so chilly that I was glad to get to the fire upstairs. We locked the doors of the drawing-rooms,—a precaution which, I should observe, we had taken with all the rooms we had searched below. The bedroom my servant had selected for me was the best on the floor,—a large one, with two windows fronting the street. The four-posted bed, which took up no inconsiderable space, was opposite to the fire, which burned clear and bright; a door in the wall to the left, between the bed and the window, communicated with the room which my servant appropriated to himself. This last was a small room with a sofa bed, and had no communication with the landing place,—no other door but that which conducted to the bedroom I was to occupy. On either side of my fireplace was a cupboard without locks, flush with the wall, and covered with the same dull-brown paper. We examined these cupboards,—only hooks to suspend female dresses, nothing else; we sounded the walls,—evidently solid, the outer walls of the building. Having finished the survey of these apartments, warmed myself a few moments, and lighted my cigar, I then, still accompanied by F——, went forth to complete my reconnoitre. In the landing place there was another door; it was closed firmly.

"Sir," said my servant, in surprise, "I unlocked this door with all the others when I first came; it cannot have got locked from the inside, for—"

Before he had finished his sentence, the door, which neither of us then was touching, opened quietly of itself. We looked at each other a single instant. The same thought seized both,— some human agency might be detected here. I rushed in first, my servant followed. A small, blank, dreary room without furniture; a few empty boxes and hampers in a corner; a small window; the shutters closed; not even a fireplace; no other door but that by which we had entered; no carpet on the floor, and the floor seemed very old, uneven, worm-eaten, mended here and there, as was shown by the whiter patches on the wood; but no living being, and no visible place in which a living being could have hidden. As we stood gazing round, the door by which we had entered closed as quietly as it had before opened; we were imprisoned.

As you can imagine, the adventure has only just begun.

THE FOREST

How many modern horror films have taken parties of campers into the woods and done nasty things to them? Harry Potter and his friends have a number of adventures involving the Forbidden Forest. Tolkien's Mirkwood is home to nests of flesh-eating giant spiders in *The Hobbit*. Our fear of the **Forest** goes back to pre-historic times, when woods and jungles were full of dangerous predators. Certainly the idea of woodland as a place of darkness and threat entered literature well before coming to flourish in the Gothic tradition. Famous Italian writer Dante begins his epic poem *The Divine Comedy* (written between 1308 and 1321, telling the story of a journey through Hell to Heaven), in a dark wood where he has lost his way. He uses words like "wild" and "harsh" to describe a terrifying situation. For Dante the **Forest**, as well as being a place of fear, is a borderland, something that has to be crossed, as it is for Bilbo Baggins and his companions in *The Hobbit*. It can play that border role in the Gothic too, but just as often it's simply nature's version of the **Castle**.

Ann Radcliffe actually gave one of her Gothic novels the title *The Romance of the Forest* (published in 1791). Near the start of the book La Motte (whom we've actually met before, in the **Ruins** segment) and his family are in a carriage being driven by their Loyal Retainer Peter, and find themselves in the woods at dusk.

It was now near sun-set, and, the prospect being closed on all sides by the forest, La Motte began to have apprehensions that his servant had mistaken the way. The road, if a road it could be called, which afforded only a slight track upon the grass, was sometimes over-run by luxuriant vegetation, and sometimes obscured by the deep shades, and Peter at length stopped uncertain of the way. La Motte, who dreaded being benighted in a scene so wild and solitary as this forest, and whose apprehensions of banditti were very sanguine, ordered him to proceed at any rate, and, if he found no track, to endeavour to gain a more open part of the forest. With these orders, Peter again set forwards, but having proceeded some way, and his views being still confined by woody glades and forest walks, he began to despair of extricating himself, and stopped for further orders. The sun was now set, but, as La Motte looked anxiously from the window, he observed upon the vivid glow of the western horizon, some dark towers rising from among the trees at a little distance, and ordered Peter to drive towards them. "If they belong to a monastery," said he, "we may probably gain admittance for the night."

The carriage drove along under the shade of melancholy boughs, through which the evening twilight, which yet coloured the air, diffused a solemnity that vibrated in thrilling sensations upon the hearts of the travellers.

It sounds like they are properly lost. Here is Radcliffe again, in her novel *The Italian* (1797), using the **Forest** to inspire fear on a journey and reinforce her **Heroine's** sense of isolation. The Forest Setting cuts her characters off from the outside world, leaving them prey to the evil that shelters in the darkness beneath the trees.

The evening of the second day was drawing on, when her guards drew near the forest, which she had long observed in the distance, spreading over the many-rising steeps of the Garganus. They entered by a track, a road it could not be called, which led among oaks and gigantic chestnuts, apparently the growth of centuries, and so thickly interwoven, that their branches formed a canopy which seldom admitted the sky. The gloom which they threw around, and the thickets of cystus, juniper, and lenticus, which flourished beneath the shade, gave a character of fearful wildness to the scene.

Having reached an eminence, where the trees were more thinly scattered, Ellena perceived the forests spreading on all sides among hills and valleys, and descending towards the Adriatic, which bounded the distance in front. The coast, bending into a bay, was rocky and bold. Lofty pinnacles, wooded to their summits, rose over the shores, and cliffs of naked marble of such gigantic proportions, that they were awful even at a distance, obtruded themselves far into the waves, breasting their eternal fury. Beyond the margin of the coast, as far as the eye could reach, appeared pointed mountains, darkened with forests, rising ridge over ridge in many successions. Ellena, as she surveyed this wild scenery, felt as if she was going into eternal banishment from society. She was tranquil, but it was with the quietness of exhausted grief, not of resignation; and she looked back upon the past, and awaited the future, with a kind of out-breathed despair.

At least for Ellena the **Forest** doesn't actually come alive. These next extracts come from *The Wendigo*, a story published in 1910 involving a party of men hunting moose in northern Canada. It is a superb evocation of the wilderness, and how overwhelming we humans can find it. We join the tale with Simpson, a Scottish student, and his local Canadian guide Défago camped by a lake. The latter has gone for a last look around before dark, leaving Simpson alone.

The dusk rapidly deepened; the glades grew dark; the crackling of the fire and the wash of little waves along the rocky lake shore were the only sounds audible. The wind had dropped with the sun, and in all that vast world of branches nothing stirred. Any moment, it seemed, the woodland gods, who are to be worshipped in silence and loneliness, might stretch their mighty and terrific outlines among the trees. In front, through doorways pillared by huge straight stems, lay the stretch of Fifty Island Water, a crescent-shaped lake some fifteen miles from tip to tip, and perhaps five miles across where they were camped.

The beauty of the scene was strangely uplifting. Simpson smoked the fish and burnt his fingers into the bargain in his efforts to enjoy it and at the same time tend the frying pan and the fire. Yet, ever at the back of his thoughts, lay that other aspect of the wilderness: the indifference to human life, the merciless spirit of desolation which took no note of man. The sense of his utter loneliness, now that even Défago had gone, came close as he looked about him and listened for the sound of his companion's returning footsteps.

There was pleasure in the sensation, yet with it a perfectly comprehensible alarm. And instinctively the thought stirred in him: "What should I—could I, do—if anything happened and he did not come back—?"

The Canadian does return, and together they eat the food Simpson has prepared. The Scotsman is being made increasingly uncomfortable by their isolation, and wants to lighten the mood.

"Sing us a song, Défago, if you're not too tired," he asked; "one of those old voyageur songs you sang the other night." He handed his tobacco pouch to the guide and then filled his own pipe, while the Canadian, nothing loth, sent his light voice across the lake in one of those plaintive, almost melancholy shanties with which lumbermen and trappers lessen the burden of their labour. The sound travelled pleasantly over the water, but the forest at their backs seemed to swallow it down with a single gulp that permitted neither echo nor resonance.

It was in the middle of the third verse that Simpson noticed something unusual—something that brought his thoughts back with a rush from faraway scenes. A curious change had come into the man's voice. Even before he knew what it was, uneasiness caught him, and looking up quickly, he saw that Défago, though still singing, was peering about him into the Bush, as though he heard or saw something. His voice grew fainter—dropped to a hush—then ceased altogether. The same instant, with a movement amazingly alert, he started to his feet and stood upright—sniffing the air. Like a dog scenting game, he drew the air into his nostrils in short, sharp breaths, turning quickly as he did so in all directions, and finally "pointing" down the lake shore, eastwards. It was a performance unpleasantly suggestive and at the same time singularly dramatic. Simpson's heart fluttered disagreeably as he watched it.

"Lord, man! How you made me jump!" he exclaimed, on his feet beside him the same instant, and peering over his shoulder into the sea of darkness. "What's up? Are you frightened—?"

Even before the question was out of his mouth he knew it was foolish, for any man with a pair of eyes in his head could see that the Canadian had turned white down to his very gills. Not even sunburn and the glare of the fire could hide that.

The student felt himself trembling a little, weakish in the knees. "What's up?" he repeated quickly. "D'you smell moose? Or anything queer, anything—wrong?" He lowered his voice instinctively.

The forest pressed round them with its encircling wall; the nearer tree stems gleamed like bronze in the firelight; beyond that—blackness, and, so far as he could tell, a silence of death. Just behind them a passing puff of wind lifted a single leaf, looked at it, then laid it softly down again without disturbing the rest of the covey. It seemed as if a million invisible causes had combined just to produce that single visible effect. Other life pulsed about them—and was gone.

It's pretty clear there's something out there. To find out what, you'll need to track down the story and read it. Its author, Algernon Blackwood, wrote a large number of excellent supernatural tales and is brilliant at slowly building an atmosphere of threatening strangeness. As well as this one, I can recommend *The Willows*, with weird events on a fishing trip on the river Danube, and his take on **Werewolves** in *The Camp of the Dog*. His "short" stories do tend not to be especially short, though.

A Young Person's Guide to the Gothic

Two: SCENERY

If the **Setting** is your bedroom, **Scenery** is the furniture and wallpaper. (Don't miss the classic story about wallpaper – yes, wallpaper – in the **Characters** section.) If the Setting is a **Castle**, Scenery might be a **Tower**, a **Haunted Room** or the **Dungeon**; in the case of the Gothic novels, it will probably include all three. Much of the time, therefore, the simplest way to think of Scenery is as an extension of Setting.

Gothic Scenery works to create an atmosphere of gloom, mystery, and suspense. There is an awful lot of darkness, for obvious reasons. It also tends to be extreme and excessive, because as we saw in the introduction, the Gothic is all about being extreme and excessive (or sublime). We have already been introduced, in earlier chapters, to the sort of over-the-top wilderness landscapes Ann Radcliffe placed around her Castle Settings. Gothic interiors are huge, empty and echoing, or old and unpleasant, dusty and musty, dripping and dank. Have I mentioned the dark?

Much of this Scenery is engineered to present **Heroes** and **Heroines** with obstacles: maze-like Castle-corridors, for instance, and winding **Forest**-trails for getting lost; or to provide **Villains** with tools to terrify their victims: Towers for **Imprisonment** and shadowy corners to jump out of. It is rare to find a door that isn't locked, the obvious exceptions being doors that swing open when nobody is there, or slam shut. Scenery plays an almost active role in the Gothic story-line. This means that as well as being an extension of the Setting, elements of Scenery bleed through into the next section: **Plot Devices**.

It's all connected!

THE TOWER

In *The Castle of Otranto* the hero is briefly held captive in the **Castle's** "black tower". The first Gothic **Towers** were often places of **Imprisonment**; readers of the time would have been very well acquainted with the story of the "Princes in the Tower", famously held and probably murdered at the Tower of London.

Much of the action of Ann Radcliffe's *A Sicilian Romance* (1790) takes place at the **Castle** of the Mazzini family. The story is set in the Sixteenth Century, and already the Castle is partly **Ruined**. The south Tower has long been abandoned and shut up, and there are rumours that it is haunted. Late one night Julia, one of two sisters who are key characters in the book, is on her way to bed and looks out of a window to admire the moonlight.

> In that situation she had not long remained, when she perceived a light faintly flash through a casement in the uninhabited part of the castle. A sudden tremor seized her, and she with difficulty supported herself. In a few moments it disappeared, and soon after a figure, bearing a lamp, proceeded from an obscure door belonging to the south tower; and stealing along the outside of the castle walls, turned round the southern angle, by which it was afterwards hid from the view.

Efforts are made to watch and explore the Tower, but locked doors and the obstructive attitude of the Castle's owner (father of the sisters and the **Villain**) make things difficult. More evidence of haunting encourages the two sisters, their Governess ("madame") and their brother Ferdinand to continue the search.

> The castle was buried in sleep when Ferdinand again joined his sisters in madame's apartment. With anxious curiosity they

followed him to the chamber. The room was hung with tapestry. Ferdinand carefully sounded the wall which communicated with the southern buildings. From one part of it a sound was returned, which convinced him there was something less solid than stone. He removed the tapestry, and behind it appeared, to his inexpressible satisfaction, a small door. With a hand trembling through eagerness, he undrew the bolts, and was rushing forward, when he perceived that a lock withheld his passage. The keys of madame and his sisters were applied in vain, and he was compelled to submit to disappointment at the very moment when he congratulated himself on success, for he had with him no means of forcing the door.

He stood gazing on the door, and inwardly lamenting, when a low hollow sound was heard from beneath. Emilia and Julia seized his arm; and almost sinking with apprehension, listened in profound silence. A footstep was distinctly heard, as if passing through the apartment below, after which all was still. Ferdinand rushed on to the door, and again tried to burst his way, but it resisted all the efforts of his strength. The ladies now rejoiced in that circumstance which they so lately lamented; for the sounds had renewed their terror, and though the night passed without further disturbance, their fears were very little abated.

Ferdinand, whose mind was wholly occupied with wonder, could with difficulty await the return of night. Emilia and Julia were scarcely less impatient. They counted the minutes as they passed; and when the family retired to rest, hastened with palpitating hearts to the apartment of madame. They were soon after joined by Ferdinand, who brought with him tools for cutting away the lock of the door. They paused a few moments in the chamber in fearful silence, but no sound disturbed the stillness of night. Ferdinand applied a knife to the door, and in a short time separated the lock. The door yielded, and disclosed a large and gloomy gallery. He took a light. Emilia and Julia, fearful of remaining in the chamber, resolved to accompany him, and each seizing an arm of madame, they followed in silence. The gallery was in many parts falling to decay, the ceiling was broke, and the window-shutters shattered, which, together with the dampness of the walls, gave the place an air of wild desolation.

They passed lightly on, for their steps ran in whispering echoes through the gallery, and often did Julia cast a fearful glance around.

The gallery terminated in a large old stair-case, which led to a hall below; on the left appeared several doors which seemed to lead to separate apartments. While they hesitated which course to pursue, a light flashed faintly up the stair-case, and in a moment after passed away; at the same time was heard the sound of a distant footstep. Ferdinand drew his sword and sprang forward; his companions, screaming with terror, ran back to madame's apartment.

Ferdinand descended a large vaulted hall; he crossed it towards a low arched door, which was left half open, and through which streamed a ray of light. The door opened upon a narrow winding passage; he entered, and the light retiring, was quickly lost in the windings of the place. Still he went on. The passage grew narrower, and the frequent fragments of loose stone made it now difficult to proceed. A low door closed the avenue, resembling that by which he had entered. He opened it, and discovered a square room, from whence rose a winding stair-case, which led up the south tower of the castle. Ferdinand paused to listen; the sound of steps was ceased, and all was profoundly silent. A door on the right attracted his notice; he tried to open it, but it was fastened. He concluded, therefore, that the person, if indeed a human being it was that bore the light he had seen, had passed up the tower. After a momentary hesitation, he determined to ascend the stair-case, but its ruinous condition made this an adventure of some difficulty. The steps were decayed and broken, and the looseness of the stones rendered a footing very insecure. Impelled by an irresistible curiosity, he was undismayed, and began the ascent. He had not proceeded very far, when the stones of a step which his foot had just quitted, loosened by his weight, gave way; and dragging with them those adjoining, formed a chasm in the stair-case that terrified even Ferdinand, who was left tottering on the suspended half of the steps, in momentary expectation of falling to the bottom with the stone on which he rested. In the terror which this occasioned, he attempted to save himself by catching at a kind of beam which projected over the stairs, when the lamp dropped from his hand, and he was left in total darkness. Terror now usurped the place of every other interest, and he was utterly perplexed how to proceed. He feared to go on, lest the steps above, as infirm as those below, should yield to his weight;—to return was impracticable, for the darkness precluded the possibility of discovering a means.

Ferdinand is rescued from this particular moment of peril, without being able to learn more about the haunting. Many adventures follow before we discover - spoiler alert - that in fact the **Villain** has imprisoned his first wife (mother of the siblings, who everybody thinks is dead) in the south **Tower** so he could marry someone else. The Tower has been a prison all along, and all the evidence of "haunting" simply follows from this secret presence in the **Castle**. This is what I call the Scooby Doo school of Gothic – which Ann Radcliffe pioneered – where what look like supernatural events provide much of the "terror" throughout the story, but turn out at the end to have a rational explanation. (In the original *Scooby Doo* cartoons the ghosts and monsters were always revealed to have been faked by criminals or other evil but human Villains.)

THE DUNGEON

The Gothic **Dungeon** is a terrible place, often found underground beneath a Castle or **Abbey**. In the Harry Potter books we are not given much detail on the prison of Azkaban (although the Dementors, its terrifyingly Gothic guardians, are very well described), but we do know it is a place of horror.

Agnes is a key character in Matthew Lewis' *The Monk*, a young noblewoman forced to become a nun by her parents, despite the love she has for Don Raymond. Don Raymond sneaks into the convent (disguised as a gardener!); the young couple lose control and share a moment of passion. Agnes becomes pregnant. The Prioress of the convent decides Agnes must be punished for her sin and tells her of her fate.

"Beneath these Vaults there exist Prisons, intended to receive such criminals as yourself: Artfully is their entrance concealed, and She who enters them, must resign all hopes of liberty. Thither must you now be conveyed. Food shall be supplied you, but not sufficient for the indulgence of appetite: You shall have just enough to keep together body and soul, and its quality shall be the simplest and coarsest. Weep, Daughter, weep, and moisten your bread with your tears: God knows that you have ample cause for sorrow! Chained down in one of these secret dungeons, shut out from the world and light for ever, with no comfort but religion, no society but repentance, thus must you groan away the remainder of your days."

Agnes later describes her life in the Dungeon, including the birth and death of her baby.

When my senses returned, I found myself in silence and solitude. I heard not even the retiring footsteps of my Persecutors. All was hushed, and all was dreadful! I had been thrown upon the bed of Straw: The heavy Chain which I had already eyed with terror, was wound around my waist, and fastened me to the Wall. A Lamp glimmering with dull, melancholy rays through my dungeon, permitted my distinguishing all its horrors: It was separated from the Cavern by a low and irregular Wall of Stone: A large Chasm was left open in it which formed the entrance, for door there was none. A leaden Crucifix was in front of my straw Couch. A tattered rug lay near me, as did also a Chaplet of Beads; and not far from me stood a pitcher of water, and a wicker Basket containing a small loaf, and a bottle of oil to supply my Lamp.

With a despondent eye did I examine this scene of suffering: When I reflected that I was doomed to pass in it the remainder of my days, my heart was rent with bitter anguish. I had once been taught to look forward to a lot so different! At one time my prospects had appeared so bright, so flattering! Now all was lost to me. Friends, comfort, society, happiness, in one moment I was deprived of all! Dead to the world, Dead to pleasure, I lived to nothing but the sense of misery. How fair did that world seem to me, from which I was for ever excluded! How many loved objects did it contain, whom I never should behold again! As I threw a look of terror round my prison, as I shrunk from the cutting wind which howled through my subterraneous dwelling, the change seemed so striking, so abrupt, that I doubted its reality.

My mental anguish, and the dreadful scenes in which I had been an Actress, advanced the period of my labour. In solitude and misery, abandoned by all, unassisted by Art, uncomforted by Friendship, with pangs which if witnessed would have touched the hardest heart, was I delivered of my wretched burthen. It came alive into the world; But I knew not how to treat it, or by what means to preserve its existence. I could only bathe it with tears, warm it in my bosom, and offer up prayers for its safety. I was soon deprived of this mournful employment: The want of proper attendance, my ignorance how to nurse it, the bitter cold of the dungeon, and the unwholesome air which inflated its lungs, terminated my sweet Babe's short and painful existence. It expired in a few hours after its birth, and I witnessed its death with agonies which beggar all description.

But my grief was unavailing. My Infant was no more; nor could all my sighs impart to its little tender frame the breath of a moment. I rent my winding-sheet, and wrapped in it my lovely Child. I placed it on my bosom, its soft arm folded round my neck, and its pale cold cheek resting upon mine. Thus did its lifeless limbs repose, while I covered it with kisses, talked to it, wept, and moaned over it without remission, day or night.

Camilla entered my prison regularly once every twenty-four hours, to bring me food. In spite of her flinty nature, She could not behold this spectacle unmoved. She feared that grief so excessive would at length turn my brain, and in truth I was not always in my proper senses. From a principle of compassion She urged me to permit the Corse to be buried: But to this I never would consent. I vowed not to part with it while I had life: Its presence was my only comfort, and no persuasion could induce me to give it up. It soon became a mass of putridity, and to every eye was a loathsome and disgusting Object; To every eye but a Mother's. In vain did human feelings bid me recoil from this emblem of mortality with repugnance: I withstood, and vanquished that repugnance. I persisted in holding my Infant to my bosom, in lamenting it, loving it, adoring it! Hour after hour have I passed upon my sorry Couch, contemplating what had once been my Child: I endeavoured to retrace its features through the livid corruption, with which they were overspread: During my confinement this sad occupation was my only delight; and at that time Worlds should not have bribed me to give it up.

Once, and once only, the Prioress visited me in my dungeon. She then treated me with the most unrelenting cruelty: She loaded me with reproaches, taunted me with my frailty, and when I implored her mercy, told me to ask it of heaven, since I deserved none on earth. She even gazed upon my lifeless Infant without emotion; and when She left me, I heard her charge Camilla to increase the hardships of my Captivity.

Thus did I drag on a miserable existence. Far from growing familiar with my prison, I beheld it every moment with new horror. The cold seemed more piercing and bitter, the air more thick and pestilential. My frame became weak, feverish, and emaciated. I was unable to rise from the bed of Straw, and exercise my limbs in the narrow limits, to which the length of my chain permitted me to move. Though exhausted, faint, and weary, I trembled to profit by the approach of Sleep: My slumbers were constantly interrupted by some obnoxious Insect crawling over me.

Sometimes I felt the bloated Toad, hideous and pampered with the poisonous vapours of the dungeon, dragging his loathsome length along my bosom: Sometimes the quick cold Lizard roused me leaving his slimy track upon my face, and entangling itself in the tresses of my wild and matted hair: Often have I at waking found my fingers ringed with the long worms which bred in the corrupted flesh of my Infant. At such times I shrieked with terror and disgust, and while I shook off the reptile, trembled with all a Woman's weakness.

Will she be rescued?

And will the prisoner in our next extract? *The Pit and the Pendulum* is one of the most famous Gothic tales by American author Edgar Allan Poe, published in 1842. Poe, who was born in 1809 and died young, at forty, was enormously influential in the development of the Gothic short-story. He was orphaned at two and had a difficult relationship with strict foster parents. Later came major problems with alcohol (which seems most likely to have caused his sudden death) and his child bride died of tuberculosis aged twenty four. All in all, he led a pretty Gothic life. If you read a few of his stories, you will realise he was obsessed with the idea of being buried, or entombed, alive. I can recommend (as well as this story and one you can read in full later in this book) *The Tell-Tale Heart*, which is all about murder and guilt, and the plague story *The Masque of the Red Death*. There are plenty more. Here the narrator has been condemned to death by the Spanish **Inquisition** and after being carried "down—down—still down—till a hideous dizziness oppressed me at the mere idea of the interminableness of the descent" describes exploring his pitch dark prison.

I thrust my arms wildly above and around me in all directions. I felt nothing; yet dreaded to move a step, lest

I should be impeded by the walls of a tomb. Perspiration burst from every pore, and stood in cold big beads upon my forehead. The agony of suspense grew at length intolerable, and I cautiously moved forward, with my arms extended, and my eyes straining from their sockets, in the hope of catching some faint ray of light. I proceeded for many paces; but still all was blackness and vacancy. I breathed more freely. It seemed evident that mine was not, at least, the most hideous of fates.

And now, as I still continued to step cautiously onward, there came thronging upon my recollection a thousand vague rumours of the horrors of Toledo. Of the dungeons there had been strange things narrated—fables I had always deemed them—but yet strange, and too ghastly to repeat, save in a whisper. Was I left to perish of starvation in this subterranean world of darkness; or what fate, perhaps even more fearful, awaited me? That the result would be death, and a death of more than customary bitterness, I knew too well the character of my judges to doubt. The mode and the hour were all that occupied or distracted me.

My outstretched hands at length encountered some solid obstruction. It was a wall, seemingly of stone masonry—very smooth, slimy, and cold. I followed it up; stepping with all the careful distrust with which certain antique narratives had inspired me. This process, however, afforded me no means of ascertaining the dimensions of my dungeon; as I might make its circuit, and return to the point whence I set out, without being aware of the fact; so perfectly uniform seemed the wall. I therefore sought the knife which had been in my pocket, when led into the inquisitorial chamber; but it was gone; my clothes had been exchanged for a wrapper of coarse serge. I had thought of forcing the blade in some minute crevice of the masonry, so as to identify my point of departure. The difficulty, nevertheless, was but trivial; although, in the disorder of my fancy, it seemed at first insuperable. I tore a part of the hem from the robe and placed the fragment at full length, and at right angles to the wall. In groping my way around the prison, I could not fail to encounter this rag upon completing the circuit. So, at least I thought: but I had not counted upon the extent of the dungeon, or upon my own weakness. The ground was moist and slippery. I staggered onward for some time, when I stumbled and fell. My excessive fatigue induced me to remain prostrate; and sleep soon overtook me as I lay.

Nothing in this **Dungeon** is as it seems, with the Inquisition trying ever more imaginative ways of killing their prisoner. Tripping over and rats (yes, rats) both save the narrator's life, but only for long enough for the next murderous mechanism to be set in motion.

The HAUNTED ROOM

The **Haunted Room** almost qualifies as a **Setting**. Located in a **Castle, Abbey** or **Haunted House**, it is the centre of supernatural disturbance and so often the key to whatever story is being told. It can also work, sometimes, as a **Plot Device**, acting as a test or challenge for the Hero.

Clara Reeve was the first writer to follow Walpole's idea for a new type of novel, with *The Old English Baron*, first published (under a different title) in 1777. Her Hero Edmund has to prove his courage by spending three nights in a Castle's haunted "apartment".

He then took a survey of his chamber; the furniture, by long neglect, was decayed and dropping to pieces; the bed was devoured by the moths, and occupied by the rats, who had built their nests there with impunity for many generations. The bedding was very damp, for the rain had forced its way through the ceiling; he determined, therefore, to lie down in his clothes. There were two doors on the further side of the room, with keys in them; being not at all sleepy, he resolved to examine them; he attempted one lock, and opened it with ease; he went into a large dining-room, the furniture of which was in the same tattered condition; out of this was a large closet with some books in it, and hung round with coats of arms, with genealogies and alliances of the house; he amused himself here some minutes, and then returned into the bed-chamber.

He recollected the other door, and resolved to see where it led to; the key was rusted into the lock, and resisted his attempts; he set the lamp on the ground, and, exerting all his strength, opened the door, and at the same instant the wind of it blew out the lamp, and left him in utter darkness. At the same moment he heard a hollow rustling noise, like that of a person coming through a narrow passage…

Will Edmund survive the challenge?

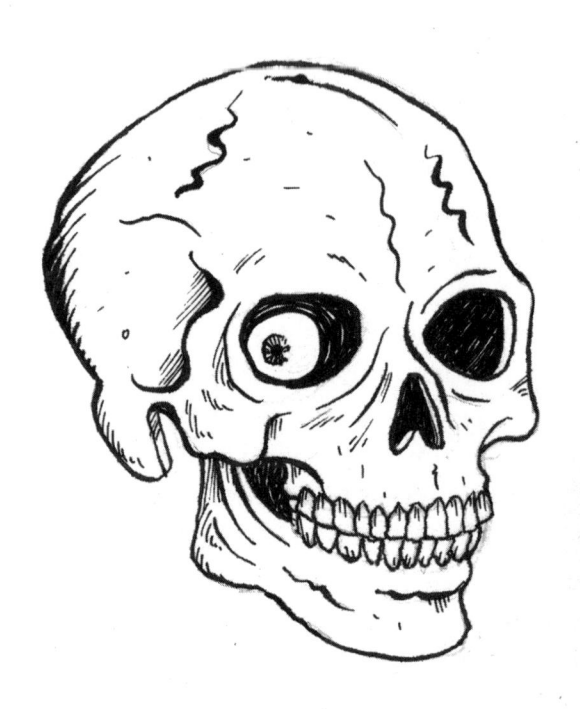

THE ROOM OF THE EVIL THOUGHT

ELIA PEATTIE

I like this story because although we are still with **Haunted Room** as **Scenery**, the room is very different to the usual cob-webbed chambers, and no ghost actually appears, or even makes spooky noises. Even so, American writer Elia Peattie's story, published in 1898, is pretty terrifying.

They called it the room of the Evil Thought. It was really the pleasantest room in the house, and when the place had been used as the rectory, was the minister's study. It looked out on a mournful clump of larches, such as may often be seen in the old-fashioned yards in Michigan, and these threw a tender gloom over the apartment.

There was a wide fireplace in the room, and it had been the young minister's habit to sit there hours and hours, staring ahead of him at the fire, and smoking moodily. The replenishing of the fire and of his pipe, it was said, would afford him occupation all the day long, and that was how it came about that his parochial duties were neglected so that, little by little, the people became dissatisfied with him, though he was an eloquent young man, who could send his congregation away drunk on his influence. However, the calmer pulsed among his parish began to whisper that it was indeed the influence of the young minister and not that of the Holy Ghost which they felt, and it was finally decided that neither animal magnetism nor hypnotism were good substitutes for religion. And so they let him go.

The new rector moved into a smart brick house on the other side of the church, and gave receptions and dinner parties, and was punctilious about making his calls. The people therefore liked him very much—so much that they raised the debt on the church and bought a chime of bells, in their enthusiasm. Everyone was lighter of heart than under the ministration of the previous rector. A burden appeared to be lifted from the community. True, there were a few who confessed the new man did not give them the food for thought which the old one had done, but, then, the former rector had made them uncomfortable! He had not only made them conscious of the sins of which they were already guilty, but also of those for which they had the latent capacity. A strange and fatal man, whom women loved to their sorrow, and whom simple men could not understand! It was generally agreed that the parish was well rid of him.

"He was a genius," said the people in commiseration. The word was an uncomplimentary epithet with them.

When the Hanscoms moved in the house which had been the old rectory, they gave Grandma Hanscom the room with the fireplace. Grandma was well pleased. The roaring fire warmed her heart as well as her chill old body, and she wept with weak joy when she looked at the larches, because they reminded her of the house she had lived in when she was first married. All the forenoon of the first day she was busy putting things away in bureau drawers and closets, but by afternoon she was ready to sit down in her high-backed rocker and enjoy the comforts of her room.

She nodded a bit before the fire, as she usually did after luncheon, and then she awoke with an awful start and sat staring before her with such a look in her gentle, filmy old eyes as had never been there before. She did not move, except to rock slightly, and the Thought grew and grew till her face was disguised as by some hideous mask of tragedy.

By and by the children came pounding at the door.

"Oh, grandma, let us in, please. We want to see your new room, and mamma gave us some ginger cookies on a plate, and we want to give some to you."

The door gave way under their assaults, and the three little ones stood peeping in, waiting for permission to enter. But it did not seem to be their grandma—their own dear grandma—who arose and tottered toward them in fierce haste, crying:

"Away, away! Out of my sight! Out of my sight before I do the thing I want to do! Such a terrible thing! Send someone to me quick, children, children! Send someone quick!"

They fled with feet shod with fear, and their mother came, and Grandma Hanscom sank down and clung about her skirts and sobbed:

"Tie me, Miranda. Make me fast to the bed or the wall. Get someone to watch me. For I want to do an awful thing!"

They put the trembling old creature in bed, and she raved there all the night long and cried out to be held, and to be kept from doing the fearful thing, whatever it was—for she never said what it was.

The next morning someone suggested taking her in the sitting-room where she would be with the family. So they laid her on the sofa, hemmed around with cushions, and before long she was her quiet self again, though exhausted, naturally, with the tumult of the previous night. Now and then, as the children played about her, a shadow crept over her face—a shadow as of cold remembrance—and then the perplexed tears followed.

When she seemed as well as ever they put her back in her room. But though the fire glowed and the lamp burned, as soon as ever she was alone they heard her shrill cries ringing to them that the Evil Thought had come again. So Hal, who was home from college, carried her up to his room, which she seemed to like very well. Then he went down to have a smoke before grandma's fire.

The next morning he was absent from breakfast. They thought he might have gone for an early walk, and waited for him a few minutes. Then his sister went to the room that looked upon the larches, and found him dressed and pacing the floor with a face set and stern. He had not been in bed at all, as she saw at once. His eyes were bloodshot, his face stricken as if with old age or sin or—but she could not make it out. When he saw her he sank in a chair and covered his face with his hands, and between the trembling fingers she could see drops of perspiration on his forehead.

"Hal!" she cried, "Hal, what is it?"

But for answer he threw his arms about the little table and clung to it, and looked at her with tortured eyes, in which she fancied she saw a gleam of hate. She ran, screaming, from the room, and her father came and went up to him and laid his hands on the boy's shoulders. And then a fearful thing happened. All the family saw it. There could be no mistake. Hal's hands found their way with frantic eagerness toward his father's throat as if they would choke him, and the look in his eyes was so like a madman's that his father raised his fist and felled him as he used to fell men years before in the college fights, and then dragged him into the sitting-room and wept over him.

By evening, however, Hal was all right, and the family said it must have been a fever,—perhaps from over study,—at which Hal covertly smiled. But his father was still too anxious about him to let him out of his sight, so he put him on a cot in his room, and thus it chanced that the mother and Grace concluded to sleep together downstairs.

The two women made a sort of festival of it, and drank little cups of chocolate before the fire, and undid and brushed their brown braids, and smiled at each other, understandingly, with that sweet intuitive sympathy which women have, and Grace told her mother a number of things which she had been waiting for just such an auspicious occasion to confide.

But the larches were noisy and cried out with wild voices, and the flame of the fire grew blue and swirled about in the draught sinuously, so that a chill crept upon the two. Something cold appeared to envelop them—such a chill as pleasure voyagers feel when a berg steals beyond Newfoundland and glows blue and threatening upon their ocean path.

Then came something else which was not cold, but hot as the flames of hell—and they saw red, and stared at each other with maddened eyes, and then ran together from the room and clasped in close embrace safe beyond the fatal place, and thanked God they had not done the thing that they dared not speak of—the thing which suddenly came to them to do.

So they called it the room of the Evil Thought. They could not account for it. They avoided the thought of it, being healthy and happy folk. But none entered it more. The door was locked.

One day, Hal, reading the paper, came across a paragraph concerning the young minister who had once lived there, and who had thought and written there and so influenced the lives of those about him that they remembered him even while they disapproved.

"He cut a man's throat on board ship for Australia," said he, "and then he cut his own, without fatal effect—and jumped overboard, and so ended it. What a strange thing!"

Then they all looked at one another with subtle looks, and a shadow fell upon them and stayed the blood at their hearts.

The next week the room of the Evil Thought was pulled down to make way for a pansy bed, which is quite gay and innocent, and blooms all the better because the larches, with their eternal murmuring, have been laid low and carted away to the sawmill.

THE GRAVEYARD

Buffy (the Vampire Slayer in the cult TV series of the late 1990s and early 2000s), when not distracted by the need to exchange witty quips with her "Scooby Gang", used to spend a lot of time hanging around the Sunnydale cemetery. She was keeping an eye on fresh graves, on the lookout for newly buried dead who might rise again as **Vampires**. **Graveyard**, churchyard, cemetery: there is no better place to find a dead body, and sometimes a not-so-dead body. The Gothic writers were bound to spend some time amongst the tombstones. In Bram Stoker's *Dracula* - published in 1897 and the most famous Vampire story of them all - a Graveyard is first presented as pleasant place.

> Between it and the town there is another church, the parish one, round which is a big graveyard, all full of tombstones. This is to my mind the nicest spot in Whitby, for it lies right over the town, and has a full view of the harbour and all up the bay to where the headland called Kettleness stretches out into the sea. It descends so steeply over the harbour that part of the bank has fallen away, and some of the graves have been destroyed.
> In one place part of the stonework of the graves stretches out over the sandy pathway far below. There are walks, with seats beside them, through the churchyard, and people go and sit there all day long looking at the beautiful view and enjoying the breeze.
> I shall come and sit here often myself and work.

This description comes from the journal, or diary, of Mina Murray, one of the main characters in the book. The churchyard becomes a favourite place for Mina and her friend Lucy Westenra, who often sit on a particular bench admiring the beautiful view; but as the story continues, we begin to get hints that this is not such a lovely place after all.

> The funeral of the poor sea captain today was most touching. Every boat in the harbour seemed to be there, and the coffin was carried by captains all the way from Tate Hill Pier up to the churchyard. Lucy came with me, and we went early to our old seat, whilst the cortege of boats went up the river to the Viaduct and came down again. We had a lovely view, and saw the procession nearly all the way. The poor fellow was laid to rest near our seat so that we stood on it, when the time came and saw everything.

A Young Person's Guide to the Gothic

Poor Lucy seemed much upset. She was restless and uneasy all the time, and I cannot but think that her dreaming at night is telling on her. She is quite odd in one thing. She will not admit to me that there is any cause for restlessness, or if there be, she does not understand it herself.

There is an additional cause in that poor Mr. Swales was found dead this morning on our seat, his neck being broken. He had evidently, as the doctor said, fallen back in the seat in some sort of fright, for there was a look of fear and horror on his face that the men said made them shudder. Poor dear old man!

Lucy is so sweet and sensitive that she feels influences more acutely than other people do. Just now she was quite upset by a little thing which I did not much heed, though I am myself very fond of animals.

One of the men who came up here often to look for the boats was followed by his dog. The dog is always with him. They are both quiet persons, and I never saw the man angry, nor heard the dog bark. During the service the dog would not come to its master, who was on the seat with us, but kept a few yards off, barking and howling. Its master spoke to it gently, and then harshly, and then angrily. But it would neither come nor cease to make a noise. It was in a fury, with its eyes savage, and all its hair bristling out like a cat's tail when puss is on the war path.

Finally the man too got angry, and jumped down and kicked the dog, and then took it by the scruff of the neck and half dragged and half threw it on the tombstone on which the seat is fixed. The moment it touched the stone the poor thing began to tremble. It did not try to get away, but crouched down, quivering and cowering, and was in such a pitiable state of terror that I tried, though without effect, to comfort it.

Lucy, as is mentioned in the fragment above, has begun to have disturbed nights, and even to sleep-walk. One night Mina awakes to find her friend has disappeared, wearing a long white nightgown.

I took a big, heavy shawl and ran out. The clock was striking one as I was in the Crescent, and there was not a soul in sight. I ran along the North Terrace, but could see no sign of the white figure which I expected. At the edge of the West Cliff above the pier I looked across the harbour to the East Cliff, in the hope or fear, I don't know which, of seeing Lucy in our favourite seat.

There was a bright full moon, with heavy black, driving clouds, which threw the whole scene into a fleeting diorama of light and shade as they sailed across. For a moment or two I could see nothing, as the shadow of a cloud obscured St. Mary's Church and all around it. Then as the cloud passed I could see the ruins of the abbey coming into view, and as the edge of a narrow band of light as sharp as a sword-cut moved along, the church and churchyard became gradually visible. Whatever my expectation was, it was not disappointed, for there, on our favourite seat, the silver light of the moon struck a half-reclining figure, snowy white. The coming of the cloud was too quick for me to see much, for shadow shut down on light almost immediately, but it seemed to me as though something dark stood behind the seat where the white figure shone, and bent over it. What it was, whether man or beast, I could not tell.

I did not wait to catch another glance, but flew down the steep steps to the pier and along by the fish-market to the bridge, which was the only way to reach the East Cliff. The town seemed as dead, for not a soul did I see. I rejoiced that it was so, for I wanted no witness of poor Lucy's condition. The time and distance seemed endless, and my knees trembled and my breath came laboured as I toiled up the endless steps to the abbey. I must have gone fast, and yet it seemed to me as if my feet were weighted with lead, and as though every joint in my body were rusty.

When I got almost to the top I could see the seat and the white figure, for I was now close enough to distinguish it even through the spells of shadow. There was undoubtedly something, long and black, bending over the half-reclining white figure. I called in fright, "Lucy! Lucy!" and something raised a head, and from where I was I could see a white face and red, gleaming eyes.

Lucy did not answer, and I ran on to the entrance of the churchyard. As I entered, the church was between me and the seat, and for a minute or so I lost sight of her. When I came in view again the cloud had passed, and the moonlight struck so brilliantly that I could see Lucy half reclining with her head lying over the back of the seat. She was quite alone, and there was not a sign of any living thing about.

We readers, unlike Mina, know that Dracula has begun to feed. One of the great strengths of the Gothic tradition is that we have become familiar with these various patterns and elements that recur within it, so we actually have a clearer idea of what is going on than the **Characters** themselves. The writers have a sort of shorthand available to them, so, for instance, we know exactly what sort of story this next one is going to be, thanks to its title.

THERE WAS A MAN DWELT BY A CHURCHYARD

M. R. JAMES

James wrote his stories to be read aloud; they were initially an entertainment for him and his friends, and we will be meeting several more later in this book. This one was published in 1924, and he has explained that it is his idea of the story a young character, Mamillius, in Shakespeare's play *The Winter's Tale*, is about to tell his mother. In the play the boy begins with the line, but is interrupted, and the story is never told. Long before the first Gothic Novel (the play was published in 1623), Shakespeare could be confident that his audience would know, just from the opening words, exactly what sort of story Mamillius was planning to tell.

There was a man dwelt by a churchyard. His house had a lower story of stone and an upper one of timber. The front windows looked out on the street and the back ones on the churchyard. It had once belonged to the parish priest, but (this was in Queen Elizabeth's days) the priest was a married man and wanted more room; besides, his wife disliked seeing the churchyard at night out of her bedroom window. She said she saw — but never mind what she said; anyhow, she gave her husband no peace till he agreed to move into a larger house in the village street, and the old one was taken by John Poole, who was a widower, and lived there alone. He was an elderly man who kept very much to himself, and people said he was something of a miser.

It was very likely true: he was morbid in other ways, certainly. In those days it was common to bury people at night and by torchlight: and it was noticed that whenever a funeral was toward, John Poole was always at his window, either on the ground floor or upstairs, according as he could get the better view from one or the other.

There came a night when an old woman was to be buried. She was fairly well to do, but she was not liked in the place. The usual thing was said of her, that she was no Christian, and that on such nights as Midsummer Eve and All Hallows, she was not to be found in her house. She was red-eyed and dreadful to look at, and no beggar ever knocked at her door. Yet when she died she left a purse of money to the Church.

There was no storm on the night of her burial; it was fair and calm. But there was some difficulty about getting bearers, and men to carry the torches, in spite of the fact that she had left larger fees than common for such as did that work. She was buried in woollen, without a coffin. No one was there but those who were actually needed — and John Poole, watching from his window. Just before the grave was filled in, the parson stooped down and cast something upon the body — something that clinked — and in a low voice he said words that sounded like "Thy money perish with thee." Then he walked quickly away, and so did the other men, leaving only one torch-bearer to light the sexton and his boy while they shovelled the earth in. They made no very neat job of it, and next day, which was a Sunday, the churchgoers were rather sharp with the sexton, saying it was the untidiest grave in the yard. And indeed, when he came to look at it himself, he thought it was worse than he had left it.

Meanwhile John Poole went about with a curious air, half exulting, as it were, and half nervous. More than once he spent an evening at the inn, which was clean contrary to his usual habit, and to those who fell into talk with him there he hinted that he had come into a little bit of money and was looking out for a somewhat better house. "Well, I don't wonder," said the smith one night, "I shouldn't care for that place of yours. I should be fancying things all night." The landlord asked him what sort of things.

"Well, maybe somebody climbing up to the chamber window, or the like of that," said the smith. "I don't know — old mother Wilkins that was buried a week ago today, eh?"

"Come, I think you might consider of a person's feelings," said the landlord. "It ain't so pleasant for Master Poole, is it now?"

"Master Poole don't mind," said the smith. "He's been there long enough to know. I only says it wouldn't be my choice. What with the passing bell, and the torches when there's a burial, and all them graves laying so quiet when there's no one about: only they say there's lights — don't you never see no lights, Master Poole?"

"No, I don't never see no lights," said Master Poole sulkily, and called for another drink, and went home late.

That night, as he lay in his bed upstairs, a moaning wind began to play about the house, and he could not go to sleep. He got up and crossed the room to a little cupboard in the wall: he took out of it something that clinked, and put it in the breast of his bedgown. Then he went to the window and looked out into the churchyard.

Have you ever seen an old brass in a church with a figure of a person in a shroud? It is bunched together at the top of the head in a curious way. Something like that was sticking up out of the earth in a spot of the churchyard which John Poole knew very well. He darted into his bed and lay there very still indeed.

Presently something made a very faint rattling at the casement. With a dreadful reluctance John Poole turned his eyes that way. Alas!

Between him and the moonlight was the black outline of the curious bunched head . . . Then there was a figure in the room. Dry earth rattled on the floor. A low cracked voice said "Where is it?" and steps went hither and thither, faltering steps as of one walking with difficulty. It could be seen now and again, peering into corners, stooping to look under chairs; finally it could be heard fumbling at the doors of the cupboard in the wall, throwing them open. There was a scratching of long nails on the empty shelves. The figure whipped round, stood for an instant at the side of the bed, raised its arms, and with a hoarse scream of "YOU'VE GOT IT!"...

The idea, since this was a story to being told by a boy to his mother, is that he would have shouted out the last words, along with a sudden lunge towards her, hoping to make her jump.

MARSHES

Swamps are evil, **Marshes** are bad. At the very least they can act as a barrier, isolating a **Character** or providing a barrier to cross. We have got used to them being part of the **Scenery** in our Gothic reading, but actually the earliest novels in the genre prefer their landscape dramatic rather dreary, mountainous rather than flat and boggy (nothing very "sublime" about a marsh), so good examples of a Gothic Marsh tend to come in later stories.

"It is a wonderful place, the moor," said he, looking round over the undulating downs, long green rollers, with crests of jagged granite foaming up into fantastic surges. "You never tire of the moor. You cannot think the wonderful secrets which it contains. It is so vast, and so barren, and so mysterious."

"You know it well, then?"

"I have only been here two years. The residents would call me a newcomer. We came shortly after Sir Charles settled. But my tastes led me to explore every part of the country round, and I should think that there are few men who know it better than I do."

"Is it hard to know?"

"Very hard. You see, for example, this great plain to the north here with the queer hills breaking out of it. Do you observe anything remarkable about that?"

"It would be a rare place for a gallop."

"You would naturally think so and the thought has cost several their lives before now. You notice those bright green spots scattered thickly over it?"

"Yes, they seem more fertile than the rest."

Stapleton laughed.

"That is the great Grimpen Mire," said he. "A false step

yonder means death to man or beast. Only yesterday I saw one of the moor ponies wander into it. He never came out. I saw his head for quite a long time craning out of the bog-hole, but it sucked him down at last. Even in dry seasons it is a danger to cross it, but after these autumn rains it is an awful place. And yet I can find my way to the very heart of it and return alive. By George, there is another of those miserable ponies!"

Something brown was rolling and tossing among the green sedges. Then a long, agonized, writhing neck shot upward and a dreadful cry echoed over the moor. It turned me cold with horror, but my companion's nerves seemed to be stronger than mine.

"It's gone!" said he. "The mire has him. Two in two days, and many more, perhaps, for they get in the way of going there in the dry weather, and never know the difference until the mire has them in its clutches. It's a bad place, the great Grimpen Mire."

Sherlock enthusiasts may have recognised a passage from Conan Doyle's classic *The Hound of the Baskervilles*, first published in instalments in 1901-2. So much attention is given to the famous sleuth's powers of detection that Conan Doyle's frequent use of Gothic devices can be overlooked. This particular story is full of them, with the **Marsh**/Moor/Mire for **Scenery**, Baskerville Hall as a **Castle**, the hound as a **Monster**, an ancestral **Curse** and plenty more.

Washington Irving, best known as the author of the *The Legend of Sleepy Hollow* – the basis of Tim Burton's 1999 film *Sleepy Hollow* – uses a Marsh (or swamp, in fact) for Scenery in his 1824 short story *The Devil and Tom Walker*.

One day that Tom Walker had been to a distant part of the neighbourhood, he took what he considered a short cut homewards through the swamp. Like most short cuts, it was an ill-chosen route. The swamp was thickly grown with great gloomy pines and hemlocks, some of them ninety feet high; which made it dark at noon-day, and a retreat for all the owls of the neighbourhood. It was full of pits and quagmires, partly covered with weeds and mosses; where the green surface often betrayed the traveller into a gulf of black smothering mud; there were also dark and stagnant pools, the abodes of the tadpole, the bull-frog, and the water-snake, and where trunks of pines and hemlocks lay half drowned, half rotting, looking like alligators, sleeping in the mire.

In the middle of the **Marsh** he meets the Devil; not surprisingly, nothing good comes of the encounter!

WEATHER

Weather can be a crucial part of the **Scenery**. The most obvious example is of course a storm, full of the drama of thunder and lightning and almost always (double whammy) arriving at night. The best Gothic storm clouds are so thick anyway, that they can make a day as dark as night. Even real storms, violent illustrations of the supreme (sublime!) power of nature, can be frightening; so when a storm is linked to a supernatural event, the power of both the storm and the event is that much greater.

Most of us imagine Frankenstein's Monster coming to life during a thunder storm, shocked into movement by a lightning strike – like the dog Sparky in Tim Burton's 2012 film *Frankenweenie*. This sequence in fact comes from the 1931 film *Frankenstein*, probably the most famous of many films inspired by the classic Gothic novel *Frankenstein* by Mary Shelley (wife of poet Percy Bysshe Shelley). In the book, first published in 1818, the way the monster comes to life is in fact left vague. Frankenstein — the creator of the monster and not the monster itself, as people often think — is so appalled when he sees what he has created ("the demoniacal corpse to which I had so miserably given life") that at first he simply runs away. He basically has a nervous breakdown, spending several months ill and then getting better, before the news that his young brother William has been murdered leads him to return home to Switzerland. Now it's time for some weather!

It was completely dark when I arrived in the environs of Geneva; the gates of the town were already shut; and I was obliged to pass the night at Secheron, a village at the distance of half a league from the city. The sky was serene; and, as I was unable to rest, I resolved to visit the spot where my poor William had been murdered. As I could not pass through the town, I was obliged to cross the lake in a boat to arrive at Plainpalais. During this short voyage I saw the lightning playing on the summit of Mont Blanc in the most beautiful figures. The storm appeared to approach rapidly, and, on landing, I ascended a low hill, that I might observe its progress. It advanced; the heavens were clouded, and I soon felt the rain coming slowly in large drops, but its violence quickly increased.

I quitted my seat, and walked on, although the darkness and storm increased every minute, and the thunder burst with a terrific crash over my head. It was echoed from Saleve, the Juras, and the Alps of Savoy; vivid flashes of lightning dazzled my eyes, illuminating the lake, making it appear like a vast sheet of fire; then for an instant every thing seemed of a pitchy darkness, until the eye recovered itself from the preceding flash. The storm, as is often the case in Switzerland, appeared at once in various parts of the heavens. The most violent storm hung exactly north of the town, over the part of the lake which lies between the promontory of Belrive and the village of Copet. Another storm enlightened Jura with faint flashes; and another darkened and sometimes disclosed the Mole, a peaked mountain to the east of the lake.

While I watched the tempest, so beautiful yet terrific, I wandered on with a hasty step. This noble war in the sky elevated my spirits; I clasped my hands, and exclaimed aloud, "William, dear angel! this is thy funeral, this thy dirge!" As I said these words, I perceived in the gloom a figure which stole from behind a clump of trees near me; I stood fixed, gazing intently: I could not be mistaken. A flash of lightning illuminated the object, and discovered its shape plainly to me; its gigantic stature, and the deformity of its aspect more hideous than belongs to humanity, instantly informed me that it was the wretch, the filthy daemon, to whom I had given life. What did he there? Could he be (I shuddered at the conception) the murderer of my brother? No sooner did that idea cross my imagination, than I became convinced of its truth; my teeth chattered, and I was forced to lean against a tree for support. The figure passed me quickly, and I lost it in the gloom.

At the other end of the **Weather** spectrum come the mists and fogs. These are useful because they conceal, in the same way as darkness, and so help build mystery and suspense. Bram Stoker, the author of *Dracula*, decided he needed the belt and braces of a storm and fog when the ship carrying the evil Count arrives in England.

Then without warning the tempest broke. With a rapidity which, at the time, seemed incredible, and even afterwards is impossible to realize, the whole aspect of nature at once became convulsed. The waves rose in growing fury, each over-topping its fellow, till in a very few minutes the lately glassy sea was like a roaring and devouring monster. White-crested waves beat madly on the level sands and rushed up the shelving cliffs. Others broke over the piers, and with their spume swept the lanthorns of the lighthouses which rise from the end of either pier of Whitby Harbour.

The wind roared like thunder, and blew with such force that it was with difficulty that even strong men kept their feet, or clung with grim clasp to the iron stanchions. It was found necessary to clear the entire pier from the mass of onlookers, or else the fatalities of the night would have increased manifold. To add to the difficulties and dangers of the time, masses of sea-fog came drifting inland. White, wet clouds, which swept by in ghostly fashion, so dank and damp and cold that it needed but little effort of imagination to think that the spirits of those lost at sea were touching their living brethren with the clammy hands of death, and many a one shuddered as the wreaths of sea-mist swept by.

At times the mist cleared, and the sea for some distance could be seen in the glare of the lightning, which came thick and fast, followed by such peals of thunder that the whole sky overhead seemed trembling under the shock of the footsteps of the storm.

Some of the scenes thus revealed were of immeasurable grandeur and of absorbing interest. The sea, running mountains high, threw skywards with each wave mighty masses of white foam, which the tempest seemed to snatch at and whirl away into space.

It's clear, from the drama above, that the ship eventually driven ashore (steered by a corpse), is carrying something seriously scary.

THE VOICE IN THE NIGHT

WILLIAM HOPE HODGSON

Our final short story for the **Scenery** section uses mist far more gently, as a barrier isolating characters from the world of normality. *The Voice in the Night* was published in 1907 and is William Hope Hodgson's most famous tale, but he wrote plenty more, often with a maritime setting – he spent many years in the Merchant Navy. He apparently came to hate and fear the sea, which may explain why his stories so often revolve around monsters from the depths – if you like this, try *A Tropical Horror*.

It was a dark, starless night. We were becalmed in the Northern Pacific. Our exact position I do not know; for the sun had been hidden during the course of a weary, breathless week, by a thin haze which had seemed to float above us, about the height of our mastheads, at whiles descending and shrouding the surrounding sea.

With there being no wind, we had steadied the tiller, and I was the only man on deck. The crew, consisting of two men and a boy, were sleeping forrard in their den; while Will — my friend, and the master of our little craft — was aft in his bunk on the port side of the little cabin.

Suddenly, from out of the surrounding darkness, there came a hail: "Schooner, ahoy!"

The cry was so unexpected that I gave no immediate answer, because of my surprise.

It came again — a voice curiously throaty and inhuman,

calling from somewhere upon the dark sea away on our port broadside: "Schooner, ahoy!"

"Hullo!" I sung out, having gathered my wits somewhat. "What are you? What do you want?"

"You need not be afraid," answered the queer voice, having probably noticed some trace of confusion in my tone. "I am only an old man."

The pause sounded oddly; but it was only afterwards that it came back to me with any significance.

"Why don't you come alongside, then?" I queried somewhat snappishly; for I liked not his hinting at my having been a trifle shaken.

"I — I — can't. It wouldn't be safe. I ——" The voice broke off, and there was silence.

"What do you mean?" I asked, growing more and more astonished. "Why not safe? Where are you?"

I listened for a moment; but there came no answer. And then, a sudden indefinite suspicion, of I knew not what, coming to me, I stepped swiftly to the binnacle, and took out the lighted lamp. At the same time, I knocked on the deck with my heel to waken Will. Then I was back at the side, throwing the yellow funnel of light out into the silent immensity beyond our rail. As I did so, I heard a slight, muffled cry, and then the sound of a splash as though someone had dipped oars abruptly. Yet I cannot say that I saw anything with certainty; save, it seemed to me, that with the first flash of the light, there had been something upon the waters, where now there was nothing.

"Hullo, there!" I called. "What foolery is this!"

But there came only the indistinct sounds of a boat being pulled away into the night.

Then I heard Will's voice, from the direction of the after scuttle: "What's up, George?"

"Come here, Will!" I said.

"What is it?" he asked, coming across the deck.

I told him the queer thing which had happened. He put several questions; then, after a moment's silence, he raised his hands to his lips, and hailed: "Boat, ahoy!"

From a long distance away there came back to us a faint reply, and my companion repeated his call. Presently, after a short period of silence, there grew on our hearing the muffled sound of oars; at which Will hailed again.

This time there was a reply: "Put away the light."

"I'm damned if I will," I muttered; but Will told me to do as the voice bade, and I shoved it down under the bulwarks.

"Come nearer," he said, and the oar-strokes continued. Then, when apparently some half-dozen fathoms distant, they again ceased.

"Come alongside," exclaimed Will. "There's nothing to be frightened of aboard here!"

"Promise that you will not show the light?"

"What's to do with you," I burst out, "that you're so infernally afraid of the light?"

"Because ——" began the voice, and stopped short.

"Because what?" I asked quickly.

Will put his hand on my shoulder.

"Shut up a minute, old man," he said, in a low voice. "Let me tackle him."

He leant more over the rail.

"See here, Mister," he said, "this is a pretty queer business, you coming upon us like this, right out in the middle of the blessed Pacific. How are we to know what sort of a hanky-panky trick you're up to? You say there's only one of you. How are we to know, unless we get a squint at you — eh? What's your objection to the light, anyway?"

As he finished, I heard the noise of the oars again, and then the voice came; but now from a greater distance, and sounding extremely hopeless and pathetic.

"I am sorry — sorry! I would not have troubled you, only I am hungry, and — so is she."

The voice died away, and the sound of the oars, dipping irregularly, was borne to us.

"Stop!" sung out Will. "I don't want to drive you away. Come back! We'll keep the light hidden, if you don't like it."

He turned to me: "It's a damned queer rig, this; but I think there's nothing to be afraid of?"

There was a question in his tone, and I replied.

"No, I think the poor devil's been wrecked around here, and gone crazy."

The sound of the oars drew nearer.

"Shove that lamp back in the binnacle," said Will; then he leaned over the rail and listened. I replaced the lamp, and came back to his side. The dipping of the oars ceased some dozen yards distant.

"Won't you come alongside now?" asked Will in an even voice. "I have had the lamp put back in the binnacle."

"I — I cannot," replied the voice. "I dare not come nearer. I dare not even pay you for the — the provisions."

"That's all right," said Will, and hesitated. "You're welcome to as much grub as you can take ——" Again he hesitated.

"You are very good," exclaimed the voice. "May God, Who understands everything, reward you ——" It broke off huskily.

"The — the lady?" said Will abruptly. "Is she ——"

"I have left her behind upon the island," came the voice.

"What island?" I cut in.

"I know not its name," returned the voice. "I would to God ——!" it began, and checked itself as suddenly.

"Could we not send a boat for her?" asked Will at this point.

"No!" said the voice, with extraordinary emphasis. "My God! No!" There was a moment's pause; then it added, in a tone which seemed a merited reproach: "It was because of our want I ventured — because her agony tortured me."

"I am a forgetful brute," exclaimed Will. "Just wait a minute, whoever you are, and I will bring you up something at once."

In a couple of minutes he was back again, and his arms were full of various edibles. He paused at the rail.

"Can't you come alongside for them?" he asked.

"No — *I dare not*," replied the voice, and it seemed to me

that in its tones I detected a note of stifled craving — as though the owner hushed a mortal desire. It came to me then in a flash, that the poor old creature out there in the darkness, was *suffering* for actual need of that which Will held in his arms; and yet, because of some unintelligible dread, refraining from dashing to the side of our little schooner, and receiving it. And with the lightning-like conviction, there came the knowledge that the Invisible was not mad; but sanely facing some intolerable horror.

"Damn it, Will!" I said, full of many feelings, over which predominated a vast sympathy. "Get a box. We must float off the stuff to him in it."

This we did — propelling it away from the vessel, out into the darkness, by means of a boathook. In a minute, a slight cry from the Invisible came to us, and we knew that he had secured the box.

A little later, he called out a farewell to us, and so heartful a blessing, that I am sure we were the better for it. Then, without more ado, we heard the ply of oars across the darkness.

"Pretty soon off," remarked Will, with perhaps just a little sense of injury.

"Wait," I replied. "I think somehow he'll come back. He must have been badly needing that food."

"And the lady," said Will. For a moment he was silent; then he continued: "It's the queerest thing ever I've tumbled across, since I've been fishing."

"Yes," I said, and fell to pondering.

And so the time slipped away — an hour, another, and still Will stayed with me; for the queer adventure had knocked all desire for sleep out of him.

The third hour was three parts through, when we heard again the sound of oars across the silent ocean.

"Listen!" said Will, a low note of excitement in his voice.

"He's coming, just as I thought," I muttered.

The dipping of the oars grew nearer, and I noted that the strokes were firmer and longer. The food had been needed.

They came to a stop a little distance off the broadside, and the queer voice came again to us through the darkness: "Schooner, ahoy!"

"That you?" asked Will.

"Yes," replied the voice. "I left you suddenly; but — but there was great need."

"The lady?" questioned Will.

"The — lady is grateful now on earth. She will be more grateful soon in — in heaven."

Will began to make some reply, in a puzzled voice; but became confused, and broke off short. I said nothing. I was wondering at the curious pauses, and, apart from my wonder, I was full of a great sympathy.

The voice continued: "We — she and I, have talked, as we shared the result of God's tenderness and yours ——"

Will interposed; but without coherence.

"I beg of you not to — to belittle your deed of Christian charity this night," said the voice. "Be sure that it has not escaped His notice."

It stopped, and there was a full minute's silence. Then it came again: "We have spoken together upon that which — which has befallen us. We had thought to go out, without telling any, of the terror which has come into our — lives. She is with me in believing that to-night's happenings are under a special ruling, and that it is God's wish that we should tell to you all that we have suffered since — since ——"

"Yes?" said Will softly.

"Since the sinking of the Albatross."

"Ah!" I exclaimed involuntarily. "She left Newcastle for 'Frisco some six months ago, and hasn't been heard of since."

"Yes," answered the voice. "But some few degrees to the North of the line she was caught in a terrible storm, and dismasted. When the day came, it was found that she was leaking badly, and, presently, it falling to a calm, the sailors took to the boats, leaving — leaving a young lady — my fiancée — and myself upon the wreck.

"We were below, gathering together a few of our belongings, when they left. They were entirely callous, through fear, and when we came up upon the deck, we saw them only as small shapes afar off upon the horizon. Yet we did not despair, but set to work and constructed a small raft. Upon this we put such few matters as it would hold including a quantity of water and some ship's biscuit. Then, the vessel being very deep in the water, we got ourselves on to the raft, and pushed off.

"It was later, when I observed that we seemed to be in the way of some tide or current, which bore us from the ship at an angle; so that in the course of three hours, by my watch, her hull became invisible to our sight, her broken masts remaining in view for a somewhat longer period. Then, towards evening, it grew misty, and so through the night. The next day we were still encompassed by the mist, the weather remaining quiet.

"For four days we drifted through this strange haze, until, on the evening of the fourth day, there grew upon our ears the murmur of breakers at a distance. Gradually it became plainer, and, somewhat after midnight, it appeared to sound upon either hand at no very great space. The raft was raised upon a swell several times, and then we were in smooth water, and the noise of the breakers was behind.

"When the morning came, we found that we were in a sort of great lagoon; but of this we noticed little at the time; for close before us, through the enshrouding mist, loomed the hull of a large sailing-vessel. With one accord, we fell upon our knees and thanked God; for we thought that here was an end to our perils. We had much to learn.

"The raft drew near to the ship, and we shouted on them to take us aboard; but none answered. Presently the raft touched against the side of the vessel, and, seeing a rope hanging downwards, I seized it and began to climb. Yet I had much ado to make my way up, because of a kind of grey, lichenous fungus which had seized upon the rope, and which blotched the side of the ship lividly.

"I reached the rail and clambered over it, on to the deck.

Here I saw that the decks were covered, in great patches, with grey masses, some of them rising into nodules several feet in height; but at the time I thought less of this matter than of the possibility of there being people aboard the ship. I shouted; but none answered. Then I went to the door below the poop deck. I opened it, and peered in. There was a great smell of staleness, so that I knew in a moment that nothing living was within, and with the knowledge, I shut the door quickly; for I felt suddenly lonely.

"I went back to the side where I had scrambled up. My — my sweetheart was still sitting quietly upon the raft. Seeing me look down she called up to know whether there were any aboard of the ship. I replied that the vessel had the appearance of having been long deserted; but that if she would wait a little I would see whether there was anything in the shape of a ladder by which she could ascend to the deck. Then we would make a search through the vessel together. A little later, on the opposite side of the decks, I found a rope side-ladder. This I carried across, and a minute afterwards she was beside me.

"Together we explored the cabins and apartments in the after part of the ship; but nowhere was there any sign of life. Here and there within the cabins themselves, we came across odd patches of that queer fungus; but this, as my sweetheart said, could be cleansed away.

"In the end, having assured ourselves that the after portion of the vessel was empty, we picked our ways to the bows, between the ugly grey nodules of that strange growth; and here we made a further search which told us that there was indeed none aboard but ourselves.

"This being now beyond any doubt, we returned to the stern of the ship and proceeded to make ourselves as comfortable as possible. Together we cleared out and cleaned two of the cabins: and after that I made examination whether there was anything eatable in the ship. This I soon found was so, and thanked God in my heart for His goodness. In addition to this I discovered the whereabouts of the fresh-water pump, and having fixed it I found the water drinkable, though somewhat unpleasant to the taste.

"For several days we stayed aboard the ship, without attempting to get to the shore. We were busily engaged in making the place habitable. Yet even thus early we became aware that our lot was even less to be desired than might have been imagined; for though, as a first step, we scraped away the odd patches of growth that studded the floors and walls of the cabins and saloon, yet they returned almost to their original size within the space of twenty-four hours, which not only discouraged us, but gave us a feeling of vague unease.

"Still we would not admit ourselves beaten, so set to work afresh, and not only scraped away the fungus, but soaked the places where it had been, with carbolic, a can-full of which I had found in the pantry. Yet, by the end of the week the growth had returned in full strength, and, in addition, it had spread to other places, as though our touching it had allowed germs from it to travel elsewhere.

"On the seventh morning, my sweetheart woke to find a small patch of it growing on her pillow, close to her face. At that, she came to me, so soon as she could get her garments upon her. I was in the galley at the time lighting the fire for breakfast.

"Come here, John," she said, and led me aft. When I saw the thing upon her pillow I shuddered, and then and there we agreed to go right out of the ship and see whether we could not fare to make ourselves more comfortable ashore.

"Hurriedly we gathered together our few belongings, and even among these I found that the fungus had been at work; for one of her shawls had a little lump of it growing near one edge. I threw the whole thing over the side, without saying anything to her.

"The raft was still alongside, but it was too clumsy to guide, and I lowered down a small boat that hung across the stern, and in this we made our way to the shore. Yet, as we drew near to it, I became gradually aware that here the vile fungus, which had driven us from the ship, was growing riot. In places it rose into horrible, fantastic mounds, which seemed almost to quiver, as with a quiet life, when the wind blew across them. Here and there it took on the forms of vast fingers, and in others it just spread out flat and smooth and treacherous. Odd places, it appeared as grotesque stunted trees, seeming extraordinarily kinked and gnarled — the whole quaking vilely at times.

"At first, it seemed to us that there was no single portion of the surrounding shore which was not hidden beneath the masses of the hideous lichen; yet, in this, I found we were mistaken; for somewhat later, coasting along the shore at a little distance, we descried a smooth white patch of what appeared to be fine sand, and there we landed. It was not sand. What it was I do not know. All that I have observed is that upon it the fungus will not grow; while everywhere else, save where the sand-like earth wanders oddly, path-wise, amid the grey desolation of the lichen, there is nothing but that loathsome greyness.

"It is difficult to make you understand how cheered we were to find one place that was absolutely free from the growth, and here we deposited our belongings. Then we went back to the ship for such things as it seemed to us we should need. Among other matters, I managed to bring ashore with me one of the ship's sails, with which I constructed two small tents, which, though exceedingly rough-shaped, served the purpose for which they were intended. In these we lived and stored our various necessities, and thus for a matter of some four weeks all went smoothly and without particular unhappiness. Indeed, I may say with much of happiness — for — for we were together.

"It was on the thumb of her right hand that the growth first showed. It was only a small circular spot, much like a little grey mole. My God! how the fear leapt to my heart when she showed me the place. We cleansed it, between us, washing it with carbolic and water. In the morning of the following day she showed her hand to me again. The grey warty thing had returned. For a little while, we looked at one another in silence. Then, still wordless, we started again to remove it. In the midst of the operation she spoke suddenly.

"'What's that on the side of your face, dear?' Her voice was sharp with anxiety. I put my hand up to feel.

"'There! Under the hair by your ear. A little to the front.' My finger rested upon the place, and then I knew.

"'Let us get your thumb done first,' I said. And she submitted, only because she was afraid to touch me until it was cleansed. I finished washing and disinfecting her thumb, and then she turned to my face. After it was finished we sat together and talked awhile of many things for there had come into our lives sudden, very terrible thoughts. We were, all at once, afraid of something worse than death. We spoke of loading the boat with provisions and water and making our way out on to the sea; yet we were helpless, for many causes, and — and the growth had attacked us already. We decided to stay. God would do with us what was His will. We would wait.

"A month, two months, three months passed and the places grew somewhat, and there had come others. Yet we fought so strenuously with the fear that its headway was but slow, comparatively speaking.

"Occasionally we ventured off to the ship for such stores as we needed. There we found that the fungus grew persistently. One of the nodules on the maindeck became soon as high as my head.

"We had now given up all thought or hope of leaving the island. We had realized that it would be unallowable to go among healthy humans, with the things from which we were suffering.

"With this determination and knowledge in our minds we knew that we should have to husband our food and water; for we did not know, at that time, but that we should possibly live for many years.

"This reminds me that I have told you that I am an old man. Judged by the years this is not so. But — but ——"

He broke off; then continued somewhat abruptly: "As I was saying, we knew that we should have to use care in the matter of food. But we had no idea then how little food there was left of which to take care. It was a week later that I made the discovery that all the other bread tanks — which I had supposed full — were empty, and that (beyond odd tins of vegetables and meat, and some other matters) we had nothing on which to depend, but the bread in the tank which I had already opened.

"After learning this I bestirred myself to do what I could, and set to work at fishing in the lagoon; but with no success. At this I was somewhat inclined to feel desperate until the thought came to me to try outside the lagoon, in the open sea.

"Here, at times, I caught odd fish; but so infrequently that they proved of but little help in keeping us from the hunger which threatened.

"It seemed to me that our deaths were likely to come by hunger, and not by the growth of the thing which had seized upon our bodies.

"We were in this state of mind when the fourth month wore out. When I made a very horrible discovery. One morning, a little before midday. I came off from the ship with a portion of the biscuits which were left. In the mouth of her tent I saw my sweetheart sitting, eating something.

"'What is it, my dear?' I called out as I leapt ashore. Yet, on hearing my voice, she seemed confused, and, turning, slyly threw something towards the edge of the little clearing. It fell short, and a vague suspicion having arisen within me, I walked across and picked it up. It was a piece of the grey fungus.

"As I went to her with it in my hand, she turned deadly pale; then rose red.

"I felt strangely dazed and frightened.

"'My dear! My dear!' I said, and could say no more. Yet at those words she broke down and cried bitterly. Gradually, as she calmed, I got from her the news that she had tried it the preceding day, and — and liked it. I got her to promise on her knees not to touch it again, however great our hunger. After she had promised she told me that the desire for it had come suddenly, and that, until the moment of desire, she had experienced nothing towards it but the most extreme repulsion.

"Later in the day, feeling strangely restless, and much

shaken with the thing which I had discovered, I made my way along one of the twisted paths — formed by the white, sand-like substance — which led among the fungoid growth. I had, once before, ventured along there; but not to any great distance. This time, being involved in perplexing thought, I went much further than hitherto.

"Suddenly I was called to myself by a queer hoarse sound on my left. Turning quickly I saw that there was movement among an extraordinarily shaped mass of fungus, close to my elbow. It was swaying uneasily, as though it possessed life of its own. Abruptly, as I stared, the thought came to me that the thing had a grotesque resemblance to the figure of a distorted human creature. Even as the fancy flashed into my brain, there was a slight, sickening noise of tearing, and I saw that one of the branch-like arms was detaching itself from the surrounding grey masses, and coming towards me. The head of the thing — a shapeless grey ball, inclined in my direction. I stood stupidly, and the vile arm brushed across my face. I gave out a frightened cry, and ran back a few paces. There was a sweetish taste upon my lips where the thing had touched me. I licked them, and was immediately filled with an inhuman desire. I turned and seized a mass of the fungus. Then more and — more. I was insatiable. In the midst of devouring, the remembrance of the morning's discovery swept into my mazed brain. It was sent by God. I dashed the fragment I held to the ground. Then, utterly wretched and feeling a dreadful guiltiness, I made my way back to the little encampment.

"I think she knew, by some marvellous intuition which love must have given, so soon as she set eyes on me. Her quiet sympathy made it easier for me, and I told her of my sudden weakness; yet omitted to mention the extraordinary thing which had gone before. I desired to spare her all unnecessary terror.

"But, for myself, I had added an intolerable knowledge, to breed an incessant terror in my brain; for I doubted not but that I had seen the end of one of those men who had come to the island in the ship in the lagoon; and in that monstrous ending I had seen our own.

"Thereafter we kept from the abominable food, though the desire for it had entered into our blood. Yet our drear punishment was upon us; for, day by day, with monstrous rapidity, the fungoid growth took hold of our poor bodies. Nothing we could do would check it materially, and so — and so — we who had been human, became — Well, it matters less each day. Only — only we had been man and maid!

"And day by day the fight is more dreadful, to withstand the hungerlust for the terrible lichen.

"A week ago we ate the last of the biscuit, and since that time I have caught three fish. I was out here fishing tonight when your schooner drifted upon me out of the mist. I hailed you. You know the rest, and may God, out of His great heart, bless you for your goodness to a — a couple of poor outcast souls."

There was the dip of an oar — another. Then the voice came again, and for the last time, sounding through the slight surrounding mist, ghostly and mournful.

"God bless you! Good-bye!"

"Good-bye," we shouted together, hoarsely, our hearts full of many emotions.

I glanced about me. I became aware that the dawn was upon us.

The sun flung a stray beam across the hidden sea; pierced the mist dully, and lit up the receding boat with a gloomy fire. Indistinctly I saw something nodding between the oars. I thought of a sponge — a great, grey nodding sponge — The oars continued to ply. They were grey — as was the boat — and my eyes searched a moment vainly for the conjunction of hand and oar. My gaze flashed back to the — head. It nodded forward as the oars went backward for the stroke. Then the oars were dipped, the boat shot out of the patch of light, and the — the thing went nodding into the mist.

A Young Person's Guide to the Gothic

Three: PLOT DEVICES

You should by now have enjoyed enough stories and excerpts to recognise that certain sorts of thing keep happening in Gothic literature. As well as the elements of **Setting** and **Scenery** that tend to be repeated (in different forms), so also do certain occurrences or events. These **Plot Devices** – not the handiest label – give the writer opportunities to stimulate fear, horror and excitement in the reader, who is (usually) identifying with one or more of the story's **Characters**. What would it feel like to be walled up alive? To realise a statue has come to life? To have your only candle blown out? The Gothic writers are here to help us find out.

CURSE & PROPHECY

Harry Potter and Lord Voldemort are the subject of a **Prophecy** revealed in the fifth book of the series. The prediction is that Harry has the power to vanquish the Dark Lord, and that one of them must defeat the other. It tells us that there will be a fight to the death – but does not say who wins!

Walpole's *The Castle of Otranto* begins with preparations being made for the marriage of Prince Manfred's son and heir, to take place on the boy's sixteenth birthday. Manfred is the book's **Villain**, the ruler of the **Castle**, and those around him know that he is in a desperate hurry for the boy to be married because he is worried about an ancient Prophecy. The prediction is that ownership of the Castle, and the title of Lord of Otranto, will "pass from the present family, whenever the real owner should be grown too large to inhabit it."

A Young Person's Guide to the Gothic

This **Prophecy** is deliberately difficult to interpret, but since Manfred's son is crushed to death, two paragraphs later, beneath a giant helmet, the reader is given a literally huge hint to the fact that the prediction may be fulfilled quite soon.

In the first chapter of Matthew Lewis' *The Monk* a gypsy woman reads the palm of Antonia, one of the main female **Characters** (her opening exclamation sounds very modern for a book written in 1796!)

> Jesus! what a palm is there!
> Chaste, and gentle, young and fair,
> Perfect mind and form possessing,
> You would be some good Man's blessing:
> But Alas! This line discovers,
> That destruction o'er you hovers;
> Lustful Man and crafty Devil
> Will combine to work your evil;
> And from earth by sorrows driven,
> Soon your Soul must speed to heaven.
> Yet your sufferings to delay,
> Well remember what I say.
> When you One more virtuous see
> Than belongs to Man to be,
> One, whose self no crimes assailing,
> Pities not his Neighbour's Failing,
> Call the Gypsy's words to mind:
> Though He seem so good and kind,
> Fair Exteriors oft will hide
> Hearts, that swell with lust and pride!
> Lovely Maid, with tears I leave you!
> Let not my prediction grieve you;
> Rather with submission bending
> Calmly wait distress impending,
> And expect eternal bliss
> In a better world than this.

Antonia is being told that she will soon die, because of a man who on the surface seems to be "good and kind". She soon forgets the **Prophecy**, but the reader, of course does not. The more we learn about how outwardly holy and pious Ambrosio (the monk of the book's title and the **Villain**) seems to be, the more we anticipate his later misbehaviour.

In these examples, Prophecy is used to whet the reader's appetite for events to come, hinting without revealing. Prophecy as **Curse** can have the same effect, but has the additional advantage of building a sense of the inevitable: however hard a **Character** – **Hero**, **Heroine** or **Villain** tries to escape, we all know that they are doomed (or are they? maybe they really will escape!). As well as the Gypsy's Prophecy above, *The Monk* includes a **Curse**, spoken by the unfortunate Agnes (see **Dungeon**). She is a nun who has committed the terrible sin of becoming pregnant, and has been pleading, unsuccessfully, for mercy from Ambrosio.

"Hear me!" She continued; "Man of an hard heart! Hear me, Proud, Stern, and Cruel! You could have saved me; you could have restored me to happiness and virtue, but would not! You are the destroyer of my Soul; You are my Murderer, and on you fall the curse of my death and my unborn Infant's! Insolent in your yet-unshaken virtue, you disdained the prayers of a Penitent; But God will show mercy, though you show none. And where is the merit of your boasted virtue? What temptations have you vanquished? Coward! you have fled from it, not opposed seduction. But the day of Trial will arrive! Oh! then when you yield to impetuous passions! when you feel that Man is weak, and born to err; When shuddering you look back upon your crimes, and solicit with terror the mercy of your God, Oh! in that fearful moment think upon me! Think upon your Cruelty! Think upon Agnes, and despair of pardon!"

By now we, as readers, are beginning to be pretty sure that Ambrosio is setting himself up for a very sticky end! And we're really looking forward to reading about it!

THE SCEPTIC

Bring together a ghost and a **Character** who does not believe in ghosts, and you create lots of potential for tension and suspense. We, as readers, know that the ghost, and the threat or message it brings, are real; the *Sceptic*, at least at first, ignores the warning signs. It's almost like the pantomime scene when the audience is supposed to shout "He's behind you!"

The **Sceptic** is so familiar to us, as a **Character** and **Plot Device**, that it may be a surprise to learn that he or she is a relative latecomer to the Gothic. The first novels of the genre seemed to have no need of the extra layer of mystery created by seeing events through the eyes of an "unbeliever." *Dracula*, on the other hand (published in 1897), makes lots of use of sceptical characters, to draw out the drama of our discoveries about the nature of **Vampires**.

Dr John Seward plays a major role in Bram Stoker's novel: he is a rational and scientific man of medicine, who tries to save the life of Lucy Westenra, the evil Count's first victim in England. In the battle against what he thinks is an illness, he calls on the help of his former teacher, Professor Van Helsing. The following extracts, theoretically from Seward's diary, come from the middle of the book. Lucy is already "dead", young children are disappearing, then re-appearing with puncture marks on their necks, Van Helsing is speaking.

"Do you mean to tell me, friend John, that you have no suspicion as to what poor Lucy died of, not after all the hints given, not only by events, but by me?"

"Of nervous prostration following a great loss or waste of blood."

"And how was the blood lost or wasted?"

I shook my head.

He stepped over and sat down beside me, and went on.

"You are a clever man, friend John. You reason well, and your wit is bold, but you are too prejudiced. You do not let your eyes see nor your ears hear, and that which is outside your daily life is not of account to you. Do you not think that there are things which you cannot understand, and yet which are, that some people see things that others cannot?

Van Helsing goes on to tell Seward that he believes the kidnapped children are in fact victims of Lucy, who is now a Vampire. The doctor refuses to believe him, so Van Helsing – the Professor – sets out to show him proof.

About ten o'clock we started from the inn. It was then very dark, and the scattered lamps made the darkness greater when we were once outside their individual radius. The Professor had evidently noted the road we were to go, for he went on unhesitatingly, but, as for me, I was in quite a mixup as to locality. As we went further, we met fewer and fewer people, till at last we were somewhat surprised when we met even the patrol of horse police going their usual suburban round. At last we reached the wall of the churchyard, which we climbed over. With some little difficulty, for it was very dark, and the whole place seemed so strange to us, we found the Westenra tomb. The Professor took the key, opened the creaky door, and standing back, politely, but quite unconsciously, motioned me to precede him. There was a delicious irony in the offer, in the courtliness of giving preference on such a ghastly occasion. My companion followed me quickly, and cautiously drew the door to, after carefully ascertaining that the lock was a falling, and not a spring one. In the latter case we should have been in a bad plight. Then he fumbled in his bag, and taking out a matchbox and a piece of candle, proceeded to make a light. The tomb in the daytime, and when wreathed with fresh flowers, had looked grim and gruesome enough, but now, some days afterwards, when the flowers hung lank and dead, their whites turning to rust and their greens to browns, when the spider and the beetle had resumed their accustomed dominance, when the time-discoloured stone, and dust-encrusted mortar, and rusty, dank iron, and tarnished brass, and clouded silver-plating gave back the feeble glimmer of a candle, the effect was more miserable and sordid than could have been imagined. It conveyed irresistibly the idea that life, animal life, was not the only thing which could pass away.

Van Helsing went about his work systematically. Holding his candle so that he could read the coffin plates, and so holding it that the wax dropped in white patches which congealed as they touched the metal, he made assurance of Lucy's coffin. Another search in his bag, and he took out a turnscrew.

"What are you going to do?" I asked.

"To open the coffin. You shall yet be convinced."

Straightway he began taking out the screws, and finally lifted off the lid, showing the casing of lead beneath. The sight was almost too much for me. It seemed to be as much an affront to the dead as it would have been to have stripped off her clothing in her sleep whilst living. I actually took hold of his hand to stop him.

He only said, "You shall see," and again fumbling in his bag took out a tiny fret saw. Striking the turnscrew through the lead with a swift downward stab, which made me wince, he made a small hole, which was, however, big enough to admit the point of the saw. I had expected a rush of gas from the week-old corpse. We doctors, who have had to study our dangers, have to become accustomed to such things, and I drew back towards the door. But the Professor never stopped for a moment. He sawed down a couple of feet along one side of the lead coffin, and then across, and down the other side. Taking the edge of the loose flange, he bent it back towards the foot of the coffin, and holding up the candle into the aperture, motioned to me to look.

I drew near and looked. The coffin was empty. It was certainly a surprise to me, and gave me a considerable shock, but Van Helsing was unmoved. He was now more sure than ever of his ground, and so emboldened to proceed in his task. "Are you satisfied now, friend John?" he asked.

I felt all the dogged argumentativeness of my nature awake within me as I answered him, "I am satisfied that Lucy's body is not in that coffin, but that only proves one thing."

"And what is that, friend John?"

"That it is not there."

"That is good logic," he said, "so far as it goes. But how do you, how can you, account for it not being there?"

"Perhaps a body-snatcher," I suggested. "Some of the undertaker's people may have stolen it." I felt that I was speaking folly, and yet it was the only real cause which I could suggest.

The Professor sighed. "Ah well!" he said, "we must have more proof. Come with me."

They go back outside the tomb to keep watch.

I took up my place behind a yew tree, and I saw Van Helsing's dark figure move until the intervening headstones and trees hid it from my sight.

It was a lonely vigil. Just after I had taken my place I heard a distant clock strike twelve, and in time came one and two. I was chilled and unnerved, and angry with the Professor for taking me on such an errand and with myself for coming. I was too cold and too sleepy to be keenly observant, and not sleepy enough to betray my trust, so altogether I had a dreary, miserable time.

Suddenly, as I turned round, I thought I saw something like a white streak, moving between two dark yew trees at the side of the churchyard farthest from the tomb. At the same time a dark mass moved from the Professor's side of the ground, and hurriedly went towards it. Then I too moved, but I had to go round headstones and railed-off tombs, and I stumbled over graves. The sky was overcast, and somewhere far off an early cock crew. A little ways off, beyond a line of scattered juniper trees, which marked the pathway to the church, a white dim figure flitted in the direction of the tomb. The tomb itself was hidden by trees, and I could not see where the figure had disappeared. I heard the rustle of actual movement where I had first seen the white figure, and coming over, found the Professor holding in his arms a tiny child. When he saw me he held it out to me, and said, "Are you satisfied now?"

"No," I said, in a way that I felt was aggressive.

"Do you not see the child?"

"Yes, it is a child, but who brought it here? And is it wounded?"

Still the **Sceptic** is not persuaded. The rescued child is handed over to a policeman, and the pair return to Lucy's tomb, this time in daylight.

The place was not so gruesome as last night, but oh, how unutterably mean looking when the sunshine streamed in. Van Helsing walked over to Lucy's coffin, and I followed. He bent over and again forced back the leaden flange, and a shock of surprise and dismay shot through me.

There lay Lucy, seemingly just as we had seen her the night before her funeral. She was, if possible, more radiantly beautiful than ever, and I could not believe that she was dead. The lips were red, nay redder than before, and on the cheeks was a delicate bloom.

"Is this a juggle?" I said to him.

"Are you convinced now?" said the Professor, in response, and as he spoke he put over his hand, and in a way that made me shudder, pulled back the dead lips and showed the white teeth. "See," he went on, "they are even sharper than before. With this and this," and he touched one of the canine teeth and that below it, "the little children can be bitten. Are you of belief now, friend John?"

Once more argumentative hostility woke within me. I could not accept such an overwhelming idea as he suggested. So, with an attempt to argue of which I was even at the moment ashamed, I said, "She may have been placed here since last night."

"Indeed? That is so, and by whom?"

"I do not know. Someone has done it."

Van Helsing does eventually succeed in convincing Seward that **Vampires** are real. It is interesting to note that the Professor is himself a man of science. His battle with this evil is based on rational processes of research and experimentation, as shown by his willingness to provide "proof" for Seward.

These next extracts come from a short story, *The Toll House* by W. W. Jacobs, first published in 1907. Most of Jacobs' writing was humorous (there is a hint of this in the business with the tea at the start of the story here), but he is best known for the excellent Gothic short story *The Monkey's Paw*, which is a gruesome twist on the "three wishes" fairy tale. Here he gives us an excellent example of the **Haunted House** Setting, and uses the **Plot Device** of the **Sceptic** to great effect, keeping us as readers guessing about whether or not we believe the house has a ghost.

"It's all nonsense," said Jack Barnes. "Of course people have died in the house; people die in every house. As for the noises-- wind in the chimney and rats in the wainscot are very convincing to a nervous man. Give me another cup of tea, Meagle."

"Lester and White are first," said Meagle, who was presiding at the tea-table of the Three Feathers Inn. "You've had two."

Lester and White finished their cups with irritating slowness, pausing between sips to sniff the aroma. Mr. Meagle served them to the brim, and then, turning to the grimly expectant Mr. Barnes, blandly requested him to ring for hot water.

"We'll try and keep your nerves in their present healthy condition," he remarked. "For my part I have a sort of half-and-half belief in the supernatural."

"All sensible people have," said Lester. "An aunt of mine saw a ghost once."

White nodded.

"I had an uncle that saw one," he said.

"It always is somebody else that sees them," said Barnes.

"Well, there is the house," said Meagle, "a large house at an absurdly low rent, and nobody will take it. It has taken toll of at least one life of every family that has lived there – however short the time – and since it has stood empty, caretaker after caretaker has died there. The last caretaker died fifteen years ago."

"Exactly," said Barnes. "Long enough ago for legends to accumulate."

"I'll bet you a sovereign you won't spend the night there alone, for all your talk," said White suddenly.

"And I," said Lester.

Of course the group leave their comfortable inn, setting out into the darkness to spend the night in the "Toll House".

"There is a window at the back where we can get in, so the landlord says," said Lester, as they stood before the hall door.

"Window?" said Meagle. "Nonsense. Let's do the thing properly. Where's the knocker?"

He felt for it in the darkness and gave a thundering rat-tat-tat at the door.

"Don't play the fool," said Barnes crossly.

"Ghostly servants are all asleep," said Meagle gravely, "but I'll wake them up before I've done with them. It's scandalous keeping us out here in the dark."

He plied the knocker again, and the noise volleyed in the emptiness beyond. Then with a sudden exclamation he put out his hands and stumbled forward.

"Why, it was open all the time," he said, with an odd catch in his voice. "Come on."

"I don't believe it was open," said Lester, hanging back. "Somebody is playing us a trick."

"Nonsense," said Meagle sharply. "Give me a candle. Thanks. Who's got a match?"

Barnes produced a box and struck one, and Meagle, shielding the candle with his hand, led the way forward to the foot of the stairs. "Shut the door, somebody," he said; "there's too much draught."

"It is shut," said White, glancing behind him.

Meagle fingered his chin. "Who shut it?" he inquired, looking from one to the other. "Who came in last?"

"I did," said Lester, "but I don't remember shutting it – perhaps I did, though."

They explore some of the house, eventually settling on an upstairs rooms to sleep in.

The others seated themselves on the floor and watched pleasantly as White drew from his pocket a small bottle of whisky and a tin cup.

"H'm! I've forgotten the water," he exclaimed.

"I'll soon get some," said Meagle.

He tugged violently at the bell-handle, and the rusty jangling of a bell sounded from a distant kitchen. He rang again.

"Don't play the fool," said Barnes roughly.

Meagle laughed. "I only wanted to convince you," he said kindly. "There ought to be, at any rate, one ghost in the servants' hall."

Barnes held up his hand for silence.

"Yes?" said Meagle, with a grin at the other two. "Is anybody coming?"

"Suppose we drop this game and go back," said Barnes suddenly. "I don't believe in spirits, but nerves are outside anybody's command. You may laugh as you like, but it really seemed to me that I heard a door open below and steps on the stairs."

His voice was drowned in a roar of laughter.

Are the others just teasing Barnes? It certainly looks like it, which reminds me of another brilliant story that puts a different twist on the **Sceptic Plot Device**: Michael Arlen's 1927 *The Gentleman from America* - track it down if you can.

IMPRISONMENT

Prisons and **Dungeons** appear regularly as **Scenery** in Gothic writing, because **Imprisonment** is a favourite **Plot Device**. To be locked up, to lose our freedom and contact with the people we love, is an awful experience. In the Gothic novel the victim is often to be locked away for ever, without hope of release. Almost always, and this makes the torture even worse, the Imprisonment is unfair. Of course the Plot Device of Imprisonment also provides opportunities for its dramatic counterpart: escape!

Theodore, the **Hero** of *The Castle of Otranto*, first appears in the story as a nameless peasant. As part of a crowd of spectators, he points out that the giant helmet (the one that has just crushed the **Villain's** son – remember?) looks like one belonging to a statue in a nearby church. Manfred, the Villain, is enraged.

> He gravely pronounced that the young man was certainly a necromancer, and that till the Church could take cognisance of the affair, he would have the Magician, whom they had thus detected, kept prisoner under the helmet itself, which he ordered his attendants to raise, and place the young man under it; declaring he should be kept there without food, with which his own infernal art might furnish him.

Theodore soon escapes (into an underground tunnel). He is later recaptured and re-imprisoned, this time in the **Castle's** "Black Tower", then escapes again with the help of one of the **Heroines**.

The poet Shelley also wrote a pair of Gothic novels. The first, *Zastrozzi: a Romance*, was written while he was seventeen and still at school, though not published till 1810, by which time he was at Oxford

University. The story begins with Zastrozzi, the **Villain**, aided by his **Henchmen** Ugo and Bernardo, kidnapping Count Verezzi and taking him to a cave in the middle of a Forest.

They had now entered the cavern. Verezzi supported himself against a fragment of rock which jutted out.

"Resistance is useless," exclaimed Zastrozzi; "following us in submissive silence can alone procure the slightest mitigation of your punishment."

Verezzi followed as fast as his frame, weakened by unnatural sleep, and enfeebled by recent illness, would permit; yet, scarcely believing that he was awake, and not thoroughly convinced of the reality of the scene before him, he viewed every thing with that kind of inexplicable horror, which a terrible dream is wont to excite.

After winding down the rugged descent for some time, they arrived at an iron door, which at first sight appeared to be part of the rock itself. Everything had till now been obscured by total darkness; and Verezzi, for the first time, saw the masked faces of his persecutors, which a torch brought by Bernardo rendered visible.

The massy door flew open.

The torches from without rendered the darkness which reigned within still more horrible; and Verezzi beheld the interior of this cavern as a place whence he was never again about to emerge – as his grave. Again he struggled with his persecutors, but his enfeebled frame was insufficient to support a conflict with the strong-nerved Ugo, and, subdued, he sank fainting into his arms.

His triumphant persecutor bore him into the damp cell, and chained him to the wall. An iron chain encircled his waist; his limbs, which not even a little straw kept from the rock, were fixed by immense staples to the flinty floor; and but one of his hands was left at liberty, to take the scanty pittance of bread and water which was daily allowed him.

Every thing was denied him but thought, which, by

comparing the present with the past, was his greatest torment.

Ugo entered the cell every morning and evening, to bring coarse bread, and a pitcher of water, seldom, yet sometimes, accompanied by Zastrozzi.

In vain did he implore mercy, pity, and even death: useless were all his enquiries concerning the cause of his barbarous imprisonment – a stern silence was maintained by his relentless gaoler.

Languishing in painful captivity, Verezzi passed days and nights seemingly countless, in the same monotonous uniformity of horror and despair. He scarcely now shuddered when the slimy lizard crossed his naked and motionless limbs. The large earth-worms, which twined themselves in his long and matted hair, almost ceased to excite sensations of horror.

There are three levels of torment: the actual imprisonment, the fact that Verezzi is innocent, and finally the fact that he has no clue why he is being imprisoned. You may want to compare this extract to the passage in Matthew Lewis' *The Monk* (published fourteen years earlier) which describes Agnes' Imprisonment and is quoted in the **Dungeon** segment of this book; it seems fairly clear where the young Shelley found some of his inspiration.

THE CASK OF AMONTILLADO

EDGAR ALLAN POE

Time for a complete story, and this one carries the **Imprisonment Plot Device** to its extreme, with a case of Immurement. This is almost a device in its own right, as a punishment often imposed on that Gothic favourite, the Pregnant Nun. Poe's *The Cask of Amontillado* was first published in 1846. Amontillado is a rare wine, and the word "pipe" means barrel in this context.

The thousand injuries of Fortunato I had borne as I best could, but when he ventured upon insult, I vowed revenge. You, who so well know the nature of my soul, will not suppose, however, that I gave utterance to a threat. At length I would be avenged; this was a point definitively settled – but the very definitiveness with which it was resolved precluded the idea of risk. I must not only punish, but punish with impunity. A wrong is unredressed when retribution overtakes its redresser. It is equally unredressed when the avenger fails to make himself felt as such to him who has done the wrong.

It must be understood that neither by word nor deed had I given Fortunato cause to doubt my good will. I continued as was my wont, to smile in his face, and he did not perceive that my smile now was at the thought of his immolation.

He had a weak point — this Fortunato — although in other regards he was a man to be respected and even feared. He prided himself on his connoisseurship in wine. Few Italians have the true virtuoso spirit. For the most part their enthusiasm is adopted to suit the time and opportunity to practise imposture upon the British and Austrian millionaires. In painting and gemmary, Fortunato, like his countrymen, was a quack, but in the matter of old wines he was sincere. In this respect I did not differ from him materially; I was skilful in the Italian vintages myself, and bought largely whenever I could.

It was about dusk, one evening during the supreme madness of the carnival season, that I encountered my friend. He accosted me with excessive warmth, for he had been drinking much. The man wore motley. He had on a tight-fitting parti-striped dress and his head was surmounted by the conical cap and bells. I was so pleased to see him, that I thought I should never have done wringing his hand.

I said to him – "My dear Fortunato, you are luckily met. How remarkably well you are looking to-day! But I have received a pipe of what passes for Amontillado, and I have my doubts."

"How?" said he, "Amontillado? A pipe? Impossible? And in the middle of the carnival?"

"I have my doubts," I replied; "and I was silly enough to pay the full Amontillado price without consulting you in the matter. You were not to be found, and I was fearful of losing a bargain."

"Amontillado!"

"I have my doubts."

"Amontillado!"

"And I must satisfy them."

"Amontillado!"

"As you are engaged, I am on my way to Luchesi. If any one has a critical turn, it is he. He will tell me…"

"Luchesi cannot tell Amontillado from Sherry."

"And yet some fools will have it that his taste is a match for your own."

"Come let us go."

"Whither?"

"To your vaults."

"My friend, no; I will not impose upon your good nature. I perceive you have an engagement. Luchesi…"

"I have no engagement; come."

"My friend, no. It is not the engagement, but the severe cold with which I perceive you are afflicted. The vaults are insufferably damp. They are encrusted with nitre."

"Let us go, nevertheless. The cold is merely nothing. Amontillado! You have been imposed upon; and as for Luchesi, he cannot distinguish Sherry from Amontillado."

Thus speaking, Fortunato possessed himself of my arm. Putting on a mask of black silk and drawing a roquelaire closely about my person, I suffered him to hurry me to my palazzo.

There were no attendants at home; they had absconded to make merry in honour of the time. I had told them that I should not return until the morning and had given them explicit orders not to stir from the house. These orders were sufficient, I well knew, to insure their immediate disappearance, one and all, as soon as my back was turned.

I took from their sconces two flambeaux, and giving one to Fortunato bowed him through several suites of rooms to the archway that led into the vaults. I passed down a long and winding staircase, requesting him to be cautious as he followed. We came at length to the foot of the descent, and stood together on the damp ground of the catacombs of the Montresors.

The gait of my friend was unsteady, and the bells upon his cap jingled as he strode.

"The pipe," said he.

"It is farther on," said I; "but observe the white webwork which gleams from these cavern walls."

He turned towards me and looked into my eyes with two filmy orbs that distilled the rheum of intoxication .

"Nitre?" he asked, at length

"Nitre," I replied. "How long have you had that cough!"

"Ugh! ugh! ugh! — ugh! ugh! ugh! — ugh! ugh! ugh! — ugh! ugh! ugh! — ugh! ugh! ugh!

My poor friend found it impossible to reply for many minutes.

"It is nothing," he said, at last.

"Come," I said, with decision, we will go back; your health is precious. You are rich, respected, admired, beloved; you are happy as once I was. You are a man to be missed. For me it is no matter. We will go back; you will be ill and I cannot be responsible. Besides, there is Luchesi..."

"Enough," he said; "the cough is a mere nothing; it will not kill me. I shall not die of a cough."

"True – true," I replied; "and, indeed, I had no intention of alarming you unnecessarily — but you should use all proper caution. A draught of this Medoc will defend us from the damps."

Here I knocked off the neck of a bottle which I drew from a long row of its fellows that lay upon the mould.

"Drink," I said, presenting him the wine.

He raised it to his lips with a leer. He paused and nodded to me familiarly, while his bells jingled.

"I drink," he said, "to the buried that repose around us."

"And I to your long life."

He again took my arm and we proceeded.

"These vaults," he said, are extensive."

"The Montresors," I replied, "were a great numerous family."

"I forget your arms."

"A huge human foot d'or, in a field azure; the foot crushes a serpent rampant whose fangs are imbedded in the heel."

"And the motto?"

"*Nemo me impune lacessit.*"

"Good!" he said.

The wine sparkled in his eyes and the bells jingled. My own fancy grew warm with the Medoc. We had passed through walls of piled bones, with casks and puncheons intermingling, into the inmost recesses of the catacombs. I paused again, and this time I made bold to seize Fortunato by an arm above the elbow.

"The nitre!" I said: see it increases. It hangs like moss upon the vaults. We are below the river's bed. The drops of moisture trickle among the bones. Come, we will go back ere it is too late. Your cough..."

"It is nothing" he said; "let us go on. But first, another draught of the Medoc."

I broke and reached him a flagon of De Grave. He emptied it at a breath. His eyes flashed with a fierce light. He laughed and threw the bottle upwards with a gesticulation I did not understand.

I looked at him in surprise. He repeated the movement – a grotesque one.

"You do not comprehend?" he said.

"Not I," I replied.

"Then you are not of the brotherhood."

"How?"

"You are not of the masons."

"Yes, yes," I said "yes! yes."

"You? Impossible! A mason?"

"A mason," I replied.

"A sign," he said.

"It is this," I answered, producing a trowel from beneath the folds of my roquelaire.

"You jest," he exclaimed, recoiling a few paces. "But let us proceed to the Amontillado."

"Be it so," I said, replacing the tool beneath the cloak, and again offering him my arm. He leaned upon it heavily. We continued our route in search of the Amontillado. We passed through a range of low arches, descended, passed on, and descending again, arrived at a deep crypt, in which the foulness of the air caused our flambeaux rather to glow than flame.

At the most remote end of the crypt there appeared another less spacious. Its walls had been lined with human remains piled to the vault overhead, in the fashion of the great catacombs of Paris. Three sides of this interior crypt were still ornamented in this manner. From the fourth the bones had been thrown down, and lay promiscuously upon the earth, forming at one point a mound of some size. Within the wall thus exposed by the displacing of the bones, we perceived a still interior recess, in depth about four feet, in width three, in height six or seven.

It seemed to have been constructed for no especial use in itself, but formed merely the interval between two of the colossal supports of the roof of the catacombs, and was backed by one of their circumscribing walls of solid granite.

It was in vain that Fortunato, uplifting his dull torch, endeavoured to pry into the depths of the recess. Its termination the feeble light did not enable us to see.

"Proceed," I said; "herein is the Amontillado. As for Luchesi…"

"He is an ignoramus," interrupted my friend, as he stepped unsteadily forward, while I followed immediately at his heels. In an instant he had reached the extremity of the niche, and finding his progress arrested by the rock, stood stupidly bewildered. A moment more and I had fettered him to the granite. In its surface were two iron staples, distant from each other about two feet, horizontally. From one of these depended a short chain. from the other a padlock. Throwing the links about his waist, it was but the work of a few seconds to secure it. He was too much astounded to resist . Withdrawing the key I stepped back from the recess.

"Pass your hand," I said, "over the wall; you cannot help feeling the nitre. Indeed it is very damp. Once more let me implore you to return. No? Then I must positively leave you. But I must first render you all the little attentions in my power."

"The Amontillado!" ejaculated my friend, not yet recovered from his astonishment.

"True," I replied; "the Amontillado."

As I said these words I busied myself among the pile of bones of which I have before spoken. Throwing them aside, I soon uncovered a quantity of building stone and mortar. With these materials and with the aid of my trowel, I began vigorously to wall up the entrance of the niche.

I had scarcely laid the first tier of my masonry when I discovered that the intoxication of Fortunato had in a great measure worn off. The earliest indication I had of this was a low moaning cry from the depth of the recess. It was not the cry of a drunken man. There was then a long and obstinate silence. I laid the second tier, and the third, and the fourth; and then I heard the furious vibrations of the chain. The noise lasted for several minutes, during which, that I might hearken to it with the more satisfaction, I ceased my labours and sat down upon the bones. When at last the clanking subsided, I resumed the trowel, and finished without interruption the fifth, the sixth, and the seventh tier. The wall was now nearly upon a level with my breast. I again paused, and holding the flambeaux over the mason-work, threw a few feeble rays upon the figure within.

A succession of loud and shrill screams, bursting suddenly from the throat of the chained form, seemed to thrust me violently back. For a brief moment I hesitated — I trembled. Unsheathing my rapier, I began to grope with it about the recess; but the thought of an instant reassured me. I placed my hand upon the solid fabric of the catacombs, and felt satisfied. I re-approached the wall. I replied to the yells of him who clamoured. I re-echoed — I aided — I surpassed them in volume and in strength. I did this, and the clamourer grew still.

It was now midnight, and my task was drawing to a close. I had completed the eighth, the ninth, and the tenth tier. I had finished a portion of the last and the eleventh; there remained but a single stone to be fitted and plastered in. I struggled with its weight; I placed it partially in its destined position. But now there came from out the niche a low laugh that erected the hairs upon my head. It was succeeded by a sad voice, which I had difficulty in recognising as that of the noble Fortunato. The voice said —

"Ha! ha! ha! — he! he! — a very good joke indeed — an excellent jest. We will have many a rich laugh about it at the palazzo — he! he! he! — over our wine — he! he! he!"

"The Amontillado!" I said.

"He! he! he! — he! he! he! — yes, the Amontillado. But is it not getting late? Will not they be awaiting us at the palazzo, the Lady Fortunato and the rest? Let us be gone."

"Yes," I said "let us be gone."

"For the love of god, Montresor!"

"Yes," I said, "for the love of God!"

But to these words I hearkened in vain for a reply. I grew impatient. I called aloud —

"Fortunato!"

No answer. I called again —

"Fortunato!"

No answer still. I thrust a torch through the remaining aperture and let it fall within. There came forth in return only a jingling of the bells. My heart grew sick -- on account of the dampness of the catacombs. I hastened to make an end of my labour. I forced the last stone into its position; I plastered it up. Against the new masonry I reerected the old rampart of bones. For the half of a century no mortal has disturbed them.

In pace requiescat!

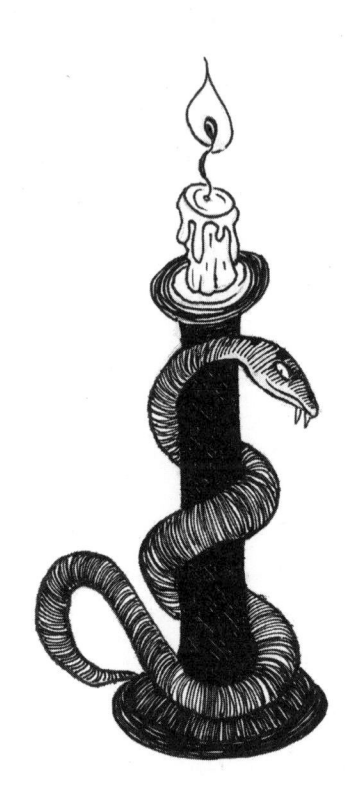

ANIMATED ART

This segment heading sounds like we should be discussing cartoons - Scooby Doo's adventures are after all full of Gothic ideas and activities – but what I really mean is the **Plot Device** where statues, or people in pictures, come to life. It is an idea that goes back as far as art itself, connecting to ancient superstitions about our attempts to copy human figures in pictures and sculpture. Roman poet Ovid tells the story of Pygmalion, who carved a female statue so beautiful he fell in love with it; so Venus, Goddess of love, brought the statue to life. Jason and his Argonauts, in Greek Myth (and the excellent 1963 film!), did battle with Talos, a giant man of bronze. The Harry Potter books are full of pictures and portraits that "come to life", or at least communicate from within the frame of the image. Doctor Who's most terrifying recent adversaries were the Weeping Angels, statues who take the playground game of Grandmother's footsteps to a lethal extreme: just don't blink!

Much of the action in *The Castle of Otranto* revolves around a statue that not only comes to life, but grows to gigantic size. In one memorable scene Manfred the Villain has to deal not only with an early glimpse of this threatening giant (the feathers on its helmet through an upstairs window), but the added complication of a portrait deciding to get involved.

Manfred's son, who was on the point of being married to Isabella has, you will remember, just been crushed to death (by the same helmet – it gets about). Our **Villain** has decided to force Isabella to marry him instead, an idea she is not at all keen on. In the circumstances, it's nice to see Isabella make successful use of what is effectively the "Look behind you!" trick as she makes her escape!

… he seized the cold hand of Isabella, who was half dead with fright and horror. She shrieked, and started from him, Manfred rose to pursue her, when the moon, which was now up, and gleamed in at the opposite casement, presented to his sight the plumes of the fatal helmet, which rose to the height of the windows, waving backwards and forwards in a tempestuous manner, and accompanied with a hollow and rustling sound. Isabella, who gathered courage from her situation, and who dreaded nothing so much as Manfred's pursuit of his declaration, cried—

"Look, my Lord! see, Heaven itself declares against your impious intentions!"

"Heaven nor Hell shall impede my designs," said Manfred, advancing again to seize the Princess.

At that instant the portrait of his grandfather, which hung over the bench where they had been sitting, uttered a deep sigh, and heaved its breast.

Isabella, whose back was turned to the picture, saw not the motion, nor knew whence the sound came, but started, and said—

"Hark, my Lord! What sound was that?" and at the same time made towards the door.

Manfred, distracted between the flight of Isabella, who had now reached the stairs, and yet unable to keep his eyes from the picture, which began to move, had, however, advanced some steps after her, still looking backwards on the portrait, when he saw it quit its panel, and descend on the floor with a grave and melancholy air.

"Do I dream?" cried Manfred, returning; "or are the devils themselves in league against me? Speak, infernal spectre! Or, if thou art my grandsire, why dost thou too conspire against thy wretched descendant, who too dearly pays for—" Ere he could finish the sentence, the vision sighed again, and made a sign to Manfred to follow him.

"Lead on!" cried Manfred; "I will follow thee to the gulf of perdition."

The spectre marched sedately, but dejected, to the end of the gallery, and turned into a chamber on the right hand. Manfred accompanied him at a little distance, full of anxiety and horror, but resolved.

So Walpole's **Animated Art** really does get involved in the action. Oscar Wilde, everybody's favourite wit, also gave a painting a life of its own, but keeps its contribution more symbolic. His only novel, *The Picture of Dorian Gray*, was published in 1890 and is strongly Gothic in flavour, even if it does not use all of the Gothic techniques on our list (no **Castle Setting**!). The story is built around a painted portrait of the protagonist, "a young man of extraordinary personal beauty". Here he is, seeing the completed picture for the first time.

> "How sad it is!" murmured Dorian Gray with his eyes still fixed upon his own portrait. "How sad it is! I shall grow old, and horrible, and dreadful. But this picture will remain always young. It will never be older than this particular day of June…. If it were only the other way! If it were I who was to be always young, and the picture that was to grow old! For that – for that – I would give everything! Yes, there is nothing in the whole world I would not give! I would give my soul for that!"

You may be able to guess that his wish is granted. Dorian Gray becomes an **Antihero** who dedicates his life to experiencing all forms of pleasure. He remains physically unchanged, but the portrait is transformed, showing the damage his choices do to his "soul". Eighteen years after the portrait was completed, Dorian shows the picture again to Basil Hallward, the artist who painted it.

> An exclamation of horror broke from the painter's lips as he saw in the dim light the hideous face on the canvas grinning at him. There was something in its expression that filled him with disgust and loathing. Good heavens! it was Dorian Gray's own face that he was looking at! The horror, whatever it was, had not yet entirely spoiled that marvellous beauty. There was still some gold in the thinning hair and some scarlet on the sensual mouth. The sodden eyes had kept something of the loveliness of their blue, the noble curves had not yet completely passed away from chiselled nostrils and from plastic throat. Yes, it was Dorian himself. But who had done it? He seemed to recognize

his own brushwork, and the frame was his own design. The idea was monstrous, yet he felt afraid. He seized the lighted candle, and held it to the picture. In the left-hand corner was his own name, traced in long letters of bright vermilion.

It was some foul parody, some infamous ignoble satire. He had never done that. Still, it was his own picture. He knew it, and he felt as if his blood had changed in a moment from fire to sluggish ice. His own picture! What did it mean? Why had it altered? He turned and looked at Dorian Gray with the eyes of a sick man. His mouth twitched, and his parched tongue seemed unable to articulate. He passed his hand across his forehead. It was dank with clammy sweat.

The young man was leaning against the mantelshelf, watching him with that strange expression that one sees on the faces of those who are absorbed in a play when some great artist is acting. There was neither real sorrow in it nor real joy. There was simply the passion of the spectator, with perhaps a flicker of triumph in his eyes. He had taken the flower out of his coat, and was smelling it, or pretending to do so.

'What does this mean?" cried Hallward, at last. His own voice sounded shrill and curious in his ears.

'Years ago, when I was a boy," said Dorian Gray, crushing the flower in his hand, "you met me, flattered me, and taught me to be vain of my good looks. One day you introduced me to a friend of yours, who explained to me the wonder of youth, and you finished a portrait of me that revealed to me the wonder of beauty. In a mad moment that, even now, I don't know whether I regret or not, I made a wish, perhaps you would call it a prayer...."

'I remember it! Oh, how well I remember it! No! the thing is impossible. The room is damp. Mildew has got into the canvas. The paints I used had some wretched mineral poison in them. I tell you the thing is impossible."

'Ah, what is impossible?" murmured the young man, going over to the window and leaning his forehead against the cold, mist-stained glass.

'You told me you had destroyed it."

'I was wrong. It has destroyed me."
'I don't believe it is my picture.'
'Can't you see your ideal in it?" said Dorian bitterly.
'My ideal, as you call it...'
'As you called it."
'There was nothing evil in it, nothing shameful. You were to me such an ideal as I shall never meet again. This is the face of a satyr.'
'It is the face of my soul."
'Christ! what a thing I must have worshipped! It has the eyes of a devil.'
'Each of us has heaven and hell in him, Basil," cried Dorian with a wild gesture of despair.
Hallward turned again to the portrait and gazed at it.
'My God! If it is true," he exclaimed, "and this is what you have done with your life, why, you must be worse even than those who talk against you fancy you to be!" He held the light up again to the canvas and examined it. The surface seemed to be quite undisturbed and as he had left it. It was from within, apparently, that the foulness and horror had come. Through some strange quickening of inner life the leprosies of sin were slowly eating the thing away. The rotting of a corpse in a watery grave was not so fearful.

From symbolising sin to using **Animated Art** almost literally to tell the story: M. R. James, who by this stage I can safely admit is my favourite writer of ghost stories, has two tales, quite similar to one another, that use this **Plot Device**. One, *The Mezzotint*, is about a picture of a country house. While it never changes when people are actually looking at it, when they return to look again, and again, after short intervals, a sinister figure appears in the corner of the image, and then begins to approach the building. A very unpleasant tale of tragedy in the house is told in a series of snapshots, almost like the frames of a cartoon. The other, similar and excellent story is *The Haunted Dolls' House*, where the observer is witness to another horrible sequence of events, unfolding when the Dolls' House "comes to life" at night. This tale was written specially for an actual Dolls' House – a magnificent building created for Queen Mary in the early 1920s (it is on display at Windsor Castle). A number of famous writers of the time provided miniature books for the miniature library, including Conan Doyle, with a Sherlock Holmes story, and **Peter Pan** author J. M. Barrie.

And finally back to **Animated Art** as **Antagonist** (which is the role the giant statue plays in *The Castle of Otranto*). Edith Nesbit is best known as the author who gave us *The Railway Children*, along with a number of other books, many of them with an element of magic. One might call her the Victorian J. K. Rowling. These extracts come from *Man-size in Marble*, a short story published in 1893 and her best-known piece of Gothic writing. A pair of newlyweds have moved to a cottage close to a church; the story is narrated by the husband.

The church was a large and lonely one, and we loved to go there, especially upon bright nights. The path skirted a wood, cut through it once, and ran along the crest of the hill through two meadows, and round the churchyard wall, over which the old yews loomed in black masses of shadow. This path, which was partly paved, was called "the bier-balk," for it had long been the way by which the corpses had been carried to burial. The churchyard was richly treed, and was shaded by great elms which stood just outside and stretched their majestic arms in benediction over the happy dead. A large, low porch let one into the building by a Norman doorway and a heavy oak door studded with iron. Inside, the arches rose into darkness, and between them the reticulated windows, which stood out white in the moonlight. In the chancel, the windows were of rich glass, which showed in faint light their noble colouring, and made the black oak of the choir pews hardly more solid than the shadows. But on each side of the altar lay a grey marble figure of a knight in full plate armour lying upon a low slab, with hands held up in everlasting prayer, and these figures, oddly enough, were always to be seen if there was any glimmer of light in the church. Their names were lost, but the peasants told of them that they had been fierce and wicked men, marauders by land

and sea, who had been the scourge of their time, and had been guilty of deeds so foul that the house they had lived in – the big house, by the way, that had stood on the site of our cottage – had been stricken by lightning and the vengeance of Heaven. But for all that, the gold of their heirs had bought them a place in the church. Looking at the bad hard faces reproduced in the marble, this story was easily believed.

The couple have a house-keeper, who insists, inconveniently, on having some time off.

"But why must you go this week?" I persisted. "Come, out with it."
Mrs. Dorman drew the little shawl, which she always wore, tightly across her bosom, as though she were cold. Then she said, with a sort of effort—
"They say, sir, as this was a big house in Catholic times, and there was a many deeds done here."
The nature of the "deeds" might be vaguely inferred from the inflection of Mrs. Dorman's voice – which was enough to make one's blood run cold. I was glad that Laura was not in the room. She was always nervous, as highly-strung natures are, and I felt that these tales about our house, told by this old peasant woman, with her impressive manner and contagious credulity, might have made our home less dear to my wife.
"Tell me all about it, Mrs. Dorman," I said; "you needn't mind about telling me. I'm not like the young people who make fun of such things."
Which was partly true.
"Well, sir' – she sank her voice – 'you may have seen in the church, beside the altar, two shapes."
"You mean the effigies of the knights in armour," I said cheerfully.
"I mean them two bodies, drawed out man-size in marble," she returned, and I had to admit that her description was a thousand times more graphic than mine, to say nothing of a

certain weird force and uncanniness about the phrase "drawed out man-size in marble."

"They do say, as on All Saints' Eve them two bodies sits up on their slabs, and gets off of them, and then walks down the aisle, in their marble' – (another good phrase, Mrs. Dorman) – 'and as the church clock strikes eleven they walks out of the church door, and over the graves, and along the bier-balk, and if it's a wet night there's the marks of their feet in the morning."

"And where do they go?" I asked, rather fascinated.

"They comes back here to their home, sir, and if any one meets them—"

"Well, what then?" I asked.

What indeed? It's interesting to see that although the story was written by a woman, she chooses to portray the female half of the young couple (at least in her husband's eyes) as "nervous" and "highly-strung".

THE LIGHTS GO OUT

Fear of the dark is something many of us share. When you can't see what might be out there coming for you, imagination takes over and decides it's something scary. Hundreds of modern films have used the shock value of the lights going out, and as a Gothic **Plot Device** the sudden arrival of darkness has been with us from the start.

In *The Castle of Otranto* the **Heroine**, Isabella, is being pursued through the **Castle** by Manfred (the **Villain**, who wants to marry her), and looks for a secret passage that leads to a church where she will be safe.

> The lower part of the castle was hollowed into several intricate cloisters; and it was not easy for one under so much anxiety to find the door that opened into the cavern. An awful

silence reigned throughout those subterraneous regions, except now and then some blasts of wind that shook the doors she had passed, and which, grating on the rusty hinges, were re-echoed through that long labyrinth of darkness. Every murmur struck her with new terror; yet more she dreaded to hear the wrathful voice of Manfred.

She trod as softly as impatience would give her leave, yet frequently stopped and listened to hear if she was followed. In one of those moments she thought she heard a sigh. She shuddered, and recoiled a few paces. In a moment she thought she heard the step of some person. Her blood curdled; she concluded it was Manfred. Every suggestion that horror could inspire rushed into her mind. Yet the sound seemed not to come from behind. If Manfred knew where she was, he must have followed her. She was still in one of the cloisters, and the steps she had heard were too distinct to proceed from the way she had come.

Cheered with this reflection, and hoping to find a friend in whoever was not the Prince, she was going to advance, when a door that stood ajar, at some distance to the left, was opened gently: but ere her lamp, which she held up, could discover who opened it, the person retreated precipitately on seeing the light.

Isabella, whom every incident was sufficient to dismay, hesitated whether she should proceed. Her dread of Manfred soon outweighed every other terror. The very circumstance of the person avoiding her gave her a sort of courage. It could only be, she thought, some domestic belonging to the castle. Fortifying herself with these reflections, and believing by what she could observe that she was near the mouth of the subterraneous cavern, she approached the door that had been opened; but a sudden gust of wind that met her at the door extinguished her lamp, and left her in total darkness.

Words cannot paint the horror of the Princess's situation.

Who (or what!) can it be, lurking in the cellars?

In this next extract, by contrast, from the classic novella *The Turn of the Screw* (published in 1898), the author turns the moment when a candle goes out on its head. Henry James had decided to apply his own, more subtle approach to the Gothic. He worked gently to build strangeness and uncertainty, rather than describing clear supernatural events to create fear. Critics still can't decide if what he wrote is a ghost story, or an exploration of obsession.

The story is narrated by a Governess who has been hired to look after two young children in an old house. Late one night, while reading, her attention is suddenly drawn away from her book.

> There was a moment during which I listened, reminded of the faint sense I had had, the first night, of there being something undefinably astir in the house, and noted the soft breath of the open casement just move the half-drawn blind. Then, with all the marks of a deliberation that must have seemed magnificent had there been anyone to admire it, I laid down my book, rose to my feet, and, taking a candle, went straight out of the room and, from the passage, on which my light made little impression, noiselessly closed and locked the door.
>
> I can say now neither what determined nor what guided me, but I went straight along the lobby, holding my candle high, till I came within sight of the tall window that presided over the great turn of the staircase. At this point I precipitately found myself aware of three things. They were practically simultaneous, yet they had flashes of succession. My candle, under a bold flourish, went out, and I perceived, by the uncovered window, that the yielding dusk of earliest morning rendered it unnecessary. Without it, the next instant, I saw that there was someone on the stair.

So in fact her candle going out makes it easier, rather than harder, to see someone (or something) that shouldn't be there. It's still pretty spooky though.

The author's second use of this **Plot Device** also sees the traditional pattern turned upside down. The Governess is speaking to the older of the two children in the story, a boy called Miles. She is convinced that something bad has happened to him, and is trying to persuade him to tell her about it.

> I waited a minute. "What happened before?"
> He gazed up at me again. "Before what?"
> "Before you came back. And before you went away."
> For some time he was silent, but he continued to meet my eyes.
> "What happened?"
> It made me, the sound of the words, in which it seemed to me that I caught for the very first time a small faint quaver of consenting consciousness—it made me drop on my knees beside the bed and seize once more the chance of possessing him.
> "Dear little Miles, dear little Miles, if you knew how I want to help you! It's only that, it's nothing but that, and I'd rather die than give you a pain or do you a wrong—I'd rather die than hurt a hair of you. Dear little Miles"—oh, I brought it out now even if I should go too far—"I just want you to help me to save you!"
> But I knew in a moment after this that I had gone too far. The answer to my appeal was instantaneous, but it came in the form of an extraordinary blast and chill, a gust of frozen air, and a shake of the room as great as if, in the wild wind, the casement had crashed in. The boy gave a loud, high shriek, which, lost in the rest of the shock of sound, might have seemed, indistinctly, though I was so close to him, a note either of jubilation or of terror. I jumped to my feet again and was conscious of darkness. So for a moment we remained, while I stared about me and saw that the drawn curtains were unstirred and the window tight.
> "Why, the candle's out!" I then cried.
> "It was I who blew it, dear!" said Miles.

Is the narrator imagining things, or is Miles the focus of powerful supernatural activity, which is all the scarier because he seems oblivious? It's clear the author wants to keep us guessing.

THE RED ROOM
H. G. WELLS

H. G. Wells is probably most famous for his novel *The War of the Worlds*, about Martians invading the Earth, which was published in 1898 (the same year as *The Turn of the Screw*); at that time the possibility of alien creatures inhabiting the planet nearest to us was still very real. It is of course labelled as science fiction, but contains some very Gothic elements, like the fact that the Martians feed themselves by draining blood from living humans and injecting it directly into their own veins. To end the section on **Plot Devices** I've chosen this tale by Wells, a wonderful example of **The Lights Go Out**. Published in 1896, it uses a **Castle Setting** and **Haunted Room Scenery** to excellent Gothic effect; you may want to compare it with Elia Peattie's *The Room of the Evil Thought* from the previous chapter.

"It's your own choosing," said the man with the withered arm once more.

I heard the faint sound of a stick and a shambling step on the flags in the passage outside. The door creaked on its hinges as a second old man entered, more bent, more wrinkled, more aged even than the first. He supported himself by the help of a crutch, his eyes were covered by a shade, and his lower lip, half averted, hung pale and pink from his decaying yellow teeth. He made straight for an armchair on the opposite side of the table, sat down clumsily, and began to cough. The man with the withered hand gave the newcomer a short glance of positive dislike; the old woman took no notice of his arrival, but remained with her eyes fixed steadily on the fire.

"I said—it's your own choosing," said the man with the withered hand, when the coughing had ceased for a while.

"It's my own choosing," I answered.

The man with the shade became aware of my presence for the first time, and threw his head back for a moment, and sidewise, to see me. I caught a momentary glimpse of his eyes, small and bright and inflamed. Then he began to cough and splutter again.

"If," said I, "you will show me to this haunted room of yours, I will make myself comfortable there."

The old man with the cough jerked his head back so suddenly that it startled me, and shot another glance of his red eyes at me from out of the darkness under the shade, but no one answered me. I waited a minute, glancing from one to the other. The old woman stared like a dead body, glaring into the fire with lack-lustre eyes.

"If," I said, a little louder, "if you will show me to this haunted room of yours, I will relieve you from the task of entertaining me."

"There's a candle on the slab outside the door," said the man with the withered hand, looking at my feet as he addressed me. "But if you go to the Red Room to-night—"

"This night of all nights!" said the old woman, softly.

"—You go alone."

"Very well," I answered, shortly, "and which way do I go?"

"You go along the passage for a bit," said he, nodding his head on his shoulder at the door, "until you come to a spiral staircase; and on the second landing is a door covered with green baize. Go through that, and down the long corridor to the end, and the Red Room is on your left up the steps."

"Have I got that right?" I said, and repeated his directions.

He corrected me in one particular.

"And you are really going?" said the man with the shade, looking at me again for the third time with that queer, unnatural tilting of the face.

"This night of all nights!" whispered the old woman.

"It is what I came for," I said, and moved toward the door. As I did so, the old man with the shade rose and staggered round the table, so as to be closer to the others and to the fire. At the door I turned and looked at them, and saw they were all close together, dark against the firelight, staring at me over their shoulders, with an intent expression on their ancient faces.

"Good-night," I said, setting the door open. "It's your own choosing," said the man with the withered arm.

I left the door wide open until the candle was well alight, and then I shut them in, and walked down the chilly, echoing passage.

I must confess that the oddness of these three old pensioners in whose charge her ladyship had left the castle, and the deep-toned, old-fashioned furniture of the housekeeper's room, in which they foregathered, had affected me curiously in spite of my effort to keep myself at a matter-of-fact phase. They seemed to belong to another age, an older age, an age when things spiritual were indeed to be feared, when common sense was uncommon, an age when omens and witches were credible, and ghosts beyond denying. Their very existence, thought I, is spectral; the cut of their clothing, fashions born in dead brains; the ornaments and conveniences in the room about them even are ghostly—the thoughts of vanished men, which still haunt rather than participate in the world of to-day. And the passage I was in, long and shadowy, with a film of moisture glistening on the wall, was as gaunt and cold as a thing that is dead and rigid. But with an effort I sent such thoughts to the right-about. The long, drafty subterranean passage was chilly and dusty, and my candle flared and made the shadows cower and quiver. The echoes rang up and down the spiral staircase, and a shadow came sweeping up after me, and another fled before me into the darkness overhead. I came to the wide landing and stopped there for a moment listening to a rustling that I fancied I heard creeping behind me, and then, satisfied of the absolute silence, pushed open the unwilling baize-covered door and stood in the silent corridor.

The effect was scarcely what I expected, for the moonlight, coming in by the great window on the grand staircase, picked out everything in vivid black shadow or reticulated silvery illumination. Everything seemed in its proper position; the house might have been deserted on the yesterday instead of twelve months ago. There were candles in the sockets of the sconces, and whatever dust had gathered on the carpets or upon the polished flooring was distributed so evenly as to be invisible in my candlelight.

The door of the Red Room and the steps up to it were in a shadowy corner. I moved my candle from side to side in order to see clearly the nature of the recess in which I stood, before opening the door. Here it was, thought I, that my predecessor was found, and the memory of that story gave me a sudden twinge of apprehension. I opened the door of the Red Room rather hastily, with my face half turned to the pallid silence of the corridor.

I entered, closed the door behind me at once, turned the key I found in the lock within, and stood with the candle held aloft surveying the scene of my vigil, the great Red Room of Lorraine Castle, in which the young Duke had died; or rather in which he had begun his dying, for he had opened the door and fallen headlong down the steps I had just ascended. That had been the end of his vigil, of his gallant attempt to conquer the ghostly tradition of the place, and never, I thought, had apoplexy better served the ends of superstition. There were other and older stories that clung to the room, back to the half-incredible beginning of it all, the tale of a timid wife and the tragic end that came to her husband's jest of frightening her. And looking round that huge shadowy room with its black window bays, its recesses and alcoves, its dusty brown-red hangings and dark gigantic furniture, one could well understand the legends that had sprouted in its black corners, its germinating darknesses. My candle was a little tongue of light in the vastness of the chamber; its rays failed to pierce to the opposite end of the room, and left an ocean of dull red mystery and suggestion, sentinel shadows and watching darknesses beyond its island of light. And the stillness of desolation brooded over it all.

I must confess some impalpable quality of that ancient room disturbed me. I tried to fight the feeling down. I resolved to make a systematic examination of the place, and so, by leaving nothing to the imagination, dispel the fanciful suggestions of the obscurity before they obtained a hold upon me. After satisfying myself of the fastening of the door, I began to walk round the room, peering round each article of furniture, tucking up the valances of the bed and opening its curtains wide. In one place there was a distinct echo to my footsteps, the noises I made seemed so little that they enhanced rather than broke the silence of the place. I pulled up the blinds and examined the fastenings of the several windows. Attracted by the fall of a particle of dust, I leaned forward and looked up the blackness of the wide chimney. Then, trying to preserve my scientific attitude of mind, I walked round and began tapping the oak panelling for any secret opening, but I desisted before reaching the alcove. I saw my face in a mirror—white.

There were two big mirrors in the room, each with a pair of sconces bearing candles, and on the mantelshelf, too, were candles in china candle-sticks. All these I lit one after the other. The fire was laid—an unexpected consideration from the old housekeeper—and I lit it, to keep down any disposition to shiver, and when it was burning well I stood round with my back to it and regarded the room again. I had pulled up a chintz-covered armchair and a table to form a kind of barricade before me. On this lay my revolver, ready to hand. My precise examination had done me a little good, but I still found the remoter darkness of the place and its perfect stillness too stimulating for the imagination. The echoing of the stir and crackling of the fire was no sort of comfort to me. The shadow in the alcove at the end of the room began to display that undefinable quality of a presence, that odd suggestion of a lurking living thing that comes so easily in silence and solitude. And to reassure myself, I walked with a candle into it and satisfied myself that there was nothing tangible there. I stood that candle upon the floor of the alcove and left it in that position.

By this time I was in a state of considerable nervous tension, although to my reason there was no adequate cause for my condition. My mind, however, was perfectly clear. I postulated quite unreservedly that nothing supernatural could happen, and to pass the time I began stringing some rhymes together, Ingoldsby fashion, concerning the original legend of the place. A few I spoke aloud, but the echoes were not pleasant. For the same reason I also abandoned, after a time, a conversation with myself upon the impossibility of ghosts and haunting. My mind reverted to the three old and distorted people downstairs, and I tried to keep it upon that topic.

The sombre reds and greys of the room troubled me; even with its seven candles the place was merely dim. The light in the alcove flaring in a draft, and the fire flickering, kept the shadows and penumbra perpetually shifting and stirring in a noiseless flighty dance. Casting about for a remedy, I recalled the wax candles I had seen in the corridor, and, with a slight effort, carrying a candle and leaving the door open, I walked out into the moonlight, and presently returned with as many as ten. These I put in the various knick-knacks of china with which the room was sparsely adorned, and lit and placed them where the shadows had lain deepest, some on the floor, some in the window recesses, arranging and rearranging them until at last my seventeen candles were so placed that not an inch of the room but had the direct light of at least one of them. It occurred to me that when the ghost came I could warn him not to trip over them. The room was now quite brightly illuminated. There was something very cheering and reassuring in these little silent streaming flames, and to notice their steady diminution of length offered me an occupation and gave me a reassuring sense of the passage of time.

Even with that, however, the brooding expectation of the vigil weighed heavily enough upon me. I stood watching the minute hand of my watch creep towards midnight.

Then something happened in the alcove. I did not see the candle go out, I simply turned and saw that the darkness was there, as one might start and see the unexpected presence of a stranger. The black shadow had sprung back to its place. "By Jove," said I aloud, recovering from my surprise, "that draft's a strong one;" and taking the matchbox from the table, I walked across the room in a leisurely manner to relight the corner again. My first match would not strike, and as I succeeded with the second, something seemed to blink on the wall before me. I turned my head involuntarily and saw that the two candles on the little table by the fireplace were extinguished. I rose at once to my feet.

"Odd," I said. "Did I do that myself in a flash of absent-mindedness?"

I walked back, relit one, and as I did so I saw the candle in the right sconce of one of the mirrors wink and go right out, and almost immediately its companion followed it. The flames vanished as if the wick had been suddenly nipped between a finger and thumb, leaving the wick neither glowing nor smoking, but black. While I stood gaping the candle at the foot of the bed went out, and the shadows seemed to take another step toward me.

"This won't do!" said I, and first one and then another candle on the mantelshelf followed.

"What's up?" I cried, with a queer high note getting into my voice somehow. At that the candle on the corner of the wardrobe went out, and the one I had relit in the alcove followed.

"Steady on!" I said, "those candles are wanted," speaking with a half-hysterical facetiousness, and scratching away at a match the while, "for the mantel candlesticks." My hands trembled so much that twice I missed the rough paper of the matchbox. As the mantel emerged from darkness again, two candles in the remoter end of the room were eclipsed. But with the same match I also relit the larger mirror candles, and those on the floor near the doorway, so that for the moment I seemed to gain on the extinctions. But then in a noiseless volley there vanished four lights at once in different corners of the room, and I struck another match in quivering haste, and stood hesitating whither to take it.

As I stood undecided, an invisible hand seemed to sweep out the two candles on the table. With a cry of terror I dashed at the alcove, then into the corner and then into the window, relighting three as two more vanished by the fireplace, and then, perceiving a better way, I dropped matches on the iron-bound deedbox in the corner, and caught up the bedroom candlestick. With this I avoided the delay of striking matches, but for all that the steady process of extinction went on, and the shadows I feared and fought against returned, and crept in upon me, first a step gained on this side of me, then on that. I was now almost frantic with the horror of the coming darkness, and my self-possession deserted me. I leaped panting from candle to candle in a vain struggle against that remorseless advance.

I bruised myself in the thigh against the table, I sent a chair headlong, I stumbled and fell and whisked the cloth from the table in my fall. My candle rolled away from me and I snatched another as I rose. Abruptly this was blown out as I swung it off the table by the wind of my sudden movement, and immediately the two remaining candles followed. But there was light still in the room, a red light, that streamed across the ceiling and staved off the shadows from me. The fire! Of course I could still thrust my candle between the bars and relight it.

I turned to where the flames were still dancing between the glowing coals and splashing red reflections upon the furniture; made two steps toward the grate, and incontinently the flames dwindled and vanished, the glow vanished, the reflections rushed together and disappeared, and as I thrust the candle between the bars darkness closed upon me like the shutting of an eye, wrapped about me in a stifling embrace, sealed my vision, and crushed the last vestiges of self-possession from my brain. And it was not only palpable darkness, but intolerable terror. The candle fell from my hands. I flung out my arms in a vain effort to thrust that ponderous blackness away from me, and lifting up my voice, screamed with all my might, once, twice, thrice. Then I think I must have staggered to my feet. I know I thought suddenly of the moonlit corridor, and with my head bowed and my arms over my face, made a stumbling run for the door.

But I had forgotten the exact position of the door, and I struck myself heavily against the corner of the bed. I staggered back, turned, and was either struck or struck myself against some other bulky furnishing. I have a vague memory of battering myself thus to and fro in the darkness, of a heavy blow at last upon my forehead, of a horrible sensation of falling that lasted an age, of my last frantic effort to keep my footing, and then I remember no more.

I opened my eyes in daylight. My head was roughly bandaged, and the man with the withered hand was watching my face. I looked about me trying to remember what had happened, and for a space I could not recollect. I rolled my eyes into the corner and saw the old woman, no longer abstracted, no longer terrible, pouring out some drops of medicine from a little blue phial into a glass. "Where am I?" I said. "I seem to remember you, and yet I can not remember who you are."

They told me then, and I heard of the haunted Red Room as one who bears a tale. "We found you at dawn," said he, "and there was blood on your forehead and lips."

I wondered that I had ever disliked him. The three of them in the daylight seemed commonplace old folk enough. The man with the green shade had his head bent as one who sleeps.

It was very slowly I recovered the memory of my experience. "You believe now," said the old man with the withered hand, "that the room is haunted?" He spoke no longer as one who greets an intruder, but as one who condoles with a friend.

"Yes," said I, "the room is haunted."

"And you have seen it. And we who have been here all our lives have never set eyes upon it. Because we have never dared. Tell us, is it truly the old earl who—"

"No," said I, "it is not."

"I told you so," said the old lady, with the glass in her hand. "It is his poor young countess who was frightened—"

"It is not," I said. "There is neither ghost of earl nor ghost of countess in that room; there is no ghost there at all, but worse, far worse, something impalpable—"

"Well?" they said.

"The worst of all the things that haunt poor mortal men," said I; "and that is, in all its nakedness—Fear! Fear that will not have light nor sound, that will not bear with reason, that deafens and darkens and overwhelms. It followed me through the corridor, it fought against me in the room—"

I stopped abruptly. There was an interval of silence. My hand went up to my bandages. "The candles went out one after another, and I fled—"

Then the man with the shade lifted his face sideways to see me and spoke.

"That is it," said he. "I knew that was it. A Power of Darkness. To put such a curse upon a home! It lurks there always. You can feel it even in the daytime, even of a bright summer's day, in the hangings, in the curtains, keeping behind you however you face about. In the dusk it creeps in the corridor and follows you, so that you dare not turn. It is even as you say. Fear itself is in that room. Black Fear.... And there it will be... so long as this house of sin endures."

A Young Person's Guide to the Gothic

Four: CHARACTERS

We all need a **Hero**, and many exciting stories rely on the antics of a **Villain**. The Hero is virtuous and noble, the Villain evil and vicious (a good word, because originally it meant full of vices, or immoral tendencies).

To be honest, there is nothing very remarkable about the Gothic Hero. He shares his qualities with heroes from other literary genres: courage, resourcefulness and honour. The original Gothic **Villain** is a more interesting **Character**, generally a patriarchal figure seeking to impose his will, and lust, on a defenceless female victim (defenceless until the Hero gets involved, of course), and prepared to commit all sorts of wicked acts to have his way. As the Gothic develops, overlapping more and more clearly with the Romantic movement, writers also explore the idea of having a lead male Character who while very far from good, is also not entirely evil: the **Antihero**.

Heroes need **Heroines**. The female protagonist in the original Gothic would struggle to match up with our current ideas of a Heroine, but I'm going to use the label anyway. There are no Lara Crofts or Katniss Everdeens in the earlier Gothic novels. Heroines are instead modelled on the "damsel in distress" pattern of fables and fairy-tales: women who need rescuing.

Female Villains, or **Villainesses**, also have a role. There are plenty of wicked women in the early Gothic novels, but William Henry Ireland, with his *The Abbess* (published 1799), was the first to make a Villainess the very centre of a novel's wrongdoing. Vittoria Bracciano is the head of a Convent, but lust and jealousy make her persecute the Hero and Heroine, inventing false accusations and handing them over to the *Inquisition*. Torture follows.

There are also other "stock" types of Character who appear

frequently in the Gothic. We don't have room to give them each a segment, but keep your eyes open for their appearances and re-appearances in the stories and extracts you read. There is, for instance, the Loyal Retainer, who generally supports a **Hero**, and has a wicked counterpart, the Evil Henchperson. A henchman was originally a servant who looked after his master's horse, but the label has evolved so that the Evil Henchman (or Henchwoman, though you don't see the word often!) has now become the **Villain's** sidekick or assistant, frequently the muscle to the Villain's brains: like Crabbe and Goyle in the Harry Potter stories. Loyal Retainers are often allowed to add some humour: *The Castle of Otranto* features a pair of incompetent servants who enrage the Villain with their stupidity, but are supposed to make the reader laugh. Then there is the Governess (or Nurse), who is sometimes just another Loyal Retainer, but sometimes more. Not forgetting the Orphan, who can be a Sinister Child (remember Miles in the previous chapter), or just a Young Victim. There is a really good story by M. R. James where Orphans are Young Victims, Sinister Children and Antagonists, all rolled into one: *Lost Hearts*. Find it and read it.

And after all of that, when does a **Character** become a **Plot Device** (remember the **Sceptic**)?

THE HERO

"I fear no man's displeasure," said Theodore, "when a woman in distress puts herself under my protection."

Theodore, the Hero of *The Castle of Otranto*, is seen to act with "a mixture of grace and humility" when he first appears. When we next meet him he offers to lay down his life to protect a woman in danger, qualities like "valour" and "bravery" are mentioned, and there is this description: "His person was noble, handsome, and commanding".

Clara Reeve's Hero Edmund, in *The Old English Baron*, is "as fine a youth as ever the sun shone upon". As he grows up and fights in the royal army he stands out by "intrepidity in action; by gentleness, humanity and modesty".

So far, so blah. These **Heroes** might sound the part, to the point of being clichés, but it is surprisingly rare to find them actually in action. More often it is the **Villains** – or **Antiheroes** – who are waving a sword or seeking a fight to the death. Heroes behave jolly well, because they are natural gentlemen, but it is often "providence", or good luck, the reward for virtue, that plays the major part in rescuing the Heroine.

Ann Radcliffe did sometimes allow a Hero to play a properly active role. In this series of passages from *A Sicilian Romance*, Hippolitus (who is also referred to as "the count") is in search of his beloved *Heroine* Julia, and manages to get properly lost – several times.

> The evening was far advanced when he discovered that he had taken a wrong direction, and that he was bewildered in a wild and solitary scene. He had wandered too far from the road to hope to regain it, and he had beside no recollection of the objects left behind him. A choice of errors, only, lay before him.

He enters a **Forest**, where night falls. He hears voices and sees a brief gleam of light which quickly disappears.

> He continued his way as nearly as he could guess, towards the place whence it had issued; and after much toil, found himself in a spot where the trees formed a circle round a kind of rude lawn. The moonlight discovered to him an edifice which appeared to have been formerly a monastery, but which now exhibited a pile of ruins, whose grandeur, heightened by decay, touched the beholder with reverential awe. Hippolitus paused to gaze upon the scene; the sacred stillness of night increased its effect, and a secret dread, he knew not wherefore, stole upon his heart.
>
> The silence and the character of the place made him doubt whether this was the spot he had been seeking; and as he stood hesitating whether to proceed or to return, he observed a figure standing under an arch-way of the ruin; it carried a light in

its hand, and passing silently along, disappeared in a remote part of the building. The courage of Hippolitus for a moment deserted him. An invincible curiosity, however, subdued his terror, and he determined to pursue, if possible, the way the figure had taken.

Radcliffe is so determined to build an atmosphere of suspense and horror, that she is quite happy to have her **Hero** feel fear.

He passed over loose stones through a sort of court till he came to the archway; here he stopped, for fear returned upon him. Resuming his courage, however, he went on, still endeavouring to follow the way the figure had passed, and suddenly found himself in an enclosed part of the ruin, whose appearance was more wild and desolate than any he had yet seen. Seized with unconquerable apprehension, he was retiring, when the low voice of a distressed person struck his ear. His heart sunk at the sound, his limbs trembled, and he was utterly unable to move.

The sound which appeared to be the last groan of a dying person, was repeated. Hippolitus made a strong effort, and sprang forward, when a light burst upon him from a shattered casement of the building, and at the same instant he heard the voices of men!

He advanced softly to the window, and beheld in a small room, which was less decayed than the rest of the edifice, a group of men, who, from the savageness of their looks, and from their dress, appeared to be banditti. They surrounded a man who lay on the ground wounded, and bathed in blood, and who it was very evident had uttered the groans heard by the count.

The obscurity of the place prevented Hippolitus from distinguishing the features of the dying man. From the blood which covered him, and from the surrounding circumstances, he appeared to be murdered; and the count had no doubt that the men he beheld were the murderers. The horror of the scene entirely overcame him; he stood rooted to the spot, and saw the assassins rifle the pockets of the dying person, who, in a voice scarcely articulate, but which despair seemed to aid, supplicated for mercy. The ruffians answered him only with execrations, and continued their plunder. His groans and his sufferings served only to aggravate their cruelty. They were proceeding to take from him a miniature picture, which was fastened round his neck, and had been hitherto concealed in his bosom; when by a sudden effort he half raised himself from the ground, and attempted to save it from their hands. The effort availed him nothing; a blow from one of the villains laid the unfortunate man on the floor without motion. The horrid barbarity of the act seized the mind of Hippolitus so entirely, that, forgetful of his own situation, he groaned aloud, and started with an instantaneous design of avenging the deed. The noise he made alarmed the banditti, who looking whence it came, discovered the count through the casement. They instantly quitted their prize, and rushed towards the door of the room. He was now returned to a sense of his danger, and endeavoured to escape to the exterior part of the ruin; but terror bewildered his senses, and he mistook his way. Instead of regaining the arch-way, he perplexed himself with fruitless wanderings, and at length found himself only more deeply involved in the secret recesses of the pile.

The steps of his pursuers gained fast upon him, and he continued to perplex himself with vain efforts at escape, till at length, quite exhausted, he sunk on the ground, and endeavoured to resign himself to his fate. He listened with a kind of stern despair, and was surprised to find all silent. On looking round, he perceived by a ray of moonlight, which streamed through a part of the ruin from above, that he was in a sort of vault, which, from the small means he had of judging, he thought was extensive.

In this situation he remained for a considerable time, ruminating on the means of escape, yet scarcely believing escape was possible. If he continued in the vault, he might continue there only to be butchered; but by attempting to rescue himself from the place he was now in, he must rush into the hands of the banditti. Judging it, therefore, the safer way of the two to remain where he was, he endeavoured to await his fate with fortitude, when suddenly the loud voices of the murderers burst upon his ear, and he heard steps advancing quickly towards the spot where he lay.

Despair instantly renewed his vigour; he started from the ground, and throwing round him a look of eager desperation, his eye caught the glimpse of a small door, upon which the moon-beam now fell. He made towards it, and passed it just as the light of a torch gleamed upon the walls of the vault.

He groped his way along a winding passage, and at length came to a flight of steps. Notwithstanding the darkness, he reached the bottom in safety.

He now for the first time stopped to listen—the sounds of pursuit were ceased, and all was silent! Continuing to wander on in effectual endeavours to escape, his hands at length touched cold iron, and he quickly perceived it belonged to a door. The door, however, was fastened, and resisted all his efforts to open it. He was giving up the attempt in despair, when a loud scream from within, followed by a dead and heavy noise, roused all his attention. Silence ensued. He listened for a considerable time at the door, his imagination filled with images of horror, and expecting to hear the sound repeated. He then sought for a decayed part of the door, through which he might discover what was beyond; but he could find none; and after waiting some time without hearing any farther noise, he was quitting the spot, when in passing his arm over the door, it struck against something hard. On examination he perceived, to his extreme surprise, that the key was in the lock. For a moment he hesitated what to do; but curiosity overcame other considerations, and with a trembling hand he turned the key. The door opened into a large and desolate apartment, dimly lighted by a lamp that stood on a table, which was almost the only furniture of the place. The count had advanced several steps before he perceived an object, which fixed all his attention. This was the figure of a young woman lying on the floor apparently dead. Her face was concealed in her robe; and the long auburn tresses which fell in beautiful luxuriance over her bosom, served to veil a part of the glowing beauty which the disorder of her dress would have revealed.

Pity, surprise, and admiration struggled in the breast of Hippolitus; and while he stood surveying the object which excited these different emotions, he heard a step advancing towards the room. He flew to the door by which he had entered, and was fortunate enough to reach it before the entrance of the persons whose steps he heard. Having turned the key, he stopped at the door to listen to their proceedings. He distinguished the voices of two men, and knew them to be those of the assassins. Presently he heard a piercing skriek, and at the same instant the voices of the ruffians grew loud and violent. One of them exclaimed that the lady was dying, and accused the other of having frightened her to death, swearing, with horrid imprecations, that she was his, and he would defend her to the last drop of his blood. The dispute grew higher; and neither of the ruffians would give up his claim to the unfortunate object of their altercation.

The clashing of swords was soon after heard, together with a violent noise. The screams were repeated, and the oaths and execrations of the disputants redoubled. They seemed to move towards the door, behind which Hippolitus was concealed; suddenly the door was shook with great force, a deep groan followed, and was instantly succeeded by a noise like that of a person whose whole weight falls at once to the ground. For a moment all was silent. Hippolitus had no doubt that one of the ruffians had destroyed the other, and was soon confirmed in the belief—for the survivor triumphed with brutal exultation over his fallen antagonist. The ruffian hastily quitted the room, and Hippolitus soon after heard the distant voices of several persons in loud dispute. The sounds seemed to come from a chamber over the place where he stood; he also heard a trampling of feet from above, and could even distinguish, at

A Young Person's Guide to the Gothic

intervals, the words of the disputants. From these he gathered enough to learn that the affray which had just happened, and the lady who had been the occasion of it, were the subjects of discourse. The voices frequently rose together, and confounded all distinction.

At length the tumult began to subside, and Hippolitus could distinguish what was said. The ruffians agreed to give up the lady in question to him who had fought for her; and leaving him to his prize, they all went out in quest of farther prey. The situation of the unfortunate lady excited a mixture of pity and indignation in Hippolitus, which for some time entirely occupied him; he revolved the means of extricating her from so deplorable a situation, and in these thoughts almost forgot his own danger. He now heard her sighs; and while his heart melted to the sounds, the farther door of the apartment was thrown open, and the wretch to whom she had been allotted, rushed in. Her screams now redoubled, but they were of no avail with the ruffian who had seized her in his arms; when the count, who was unarmed, insensible to every pulse but that of a generous pity, burst into the room, but became fixed like a statue when he beheld his Julia struggling in the grasp of the ruffian. On discovering Hippolitus, she made a sudden spring, and liberated herself; when, running to him, she sunk lifeless in his arms.

Surprise and fury sparkled in the eyes of the ruffian, and he turned with a savage desperation upon the count; who, relinquishing Julia, snatched up the sword of the dead ruffian, which lay upon the floor, and defended himself. The combat was furious, but Hippolitus laid his antagonist senseless at his feet.

Thank goodness for that! Hippolitus, after all that running away, hiding and getting lost in the dark in a most un-heroic fashion, manages to rescue his Julia. Or does he?

A Young Person's Guide to the Gothic

After some little consideration, Hippolitus judged it most prudent to seek an outlet through the passage by which he entered; he therefore took the lamp, and led Julia to the door. They entered the avenue, and locking the door after them, sought the flight of steps down which the count had before passed; but having pursued the windings of the avenue a considerable time without finding them, he became certain he had mistaken the way. They, however, found another flight, which they descended and entered upon a passage so very narrow and low, as not to admit of a person walking upright. This passage was closed by a door, which on examination was found to be chiefly of iron. Hippolitus was startled at the sight, but on applying his strength found it gradually yield, when the imprisoned air rushed out, and had nearly extinguished the light. They now entered upon a dark abyss; and the door which moved upon a spring, suddenly closed upon them. On looking round they beheld a large vault; and it is not easy to imagine their horror on discovering they were in a receptacle for the murdered bodies of the unfortunate people who had fallen into the hands of the banditti.

The count could scarcely support the fainting spirits of Julia; he ran to the door, which he endeavoured to open, but the lock was so constructed that it could be moved only on the other side, and all his efforts were useless. He was constrained, therefore, to seek for another door, but could find none. Their situation was the most deplorable that can be imagined; for they were now enclosed in a vault strewn with the dead bodies of the murdered, and must there become the victims of famine, or of the sword. The earth was in several places thrown up, and marked the boundaries of new-made graves. The bodies which remained unburied were probably left either from hurry or negligence, and exhibited a spectacle too shocking for humanity.

The words frying-pan and fire spring to mind.

THE HEROINE

The main female **Character** in the original Gothic novel is almost always a "damsel in distress". She is pursued, oppressed and sometimes murdered by the **Villain**. In these earlier Gothic works, attitudes to women meant the **Heroine** was expected to be virtuous (and so a virgin according to the values of the time) and a passive victim, powerless to resist the sexual, or at least marital, advances of the Villain. Interestingly, similar criticisms have been made of a modern Heroine – Bella Swan in the *Twilight* series – but author Stephanie Meyer argues that while Bella does find herself a frequent damsel in distress, she is also empowered to make her own choices about how to act.

The poet Shelley wrote a second Gothic tale, *St Irvyne; or, the Rosicrucian,* published the year after *Zastrozzi*, in 1811. In the first section of the story his female protagonist, a prisoner of bandits who have killed her father, behaves in the way we expect of the Gothic Heroine.

> The wretched Megalena, a prey to despair and terror, endeavoured to revolve in her mind the events which had brought her to this spot, but an unconnected stream of ideas pressed upon her brain. The sole light in her cell was that of a dismal lamp, which, by its uncertain flickering, only dissipated the almost palpable obscurity, in a sufficient degree more assuredly to point out the circumambient horrors. She gazed wistfully around, to see if there were any outlet; none there was, save the door which was strongly barred on the outside. In despair she threw herself on the wretched pallet.
>
> "For what cause, then, am I thus entombed alive?" soliloquized the hapless Megalena; "would it not be preferable at once to annihilate the spark of life which burns but faintly within my bosom? O my father! where art thou? Thy tombless corse, perhaps, is torn

into a thousand pieces by the fury of the mountain cataract. Little didst thou presage misfortunes such as these! Little didst thou suppose that our last journey would have caused thy immature dissolution – my infamy and misery, not to end but with my hapless existence! Here there is none to comfort me, none to participate my miseries!" Thus speaking, overcome by a paroxysm of emotion, she sank on the bed, and bedewed her fair face with tears.

If you read the rest of the book, Megalena does, however, undergo something of a transformation!

Ann Radcliffe is admired for the relative toughness of her *Heroines*, earlier versions of today's more effective female Characters – along the lines of Hermione in the Harry Potter books. They are often damsels in distress, but are still able to show intelligence and determination. Emily St Aubert, in *The Mysteries of Udolpho*, is certainly frightened, but keeps (relatively) calm and carries on. She has been Imprisoned in a **Castle** by the **Villain** Montoni.

From the disturbed slumber, into which she then sunk, she was soon awakened by a noise, which seemed to arise within her chamber; but the silence, that prevailed, as she fearfully listened, inclined her to believe, that she had been alarmed by such sounds as sometimes occur in dreams, and she laid her head again upon the pillow.

A return of the noise again disturbed her; it seemed to come from that part of the room, which communicated with the private stair-case, and she instantly remembered the odd circumstance of the door having been fastened, during the preceding night, by some unknown hand. Her late alarming suspicion, concerning its communication, also occurred to her. Her heart became faint with terror. Half raising herself from the bed, and gently drawing aside the curtain, she looked towards the door of the stair-case, but the lamp, that burnt on the hearth, spread so feeble a light through the apartment, that the remote parts of it were lost in shadow. The noise, however, which, she was convinced, came from the door, continued. It seemed like that made by the undrawing of rusty bolts, and often ceased, and was then renewed more gently, as if the hand, that occasioned it, was restrained by a fear of discovery.

While Emily kept her eyes fixed on the spot, she saw the door move, and then slowly open, and perceived something enter the room, but the extreme duskiness prevented her distinguishing what it was. Almost fainting with terror, she had yet sufficient command over herself, to check the shriek, that was escaping from her lips, and, letting the curtain drop from her hand, continued to observe in silence the motions of the mysterious form she saw. It seemed to glide along the remote obscurity of the apartment, then paused, and, as it approached the hearth, she perceived, in the stronger light, what appeared to be a human figure. Certain remembrances now struck upon her heart, and almost subdued the feeble remains of her spirits; she continued, however, to watch the figure, which remained for some time motionless, but then, advancing slowly towards the bed, stood silently at the feet, where the curtains, being a little open, allowed her still to see it; terror, however, had now deprived her of the power of discrimination, as well as of that of utterance.

Having continued there a moment, the form retreated towards the hearth, when it took the lamp, held it up, surveyed the chamber, for a few moments, and then again advanced towards the bed. The light at that instant awakening the dog, that had slept at Emily's feet, he barked loudly, and, jumping to the floor, flew at the stranger, who struck the animal smartly with a sheathed sword, and, springing towards the bed, Emily discovered – Count Morano!

The **Villain** Montoni had earlier promised to force Emily to marry Morano, basically selling her to him. He then changed his mind, but Morano has fallen in love with her, so has come to steal her away.

She gazed at him for a moment in speechless affright, while he, throwing himself on his knee at the bed-side, besought her to fear nothing, and, having thrown down his sword, would have taken her hand, when the faculties, that terror had suspended, suddenly returned, and she sprung from the bed, in the dress, which surely a kind of prophetic apprehension had prevented her, on this night, from throwing aside.

Morano rose, followed her to the door, through which he had entered, and caught her hand, as she reached the top of the stair-case, but not before she had discovered, by the gleam of a lamp, another man half-way down the steps. She now screamed in despair, and, believing herself given up by Montoni, saw, indeed, no possibility of escape.

The Count, who still held her hand, led her back into the chamber.

"Why all this terror?" said he, in a tremulous voice. "Hear me, Emily: I come not to alarm you; no, by Heaven! I love you too well – too well for my own peace."

Emily looked at him for a moment, in fearful doubt.

"Then leave me, sir," said she, "leave me instantly."

"Hear me, Emily," resumed Morano, "hear me! I love, and am in despair – yes – in despair. How can I gaze upon you, and know, that it is, perhaps, for the last time, without suffering all the frenzy of despair? But it shall not be so; you shall be mine, in spite of Montoni and all his villany."

"In spite of Montoni!" cried Emily eagerly: "what is it I hear?"

"You hear, that Montoni is a villain," exclaimed Morano with vehemence, – "a villain who would have sold you to my love!—Who…"

"And is he less, who would have bought me?" said Emily, fixing on the Count an eye of calm contempt. "Leave the room, sir, instantly," she continued in a voice, trembling between joy and fear, "or I will alarm the family, and you may receive that from Signor Montoni's vengeance, which I have vainly supplicated from his pity."

She may be dealing with an uninvited man waving a sword in her bedroom, but she can still look at him with "calm contempt" and give him his marching orders.

THE YELLOW WALLPAPER
CHARLOTTE PERKINS GILMAN

The **Heroine** – and narrator - of this story, which was first published in 1892, may not seem to share much with our earlier damsels in distress, but she is in fact very much the powerless victim of a dominant male. The author, Charlotte Perkins Gilman was an outspoken feminist, and the story was to some extent autobiographical; Gilman separated from her first husband following a severe bout of depression which was initially treated with a "rest cure" she judged had made things worse.

It is very seldom that mere ordinary people like John and myself secure ancestral halls for the summer.

A colonial mansion, a hereditary estate, I would say a haunted house, and reach the height of romantic felicity—but that would be asking too much of fate!

Still I will proudly declare that there is something queer about it.

Else, why should it be let so cheaply? And why have stood so long untenanted?

John laughs at me, of course, but one expects that in marriage.

John is practical in the extreme. He has no patience with faith, an intense horror of superstition, and he scoffs openly at any talk of things not to be felt and seen and put down in figures.

John is a physician, and perhaps—(I would not say it to a living soul, of course, but this is dead paper and a great relief to my mind)—perhaps that is one reason I do not get well faster.

You see he does not believe I am sick!

And what can one do?

If a physician of high standing, and one's own husband, assures friends and relatives that there is really nothing the matter with one but temporary nervous depression—a slight hysterical tendency—what is one to do?

My brother is also a physician, and also of high standing, and he says the same thing.

So I take phosphates or phosphites—whichever it is, and tonics, and journeys, and air, and exercise, and am absolutely forbidden to "work" until I am well again.

Personally, I disagree with their ideas.

Personally, I believe that congenial work, with excitement and change, would do me good.

But what is one to do?

I did write for a while in spite of them; but it does exhaust me a good deal—having to be so sly about it, or else meet with heavy opposition.

I sometimes fancy that in my condition if I had less opposition and more society and stimulus—but John says the very worst thing I can do is to think about my condition, and I confess it always makes me feel bad.

So I will let it alone and talk about the house.

The most beautiful place! It is quite alone, standing well back from the road, quite three miles from the village. It makes me think of English places that you read about, for there are hedges and walls and gates that lock, and lots of separate little houses for the gardeners and people.

There is a delicious garden! I never saw such a garden—large and shady, full of box-bordered paths, and lined with long grape-covered arbours with seats under them.

There were greenhouses, too, but they are all broken now.

There was some legal trouble, I believe, something about the heirs and coheirs; anyhow, the place has been empty for years.

That spoils my ghostliness, I am afraid, but I don't care—there is something strange about the house—I can feel it.

I even said so to John one moonlight evening, but he said what I felt was a draught, and shut the window.

I get unreasonably angry with John sometimes. I'm sure I never used to be so sensitive. I think it is due to this nervous condition.

But John says if I feel so, I shall neglect proper self-control; so I take pains to control myself—before him, at least, and that makes me very tired.

I don't like our room a bit. I wanted one downstairs that opened on the piazza and had roses all over the window, and such pretty old-fashioned chintz hangings! but John would not hear of it.

He said there was only one window and not room for two beds, and no near room for him if he took another.

He is very careful and loving, and hardly lets me stir without special direction.

I have a schedule prescription for each hour in the day; he takes all care from me, and so I feel basely ungrateful not to value it more.

He said we came here solely on my account, that I was to have perfect rest and all the air I could get. "Your exercise depends on your strength, my dear," said he, "and your food somewhat on your appetite; but air you can absorb all the time." So we took the nursery at the top of the house.

It is a big, airy room, the whole floor nearly, with windows that look all ways, and air and sunshine galore. It was nursery first and then playroom and gymnasium, I should judge; for the windows are barred for little children, and there are rings and things in the walls.

The paint and paper look as if a boys' school had used it. It is stripped off—the paper—in great patches all around the head of my bed, about as far as I can reach, and in a great place on the other side of the room low down. I never saw a worse paper in my life.

One of those sprawling flamboyant patterns committing every artistic sin.

A Young Person's Guide to the Gothic

It is dull enough to confuse the eye in following, pronounced enough to constantly irritate and provoke study, and when you follow the lame uncertain curves for a little distance they suddenly commit suicide—plunge off at outrageous angles, destroy themselves in unheard of contradictions.

The colour is repellent, almost revolting; a smouldering unclean yellow, strangely faded by the slow-turning sunlight.

It is a dull yet lurid orange in some places, a sickly sulphur tint in others.

No wonder the children hated it! I should hate it myself if I had to live in this room long.

There comes John, and I must put this away,—he hates to have me write a word.

We have been here two weeks, and I haven't felt like writing before, since that first day.

I am sitting by the window now, up in this atrocious nursery, and there is nothing to hinder my writing as much as I please, save lack of strength.

John is away all day, and even some nights when his cases are serious.

I am glad my case is not serious!

But these nervous troubles are dreadfully depressing.

John does not know how much I really suffer. He knows there is no reason to suffer, and that satisfies him.

Of course it is only nervousness. It does weigh on me so not to do my duty in any way!

I meant to be such a help to John, such a real rest and comfort, and here I am a comparative burden already!

Nobody would believe what an effort it is to do what little I am able,—to dress and entertain, and order things.

It is fortunate Mary is so good with the baby. Such a dear baby!

And yet I cannot be with him, it makes me so nervous.

I suppose John never was nervous in his life. He laughs at me so about this wall-paper!

At first he meant to repaper the room, but afterwards he

said that I was letting it get the better of me, and that nothing was worse for a nervous patient than to give way to such fancies.

He said that after the wall-paper was changed it would be the heavy bedstead, and then the barred windows, and then that gate at the head of the stairs, and so on.

"You know the place is doing you good," he said, "and really, dear, I don't care to renovate the house just for a three months' rental."

"Then do let us go downstairs," I said, "there are such pretty rooms there."

Then he took me in his arms and called me a blessed little goose, and said he would go down to the cellar, if I wished, and have it whitewashed into the bargain.

But he is right enough about the beds and windows and things.

It is an airy and comfortable room as any one need wish, and, of course, I would not be so silly as to make him uncomfortable just for a whim.

I'm really getting quite fond of the big room, all but that horrid paper.

Out of one window I can see the garden, those mysterious deepshaded arbours, the riotous old-fashioned flowers, and bushes and gnarly trees.

Out of another I get a lovely view of the bay and a little private wharf belonging to the estate. There is a beautiful shaded lane that runs down there from the house. I always fancy I see people walking in these numerous paths and arbours, but John has cautioned me not to give way to fancy in the least. He says that with my imaginative power and habit of story-making, a nervous weakness like mine is sure to lead to all manner of excited fancies, and that I ought to use my will and good sense to check the tendency. So I try.

I think sometimes that if I were only well enough to write a little it would relieve the press of ideas and rest me.

But I find I get pretty tired when I try.

It is so discouraging not to have any advice and

companionship about my work. When I get really well, John says we will ask Cousin Henry and Julia down for a long visit; but he says he would as soon put fireworks in my pillow-case as to let me have those stimulating people about now.

I wish I could get well faster.

But I must not think about that. This paper looks to me as if it knew what a vicious influence it had!

There is a recurrent spot where the pattern lolls like a broken neck and two bulbous eyes stare at you upside down.

I get positively angry with the impertinence of it and the everlastingness. Up and down and sideways they crawl, and those absurd, unblinking eyes are everywhere. There is one place where two breadths didn't match, and the eyes go all up and down the line, one a little higher than the other.

I never saw so much expression in an inanimate thing before, and we all know how much expression they have! I used to lie awake as a child and get more entertainment and terror out of blank walls and plain furniture than most children could find in a toy store.

I remember what a kindly wink the knobs of our big, old bureau used to have, and there was one chair that always seemed like a strong friend.

I used to feel that if any of the other things looked too fierce I could always hop into that chair and be safe.

The furniture in this room is no worse than inharmonious, however, for we had to bring it all from downstairs. I suppose when this was used as a playroom they had to take the nursery things out, and no wonder! I never saw such ravages as the children have made here.

The wall-paper, as I said before, is torn off in spots, and it sticketh closer than a brother—they must have had perseverance as well as hatred.

Then the floor is scratched and gouged and splintered, the plaster itself is dug out here and there, and this great heavy bed which is all we found in the room, looks as if it had been through the wars.

But I don't mind it a bit—only the paper.

There comes John's sister. Such a dear girl as she is, and so careful of me! I must not let her find me writing.

She is a perfect and enthusiastic housekeeper, and hopes for no better profession. I verily believe she thinks it is the writing which made me sick!

But I can write when she is out, and see her a long way off from these windows.

There is one that commands the road, a lovely shaded winding road, and one that just looks off over the country. A lovely country, too, full of great elms and velvet meadows.

This wall-paper has a kind of sub-pattern in a different shade, a particularly irritating one, for you can only see it in certain lights, and not clearly then.

But in the places where it isn't faded and where the sun is just so—I can see a strange, provoking, formless sort of figure, that seems to skulk about behind that silly and conspicuous front design.

There's sister on the stairs!

Well, the Fourth of July is over! The people are gone and I am tired out. John thought it might do me good to see a little company, so we just had mother and Nellie and the children down for a week.

Of course I didn't do a thing. Jennie sees to everything now.

But it tired me all the same.

John says if I don't pick up faster he shall send me to Weir Mitchell in the fall.

But I don't want to go there at all. I had a friend who was in his hands once, and she says he is just like John and my brother, only more so!

Besides, it is such an undertaking to go so far.

I don't feel as if it was worth while to turn my hand over for anything, and I'm getting dreadfully fretful and querulous.

I cry at nothing, and cry most of the time.

Of course I don't when John is here, or anybody else, but when I am alone.

And I am alone a good deal just now. John is kept in town very often by serious cases, and Jennie is good and lets me alone when I want her to.

So I walk a little in the garden or down that lovely lane, sit on the porch under the roses, and lie down up here a good deal.

I'm getting really fond of the room in spite of the wall-paper. Perhaps because of the wall-paper.

It dwells in my mind so!

I lie here on this great immovable bed—it is nailed down, I believe—and follow that pattern about by the hour. It is as good as gymnastics, I assure you. I start, we'll say, at the bottom, down in the corner over there where it has not been touched, and I determine for the thousandth time that I will follow that pointless pattern to some sort of a conclusion.

I know a little of the principle of design, and I know this thing was not arranged on any laws of radiation, or alternation, or repetition, or symmetry, or anything else that I ever heard of.

It is repeated, of course, by the breadths, but not otherwise.

Looked at in one way each breadth stands alone, the bloated curves and flourishes—a kind of "debased Romanesque" with delirium tremens—go waddling up and down in isolated columns of fatuity.

But, on the other hand, they connect diagonally, and the sprawling outlines run off in great slanting waves of optic horror, like a lot of wallowing seaweeds in full chase.

The whole thing goes horizontally, too, at least it seems so, and I exhaust myself in trying to distinguish the order of its going in that direction.

They have used a horizontal breadth for a frieze, and that adds wonderfully to the confusion.

There is one end of the room where it is almost intact, and there, when the crosslights fade and the low sun shines directly upon it, I can almost fancy radiation after all,—the interminable grotesques seem to form around a common centre and rush off in headlong plunges of equal distraction.

It makes me tired to follow it. I will take a nap I guess.

I don't know why I should write this.

I don't want to.

I don't feel able.

And I know John would think it absurd. But I must say what I feel and think in some way—it is such a relief!

But the effort is getting to be greater than the relief.

Half the time now I am awfully lazy, and lie down ever so much.

John says I mustn't lose my strength, and has me take cod liver oil and lots of tonics and things, to say nothing of ale and wine and rare meat.

Dear John! He loves me very dearly, and hates to have me sick. I tried to have a real earnest reasonable talk with him the other day, and tell him how I wish he would let me go and make a visit to Cousin Henry and Julia.

But he said I wasn't able to go, nor able to stand it after I got there; and I did not make out a very good case for myself, for I was crying before I had finished.

It is getting to be a great effort for me to think straight. Just this nervous weakness I suppose.

And dear John gathered me up in his arms, and just carried me upstairs and laid me on the bed, and sat by me and read to me till it tired my head.

He said I was his darling and his comfort and all he had, and that I must take care of myself for his sake, and keep well.

He says no one but myself can help me out of it, that I must use my will and self-control and not let any silly fancies run away with me.

There's one comfort, the baby is well and happy, and does not have to occupy this nursery with the horrid wall-paper.

If we had not used it, that blessed child would have! What a fortunate escape! Why, I wouldn't have a child of mine, an impressionable little thing, live in such a room for worlds.

I never thought of it before, but it is lucky that John kept me here after all, I can stand it so much easier than a baby, you see.

Of course I never mention it to them any more—I am too wise,—but I keep watch of it all the same.

There are things in that paper that nobody knows but me, or ever will.

Behind that outside pattern the dim shapes get clearer every day.

It is always the same shape, only very numerous.

And it is like a woman stooping down and creeping about behind that pattern. I don't like it a bit. I wonder—I begin to think—I wish John would take me away from here!

It is so hard to talk with John about my case, because he is so wise, and because he loves me so.

But I tried it last night.

It was moonlight. The moon shines in all around just as the sun does.

I hate to see it sometimes, it creeps so slowly, and always comes in by one window or another.

John was asleep and I hated to waken him, so I kept still and watched the moonlight on that undulating wall-paper till I felt creepy.

The faint figure behind seemed to shake the pattern, just as if she wanted to get out.

I got up softly and went to feel and see if the paper did move, and when I came back John was awake.

"What is it, little girl?" he said. "Don't go walking about like that—you'll get cold."

I thought it was a good time to talk, so I told him that I really was not gaining here, and that I wished he would take me away.

"Why darling!" said he, "our lease will be up in three weeks, and I can't see how to leave before.

"The repairs are not done at home, and I cannot possibly leave town just now. Of course if you were in any danger, I could and would, but you really are better, dear, whether you can see it or not. I am a doctor, dear, and I know. You are gaining flesh and colour, your appetite is better, I feel really much easier about you."

"I don't weigh a bit more," said I, "nor as much; and my appetite may be better in the evening when you are here, but it is worse in the morning when you are away!"

"Bless her little heart!" said he with a big hug, "she shall be as sick as she pleases! But now let's improve the shining hours by going to sleep, and talk about it in the morning!"

"And you won't go away?" I asked gloomily.

"Why, how can I, dear? It is only three weeks more and then we will take a nice little trip of a few days while Jennie is getting the house ready. Really dear you are better!"

"Better in body perhaps—" I began, and stopped short, for he sat up straight and looked at me with such a stern, reproachful look that I could not say another word.

"My darling," said he, "I beg of you, for my sake and for our child's sake, as well as for your own, that you will never for one instant let that idea enter your mind! There is nothing so dangerous, so fascinating, to a temperament like yours. It is a false and foolish fancy. Can you not trust me as a physician when I tell you so?"

So of course I said no more on that score, and we went to sleep before long. He thought I was asleep first, but I wasn't, and lay there for hours trying to decide whether that front pattern and the back pattern really did move together or separately.

On a pattern like this, by daylight, there is a lack of sequence, a defiance of law, that is a constant irritant to a normal mind.

The colour is hideous enough, and unreliable enough, and infuriating enough, but the pattern is torturing.

You think you have mastered it, but just as you get well underway in following, it turns a back-somersault and there you are. It slaps you in the face, knocks you down, and tramples upon you. It is like a bad dream.

The outside pattern is a florid arabesque, reminding one of a fungus. If you can imagine a toadstool in joints, an interminable string of toadstools, budding and sprouting in endless convolutions—why, that is something like it.

That is, sometimes!

There is one marked peculiarity about this paper, a thing nobody seems to notice but myself, and that is that it changes as the light changes.

When the sun shoots in through the east window—I always watch for that first long, straight ray—it changes so quickly that I never can quite believe it.

That is why I watch it always.

By moonlight—the moon shines in all night when there is a moon—I wouldn't know it was the same paper.

At night in any kind of light, in twilight, candle light, lamplight, and worst of all by moonlight, it becomes bars! The outside pattern I mean, and the woman behind it is as plain as can be.

I didn't realize for a long time what the thing was that showed behind, that dim sub-pattern, but now I am quite sure it is a woman.

By daylight she is subdued, quiet. I fancy it is the pattern that keeps her so still. It is so puzzling. It keeps me quiet by the hour.

I lie down ever so much now. John says it is good for me, and to sleep all I can.

Indeed he started the habit by making me lie down for an hour after each meal.

It is a very bad habit I am convinced, for you see I don't sleep.

And that cultivates deceit, for I don't tell them I'm awake—O no!

The fact is I am getting a little afraid of John.

He seems very queer sometimes, and even Jennie has an inexplicable look.

It strikes me occasionally, just as a scientific hypothesis,—that perhaps it is the paper!

I have watched John when he did not know I was looking, and come into the room suddenly on the most innocent excuses, and I've caught him several times looking at the paper! And

Jennie too. I caught Jennie with her hand on it once.

She didn't know I was in the room, and when I asked her in a quiet, a very quiet voice, with the most restrained manner possible, what she was doing with the paper—she turned around as if she had been caught stealing, and looked quite angry—asked me why I should frighten her so!

Then she said that the paper stained everything it touched, that she had found yellow smooches on all my clothes and John's, and she wished we would be more careful!

Did not that sound innocent? But I know she was studying that pattern, and I am determined that nobody shall find it out but myself!

Life is very much more exciting now than it used to be. You see I have something more to expect, to look forward to, to watch. I really do eat better, and am more quiet than I was.

John is so pleased to see me improve! He laughed a little the other day, and said I seemed to be flourishing in spite of my wall-paper.

I turned it off with a laugh. I had no intention of telling him it was because of the wall-paper—he would make fun of me. He might even want to take me away.

I don't want to leave now until I have found it out. There is a week more, and I think that will be enough.

I'm feeling ever so much better! I don't sleep much at night, for it is so interesting to watch developments; but I sleep a good deal in the daytime.

In the daytime it is tiresome and perplexing.

There are always new shoots on the fungus, and new shades of yellow all over it. I cannot keep count of them, though I have tried conscientiously.

It is the strangest yellow, that wall-paper! It makes me think of all the yellow things I ever saw—not beautiful ones like buttercups, but old foul, bad yellow things.

But there is something else about that paper—the smell! I noticed it the moment we came into the room, but with so much air and sun it was not bad. Now we have had a week of fog and rain, and whether the windows are open or not, the smell is here.

It creeps all over the house.

I find it hovering in the dining-room, skulking in the parlour, hiding in the hall, lying in wait for me on the stairs.

It gets into my hair.

Even when I go to ride, if I turn my head suddenly and surprise it—there is that smell!

Such a peculiar odour, too! I have spent hours in trying to analyze it, to find what it smelled like.

It is not bad—at first, and very gentle, but quite the subtlest, most enduring odour I ever met.

In this damp weather it is awful, I wake up in the night and find it hanging over me.

It used to disturb me at first. I thought seriously of burning the house—to reach the smell.

But now I am used to it. The only thing I can think of that it is like is the colour of the paper! A yellow smell.

There is a very funny mark on this wall, low down, near the mopboard. A streak that runs round the room. It goes behind every piece of furniture, except the bed, a long, straight, even smooch, as if it had been rubbed over and over.

I wonder how it was done and who did it, and what they did it for. Round and round and round—round and round and round—it makes me dizzy!

I really have discovered something at last.

Through watching so much at night, when it changes so, I have finally found out.

The front pattern does move—and no wonder! The woman behind shakes it!

Sometimes I think there are a great many women behind, and sometimes only one, and she crawls around fast, and her crawling shakes it all over.

Then in the very bright spots she keeps still, and in the very shady spots she just takes hold of the bars and shakes them hard.

And she is all the time trying to climb through. But nobody could climb through that pattern—it strangles so; I think that is why it has so many heads.

They get through, and then the pattern strangles them off and turns them upside down, and makes their eyes white!

If those heads were covered or taken off it would not be half so bad.

I think that woman gets out in the daytime!

And I'll tell you why—privately—I've seen her!

I can see her out of every one of my windows!

It is the same woman, I know, for she is always creeping, and most women do not creep by daylight.

I see her on that long road under the trees, creeping along, and when a carriage comes she hides under the blackberry vines.

I don't blame her a bit. It must be very humiliating to be caught creeping by daylight!

I always lock the door when I creep by daylight. I can't do it at night, for I know John would suspect something at once.

And John is so queer now, that I don't want to irritate him. I wish he would take another room! Besides, I don't want anybody to get that woman out at night but myself.

I often wonder if I could see her out of all the windows at once.

But, turn as fast as I can, I can only see out of one at one time.

And though I always see her, she may be able to creep faster than I can turn!

I have watched her sometimes away off in the open country, creeping as fast as a cloud shadow in a high wind.

If only that top pattern could be gotten off from the under one! I mean to try it, little by little.

I have found out another funny thing, but I shan't tell it this time! It does not do to trust people too much.

There are only two more days to get this paper off, and I believe John is beginning to notice. I don't like the look in his eyes.

And I heard him ask Jennie a lot of professional questions about me. She had a very good report to give.

She said I slept a good deal in the daytime.

John knows I don't sleep very well at night, for all I'm so quiet!

He asked me all sorts of questions, too, and pretended to be very loving and kind.

As if I couldn't see through him!

Still, I don't wonder he acts so, sleeping under this paper for three months.

It only interests me, but I feel sure John and Jennie are secretly affected by it.

Hurrah! This is the last day, but it is enough. John is to stay in town over night, and won't be out until this evening.

Jennie wanted to sleep with me—the sly thing! but I told her I should undoubtedly rest better for a night all alone.

That was clever, for really I wasn't alone a bit! As soon as it was moonlight and that poor thing began to crawl and shake the pattern, I got up and ran to help her.

I pulled and she shook, I shook and she pulled, and before morning we had peeled off yards of that paper.

A strip about as high as my head and half around the room.

And then when the sun came and that awful pattern began to laugh at me, I declared I would finish it to-day!

We go away to-morrow, and they are moving all my furniture down again to leave things as they were before.

Jennie looked at the wall in amazement, but I told her merrily that I did it out of pure spite at the vicious thing.

She laughed and said she wouldn't mind doing it herself, but I must not get tired.

How she betrayed herself that time!

But I am here, and no person touches this paper but me—not alive!

She tried to get me out of the room—it was too patent! But I said it was so quiet and empty and clean now that I believed I would lie down again and sleep all I could; and not to wake me even for dinner—I would call when I woke.

So now she is gone, and the servants are gone, and the things are gone, and there is nothing left but that great bedstead nailed down, with the canvas mattress we found on it.

We shall sleep downstairs to-night, and take the boat home to-morrow.

I quite enjoy the room, now it is bare again.

How those children did tear about here!

This bedstead is fairly gnawed!

But I must get to work.

I have locked the door and thrown the key down into the front path.

I don't want to go out, and I don't want to have anybody come in, till John comes.

I want to astonish him.

I've got a rope up here that even Jennie did not find. If that woman does get out, and tries to get away, I can tie her!

But I forgot I could not reach far without anything to stand on!

This bed will not move!

I tried to lift and push it until I was lame, and then I got so angry I bit off a little piece at one corner—but it hurt my teeth.

Then I peeled off all the paper I could reach standing on the floor. It sticks horribly and the pattern just enjoys it! All those strangled heads and bulbous eyes and waddling fungus growths just shriek with derision!

I am getting angry enough to do something desperate. To jump out of the window would be admirable exercise, but the bars are too strong even to try.

Besides I wouldn't do it. Of course not. I know well enough that a step like that is improper and might be misconstrued.

I don't like to look out of the windows even—there are so many of those creeping women, and they creep so fast.

I wonder if they all come out of that wall-paper as I did?

But I am securely fastened now by my well-hidden rope—you don't get me out in the road there!

I suppose I shall have to get back behind the pattern when it comes night, and that is hard!

It is so pleasant to be out in this great room and creep around as I please!

I don't want to go outside. I won't, even if Jennie asks me to.

For outside you have to creep on the ground, and everything is green instead of yellow.

But here I can creep smoothly on the floor, and my shoulder just fits in that long smooch around the wall, so I cannot lose my way.

Why there's John at the door!

It is no use, young man, you can't open it!

How he does call and pound!

Now he's crying for an axe.

It would be a shame to break down that beautiful door!

"John dear!" said I in the gentlest voice, "the key is down by the front steps, under a plantain leaf!"

That silenced him for a few moments.

Then he said—very quietly indeed, "Open the door, my darling!"

"I can't," said I. "The key is down by the front door under a plantain leaf!"

And then I said it again, several times, very gently and slowly, and said it so often that he had to go and see, and he got it of course, and came in. He stopped short by the door.

"What is the matter?" he cried. "For God's sake, what are you doing!"

I kept on creeping just the same, but I looked at him over my shoulder.

"I've got out at last," said I, "in spite of you and Jane. And I've pulled off most of the paper, so you can't put me back!"

Now why should that man have fainted? But he did, and right across my path by the wall, so that I had to creep over him every time!

THE VILLAINESS

The full-on female **Villain**, or **Villainess** (as opposed to an Evil Henchwoman), is quite rare in the early Gothic novels, which are more comfortable with women as victims. Matthew Lewis however, in *The Monk*, gives us a very fine example, on which many later wicked temptresses will be modelled. Matilda has fallen in love with Ambrosio, who is the Monk of the title (and the **Villain**), and actually pretends to be a boy, becoming a novice monk, in order to get close to him. She eventually succeeds in seducing him and although he is initially appalled at what he has done, Matilda is soon able get him back into bed!

"Dangerous Woman!" said He; "Into what an abyss of misery have you plunged me! Fool that I was, to trust myself to your seductions! What can now be done? How can my offence be expiated? What atonement can purchase the pardon of my crime? Wretched Matilda, you have destroyed my quiet for ever!"

"To me these reproaches, Ambrosio? To me, who have sacrificed for you the world's pleasures, the luxury of wealth, the delicacy of sex, my Friends, my fortune, and my fame? What have you lost, which *I* preserved? Have *I* not shared in *your* guilt? Have *you* not shared in *my* pleasure? Guilt, did I say? In what consists ours, unless in the opinion of an ill-judging World? Let that World be ignorant of them, and our joys become divine and blameless! Unnatural were your vows of Celibacy; Man was not created for such a state; And were Love a crime, God never would have made it so sweet, so irresistible! Then banish those clouds from your brow, my Ambrosio! Indulge in those pleasures freely, without which life is a worthless gift: Cease to reproach me with having taught you what is bliss, and feel equal transports with the Woman who adores you!"

As She spoke, her eyes were filled with a delicious languor. Her bosom panted: She twined her arms voluptuously round him, drew him towards her, and glued her lips to his. Ambrosio again raged with desire: The die was thrown: His vows were already broken; He had already committed the crime, and why should He refrain from enjoying its reward? He clasped her to his breast with redoubled ardour. No longer repressed by the sense of shame, He gave a loose to his intemperate appetites. While the fair Wanton put every invention of lust in practice, every refinement in the art of pleasure which might heighten the bliss of her possession, and render her Lover's transports still more exquisite, Ambrosio rioted in delights till then unknown to him: Swift fled the night, and the Morning blushed to behold him still clasped in the embraces of Matilda.

This is hardcore stuff by the standards of the time. Later Matilda persuades Ambrosio to join her as she uses black magic to summon a demon: her unembarrassed commitment to evil makes her more honest than the hypocritical monk. They are together in the cellars under the monastery; the ritual and accompanying "special effects" seem familiar because they have inspired so many subsequent books and films.

The light of the returning Lamp gilded the walls, and in a few moments after Matilda stood beside him. She had quitted her religious habit: She was now clothed in a long sable Robe, on which was traced in gold embroidery a variety of unknown characters: It was fastened by a girdle of precious stones, in which was fixed a poignard. Her neck and arms were uncovered. In her hand She bore a golden wand. Her hair was loose and flowed wildly upon her shoulders; Her eyes sparkled with terrific expression; and her whole Demeanour was calculated to inspire the beholder with awe and admiration.

"Follow me!" She said to the Monk in a low and solemn

voice; "All is ready!"

His limbs trembled, while He obeyed her. She led him through various narrow passages; and on every side as they passed along, the beams of the Lamp displayed none but the most revolting objects; Skulls, Bones, Graves, and Images whose eyes seemed to glare on them with horror and surprise. At length they reached a spacious Cavern, whose lofty roof the eye sought in vain to discover. A profound obscurity hovered through the void. Damp vapours struck cold to the Friar's heart; and He listened sadly to the blast while it howled along the lonely Vaults. Here Matilda stopped. She turned to Ambrosio. His cheeks and lips were pale with apprehension. By a glance of mingled scorn and anger She reproved his pusillanimity, but She spoke not. She placed the Lamp upon the ground, near the Basket. She motioned that Ambrosio should be silent, and began the mysterious rites. She drew a circle round him, another round herself, and then taking a small Phial from the Basket, poured a few drops upon the ground before her. She bent over the place, muttered some indistinct sentences, and immediately a pale sulphurous flame arose from the ground. It increased by degrees, and at length spread its waves over the whole surface, the circles alone excepted in which stood Matilda and the Monk. It then ascended the huge Columns of unhewn stone, glided along the roof, and formed the Cavern into an immense chamber totally covered with blue trembling fire. It emitted no heat: On the contrary, the extreme chillness of the place seemed to augment with every moment. Matilda continued her incantations: At intervals She took various articles from the Basket, the nature and name of most of which were unknown to the Friar: But among the few which He distinguished, He particularly observed three human fingers, and an Agnus Dei which She broke in pieces. She threw them all into the flames which burned before her, and they were instantly consumed.

The Monk beheld her with anxious curiosity. Suddenly She uttered a loud and piercing shriek. She appeared to be seized with an access of delirium; She tore her hair, beat her bosom, used the most frantic gestures, and drawing the poignard from her girdle plunged it into her left arm. The blood gushed out plentifully, and as She stood on the brink of the circle, She took care that it should fall on the outside. The flames retired from the spot on which the blood was pouring. A volume of dark clouds rose slowly from the ensanguined earth, and ascended gradually, till it reached the vault of the Cavern. At the same time a clap of thunder was heard: The echo pealed fearfully along the subterraneous passages, and the ground shook beneath the feet of the Enchantress.

It was now that Ambrosio repented of his rashness. The solemn singularity of the charm had prepared him for something strange and horrible. He waited with fear for the Spirit's appearance, whose coming was announced by thunder and earthquakes. He looked wildly round him, expecting that some dreadful Apparition would meet his eyes, the sight of which would drive him mad. A cold shivering seized his body, and He sank upon one knee, unable to support himself.

"He comes!" exclaimed Matilda in a joyful accent.

The demon she has summoned appears in the form of a beautiful young man – naked, with red wings. In contrast, the spirit stalking this next extract (from short story *The Cedar Closet*, published in 1874) is a "hideous" and "deformed" woman, a **Villainess** who has become a ghost and haunts the narrator, a Gothic-style **Heroine**. The "closet" of the title is a **Haunted Room**, panelled with cedar wood. Lafcadio Hearn, the author, began his writing career with lurid accounts of murders and other sensational stories in an American newspaper, but later moved to Japan and became a leading western authority on Japanese legends and tales of the supernatural.

I do not know how long I had been asleep, when I was suddenly, as it were, wrenched back to consciousness. The moon had set, the room was quite dark; I could just distinguish the glimmer of a clouded, starless sky through the open window.

I could not see or hear anything unusual, but not the less was I conscious of an unwonted, a baleful presence near; an indescribable horror cramped the very beatings of my heart; with every instant the certainty grew that my room was shared by some evil being. I could not cry for help, though Archie's room was so close, and I knew that one call through the death-like stillness would bring him to me; all I could do was to gaze, gaze, gaze into the darkness. Suddenly – and a throb stung through every nerve – I heard distinctly from behind the wainscot against which the head of my bed was placed a low, hollow moan, followed on the instant by a cackling, malignant laugh from the other side of the room. If I had been one of the monumental figures in the little churchyard on which I had seen the quiet moonbeams shine a few hours before I could not have been more utterly unable to move or speak; every other faculty seemed to be lost in the one intent strain of eye and ear. There came at last the sound of a halting step, the tapping of a crutch upon the floor, then stillness, and slowly, gradually the room filled with light – a pale, cold, steady light. Everything around was exactly as I had last seen it in the mingled shine of the moon and fire, and though I heard at intervals the harsh laugh, the curtain at the foot of the bed hid from me whatever uttered it. Again, low but distinct, the piteous moan broke forth, followed by some words in a foreign tongue, and with the sound a figure started from behind the curtain – a dwarfed, deformed woman, dressed in a loose robe of black, sprinkled with golden stars, which gave forth a dull, fiery gleam, in the mysterious light; one lean, yellow hand clutched the curtain of my bed; it glittered with jewelled rings; – long black hair fell in heavy masses from a golden circlet over the stunted form. I saw it all clearly as I now see the pen which writes these words and the hand which guides it. The face was turned from me, bent aside, as if greedily drinking in those astonished moans; I noted even the streaks of gray in the long tresses, as I lay helpless in dumb, bewildered horror.

"Again!" she said hoarsely, as the sounds died away into

indistinct murmurs, and advancing a step she tapped sharply with a crutch on the cedar wainscot; then again louder and more purposeful rose the wild beseeching voice; this time the words were English.

"Mercy, have mercy! not on me, but on my child, my little one; she never harmed you. She is dying – she is dying here in darkness; let me but see her face once more. Death is very near, nothing can save her now; but grant one ray of light, and I will pray that you may be forgiven, if forgiveness there be for such as you."

"What, you kneel at last! Kneel to Gerda, and kneel in vain. A ray of light; Not if you could pay for it in diamonds. You are mine! Shriek and call as you will, no other ears can hear. Die together. You are mine to torture as I will; mine, mine, mine!" and again an awful laugh rang through the room. At the instant she turned. O the face of malign horror that met my gaze! The green eyes flamed, and with something like the snarl of a savage beast she sprang toward me; that hideous face almost touched mine; the grasp of the skinny jewelled hand was all but on me; then – I suppose I fainted.

Who is trapped behind the cedar panels? Why is Gerda torturing them? Who is this evil **Villainess**?

THE VILLAIN

If the Gothic **Heroine** is a damsel in distress, the **Villain** is the one causing the distress. Manfred, the lord and Villain of *The Castle of Otranto*, is a man with a violent temper, who does his best to protect his position of power however he can. Unfortunately for him, ancient **Prophecy**, supernatural events and bad luck (which all come to the same thing in this context) drive him to disown his dead son, divorce his wife, pursue a reluctant potential wife and kill his daughter. And yet we are told:

> Manfred was not one of those savage tyrants who wanton in cruelty unprovoked. The circumstances of his fortune had given an asperity to his temper, which was naturally humane; and his virtues were always ready to operate, when his passions did not obscure his reason.

This makes him sound a bit like The Hulk: perfectly sensible until he gets angry. It would be a stretch to call him an **Antihero** – his behaviour is too consistently bad ("he curbed the yearnings of his heart, and did not dare to lean even towards pity. The next transition of his soul was to exquisite villainy."), but he is not pure evil. Walpole, as we saw with his **Castle**, is not one for specific physical description – we can make up our own minds about what Manfred looks like.

Ann Radcliffe, on the other hand, in *The Italian* (1797), gives a very detailed account of her Villain's appearance.

> His figure was striking, but not so from grace; it was tall, and, though extremely thin, his limbs were large and uncouth, and as he stalked along, wrapt in the black garments of his order, there was something terrible in its air; something almost superhuman. His cowl, too, as it threw a shade over the livid

paleness of his face, encreased its severe character, and gave an effect to his large melancholy eye, which approached to horror. His was not the melancholy of a sensible and wounded heart, but apparently that of a gloomy and ferocious disposition. There was something in his physiognomy extremely singular, and that can not easily be defined. It bore the traces of many passions, which seemed to have fixed the features they no longer animated. An habitual gloom and severity prevailed over the deep lines of his countenance; and his eyes were so piercing that they seemed to penetrate, at a single glance into the hearts of men, and to read their most secret thoughts; few persons could support their scrutiny, or even endure to meet them twice. Yet, notwithstanding all this gloom and austerity, some rare occasions of interest had called forth a character upon his countenance entirely different; and he could adapt himself to the tempers and passions of persons, whom he wished to conciliate, with astonishing facility, and generally with complete triumph. This monk, this Schedoni, was the confessor and secret adviser of the Marchesa di Vivaldi.

Schedoni may look grim, and does indeed perpetrate much wickedness, but he is still given human drives and motivations (pride, greed and revenge, mostly). For pure evil it is difficult to do better –or worse – than Bram Stoker's Count Dracula. Here is the introductory description that hints at the truth:

His face was a strong, a very strong, aquiline, with high bridge of the thin nose and peculiarly arched nostrils, with lofty domed forehead, and hair growing scantily round the temples but profusely elsewhere. His eyebrows were very massive, almost meeting over the nose, and with bushy hair that seemed to curl in its own profusion. The mouth, so far as I could see it under the heavy moustache, was fixed and rather cruel-looking, with peculiarly sharp white teeth. These protruded over the lips, whose remarkable ruddiness showed astonishing vitality in a man of his years. For the rest, his ears were pale, and at the tops extremely pointed. The chin was broad and strong, and the cheeks firm though thin. The general effect was one of extraordinary pallor.

Hitherto I had noticed the backs of his hands as they lay on his knees in the firelight, and they had seemed rather white and fine. But seeing them now close to me, I could not but notice that they were rather coarse, broad, with squat fingers. Strange to say, there were hairs in the centre of the palm. The nails were long and fine, and cut to a sharp point. As the Count leaned over me and his hands touched me, I could not repress a shudder. It may have been that his breath was rank, but a horrible feeling of nausea came over me, which, do what I would, I could not conceal.

Later in the book we see him in his true condition.

There lay the Count, but looking as if his youth had been half restored. For the white hair and moustache were changed to dark iron-grey. The cheeks were fuller, and the white skin seemed ruby-red underneath. The mouth was redder than ever, for on the lips were gouts of fresh blood, which trickled from the corners of the mouth and ran down over the chin and neck. Even the deep, burning eyes seemed set amongst swollen flesh, for the lids and pouches underneath were bloated. It seemed as if the whole awful creature were simply gorged with blood. He lay like a filthy leech, exhausted with his repletion. … There was a mocking smile on the face which seemed to drive me mad. This was the being I was helping to transfer to London, where, perhaps, for centuries to come he might, amongst its teeming millions, satiate his lust for blood, and create a new and ever-widening circle of semi-demons to batten on the helpless.

A Young Person's Guide to the Gothic

The ANTIHERO

A Gothic **Villain** who does not retain a spark of goodness somewhere deep down is actually quite rare, as we have just seen with the very first: Manfred from *The Castle of Otranto*. In the TV series *Buffy the Vampire Slayer*, the **Vampire** Angel has a villainous past, but with his soul returned to him now feels guilt and remorse; he mostly sides with the "good guys", but does suffer relapses. Spike, in the same programme, is initially pure evil, but also evolves to achieve **Antihero** status. Eoin Colfer's *Artemis Fowl*, a teenage criminal mastermind, starts out ruthless and selfish, plotting kidnap for ransom, but gradually learns the value of at least a Robin Hood sort of morality. Good writers have always known that a **Character** who experiences some internal conflict is more interesting than a simple caricature of good or evil. **Antiheroes** fascinate us because we can recognise that we too are sometimes bad and might experience the same urges they do.

William Beckford's *Vathek* was originally written in French in 1782. The author was twenty-one and variously claimed the novel took him two days and a night, or three days and two nights to complete. The title character is a middle-eastern Caliph (a sort of king), whose adventures are very much inspired by the tales of the Arabian Nights.

> Vathek, ninth Caliph of the race of the Abassides, was the son of Motassem, and the grandson of Haroun Al Raschid. From an early accession to the throne, and the talents he possessed to adorn it, his subjects were induced to expect that his reign would be long and happy. His figure was pleasing and majestic; but when he was angry one of his eyes became so terrible that no person could bear to behold it, and the wretch upon whom it was fixed instantly fell backward, and sometimes expired. For fear, however, of depopulating his dominions and making his palace desolate he but rarely gave way to his anger.

Vathek is an **Antihero** almost by default. There is no traditional **Hero** in the story, so the reader's interest lies in following the actions and escapades of the protagonist Caliph. Early in the book he decides to build a huge tower, to get closer to the sky and discover the secrets of Heaven.

> His pride arrived at its height when, having ascended for the first time the eleven thousand stairs of his tower, he cast his eyes below, and beheld men not larger than pismires [ants], mountains than shells, and cities than bee-hives. The idea which such an elevation inspired of his own grandeur completely bewildered him; he was almost ready to adore himself, till, lifting his eyes upward, he saw the stars as high above him as they appeared when he stood on the surface of the earth. He consoled himself, however, for this transient perception of his littleness with the thought of being great in the eyes of others, and flattered himself that the light of his mind would extend beyond the reach of his sight, and transfer to the stars the decrees of his destiny.

His unquenchable thirst for knowledge leads him through pride and pleasure-seeking to an ultimately very sticky end. He is tricked and persuaded towards Hell by his own arrogance and the servants of Eblis – the Islamic equivalent of the Devil.

Romantic poet Lord Byron is so much associated with a certain type of **Antihero** (both through his writing and his own life) that the label "Byronic Hero" is given to a certain sort of literary protagonist, who shows great passion and intelligence, is a proud outsider, and ultimately self-destructive. The Brontë sisters were clearly much interested in the Byronic type, with both Heathcliff in *Wuthering Heights* and Rochester in *Jane Eyre* identified as classic examples, even if the latter is redeemed from his questionable past. These two novels are better defined as Romantic (with a capital R) than Gothic, but do make use of a number of Gothic devices: bleak and stormy moorland **Scenery** with a ghost knocking at the window in *Wuthering Heights*, while Jane Eyre hears a variety of strange noises in the night.

A Young Person's Guide to the Gothic

In Charles Maturin's *Melmoth the Wanderer* (1820), the title character is very much an Antihero, travelling the world in search of someone to take his place in a pact with the Devil.

"The secret of my destiny rests with myself. If all that fear has invented, and credulity believed of me be true, to what does it amount? That if my crimes have exceeded those of mortality, so will my punishment. I have been on earth a terror, but not an evil to its inhabitants. None can participate in my destiny but with his own consent—none have consented—none can be involved in its tremendous penalties, but by participation. I alone must sustain the penalty. If I have put forth my hand, and eaten of the fruit of the interdicted tree, am I not driven from the presence of God and the region of paradise, and sent to wander amid worlds of barrenness and curse for ever and ever?"

At the end there Melmoth is comparing himself to Adam in the Garden of Eden, basically claiming that all he did wrong was seek knowledge, and that he has been punished for it. In fact the Devil gave him a longer life (150 years) and special powers, on the condition that he used them to tempt others into making the same deal, changing places with him. Melmoth clearly believed he would be able to enjoy the benefits of the pact, before easily persuading someone to take his place. Instead he finds himself alone and isolated, forced to behave wickedly, and unable to escape his fate. Yet deep down, his human potential for good still flickers. In the following brief fragment we see him ("the stranger") soon after he first meets with the book's **Heroine** (who is called both Immalee and Isidora), an innocent young woman.

The stranger gazed at her for some time, and thoughts it would be difficult for man to penetrate into, threw their varying expression over his features for a moment. It was the first of his intended victims he had ever beheld with compunction. The joy, too, with which Immalee received him, almost brought back human feelings to a heart that had long renounced them;

and, for a moment, he experienced a sensation like that of his master when he visited paradise,–pity for the flowers he resolved to wither for ever.

This brief passage makes clear that a degree of self-knowledge is a key part of the **Antihero** Character. They know their actions are wrong, and even experience guilt and regret, but cannot resist the strength of the urges that drive them.

THE CONE
H. G. WELLS

Passions run high in this final short story for the **Characters** chapter (it was published in 1895). Horrocks, betrayed by his wife and friend Raut, is definitely the **Antihero** of the piece, driven to extreme action for which he feels immediately guilty. It is interesting to see how the author uses his industrial **Setting** (an iron foundry near Stoke-on-Trent – the location names in the story are suburbs of the city) in the same way as a Gothic **Castle**.

The night was hot and overcast, the sky red-rimmed with the lingering sunset of midsummer. They sat at the open window, trying to fancy the air was fresher there. The trees and shrubs of the garden stood stiff and dark; beyond in the roadway a gas-lamp burnt, bright orange against the hazy blue of the evening. Farther were the three lights of the railway signal against the lowering sky. The man and woman spoke to one another in low tones.

"He does not suspect?" said the man, a little nervously.

"Not he," she said peevishly, as though that too irritated her. "He thinks of nothing but the works and the prices of fuel. He has no imagination, no poetry."

"None of these men of iron have," he said sententiously. "They have no hearts."

"He has not," she said. She turned her discontented face towards the window. The distant sound of a roaring and rushing drew nearer and grew in volume; the house quivered; one heard the metallic rattle of the tender. As the train passed, there was a glare of light above the cutting and a driving tumult of smoke;

one, two, three, four, five, six, seven, eight black oblongs – eight trucks – passed across the dim grey of the embankment, and were suddenly extinguished one by one in the throat of the tunnel, which, with the last, seemed to swallow down train, smoke, and sound in one abrupt gulp.

"This country was all fresh and beautiful once," he said; "and now – it is Gehenna. Down that way – nothing but pot-banks and chimneys belching fire and dust into the face of heaven... But what does it matter? An end comes, an end to all this cruelty... Tomorrow." He spoke the last word in a whisper.

"*Tomorrow*," she said, speaking in a whisper too, and still staring out of the window.

"Dear!" he said, putting his hand on hers.

She turned with a start, and their eyes searched one another's. Hers softened to his gaze. "My dear one!" she said, and then: "It seems so strange – that you should have come into my life like this – to open – " She paused.

"To open?" he said.

"All this wonderful world' – she hesitated, and spoke still more softly – "this world of love to me."

Then suddenly the door clicked and closed. They turned their heads, and he started violently back. In the shadow of the room stood a great shadowy figure - silent. They saw the face dimly in the half-light, with unexpressive dark patches under the pent-house brows. Every muscle in Raut's body suddenly became tense. When could the door have opened? What had he heard? Had he heard all? What had he seen? A tumult of questions.

The new-comer's voice came at last, after a pause that seemed interminable. "Well?" he said.

"I was afraid I had missed you, Horrocks," said the man at the window, gripping the window-ledge with his hand. His voice was unsteady.

The clumsy figure of Horrocks came forward out of the shadow. He made no answer to Raut's remark. For a moment he stood above them.

The woman's heart was cold within her. "I told Mr. Raut it was just possible you might come back," she said in a voice that never quivered.

Horrocks, still silent, sat down abruptly in the chair by her little work-table. His big hands were clenched; one saw now the fire of his eyes under the shadow of his brows. He was trying to get his breath. His eyes went from the woman he had trusted to the friend he had trusted, and then back to the woman.

By this time and for the moment all three half understood one another. Yet none dared say a word to ease the pent-up things that choked them.

It was the husband's voice that broke the silence at last.

"You wanted to see me?" he said to Raut.

Raut started as he spoke. "I came to see you," he said, resolved to lie to the last.

"Yes," said Horrocks.

"You promised," said Raut, "to show me some fine effects of moonlight and smoke."

"I promised to show you some fine effects of moonlight and smoke," repeated Horrocks in a colourless voice.

"And I thought I might catch you to-night before you went down to the works," proceeded Raut, "and come with you."

There was another pause. Did the man mean to take the thing coolly? Did he, after all, know? How long had he been in the room? Yet even at the moment when they heard the door, their attitudes ... Horrocks glanced at the profile of the woman, shadowy pallid in the half-light. Then he glanced at Raut, and seemed to recover himself suddenly. "Of course," he said, "I promised to show you the works under their proper dramatic conditions. It's odd how I could have forgotten."

"If I am troubling you – " began Raut.

Horrocks started again. A new light had suddenly come into the sultry gloom of his eyes. "Not in the least." he said.

"Have you been telling Mr. Raut of all these contrasts of flame and shadow you think so splendid?" said the woman, turning now to her husband for the first time, her confidence creeping back again, her voice just one half-note too high – "that dreadful theory of yours that machinery is beautiful, and everything else in the world ugly. I thought he would not spare you, Mr. Raut. It's his great theory, his one discovery in art."

"I am slow to make discoveries," said Horrocks grimly, damping her suddenly. "But what I discover ..." He stopped.

"Well?" she said.

"Nothing;" and suddenly he rose to his feet.

"I promised to show you the works," he said to Raut, and put his big, clumsy hand on his friend's shoulder. "And you are ready to go?"

"Quite," said Raut, and stood up also.

There was another pause. Each of them peered through the indistinctness of the dusk at the other two.

Horrocks' hand still rested on Raut's shoulder. Raut half fancied still that the incident was trivial after all. But Mrs. Horrocks knew her husband better, knew that grim quiet in his voice, and the confusion in her mind took a vague shape of physical evil. "Very well," said Horrocks, and, dropping his hand, turned towards the door.

"My hat?" Raut looked round in the half-light.

"That's my work-basket," said Mrs. Horrocks with a gust of hysterical laughter. Their hands came together on the back of the chair. "Here it is!" he said. She had an impulse to warn him in an undertone, but she could not frame a word. "Don't go!" and "Beware of him!" struggled in her mind, and the swift moment passed.

"Got it?" said Horrocks, standing with the door half open.

Raut stepped towards him. "Better say goodbye to Mrs. Horrocks," said the ironmaster, even more grimly quiet in his tone than before.

Raut started and turned. "Good-evening, Mrs. Horrocks," he said, and their hands touched.

Horrocks held the door open with a ceremonial politeness unusual in him towards men. Raut went out, and then, after a wordless look at her, her husband followed. She stood motionless while Raut's light footfall and her husband's heavy tread, like bass and treble, passed down the passage together. The front door slammed heavily. She went to the window, moving slowly, and stood watching, leaning forward. The two men appeared for a moment at the gateway in the road, passed under the street lamp, and were hidden by the black masses of the shrubbery. The lamplight fell for a moment on their faces, showing only unmeaning pale patches, telling nothing of what she still feared, and doubted, and craved vainly to know. Then she sank down into a crouching attitude in the big arm-chair, her eyes-wide open and staring out at the red lights from the furnaces that flickered in the sky. An hour after she was still there, her attitude scarcely changed.

The oppressive stillness of the evening weighed heavily upon Raut. They went side by side down the road in silence, and in silence turned into the cinder-made byway that presently opened out the prospect of the valley.

A blue haze, half dust, half mist, touched the long valley with mystery. Beyond were Hanley and Etruria , grey and dark masses, outlined thinly by the rare golden dots of the street lamps, and here and there a gas-lit window, or the yellow glare of some late-working factory or crowded public-house. Out of the masses, clear and slender against the evening sky, rose a multitude of tall chimneys, many of them reeking, a few smokeless during a season of "play." Here and there a pallid patch and ghostly stunted beehive shapes showed the position of a pot-bank or a wheel, black and sharp against the hot lower sky, marked some colliery where they raise the iridescent coal of the place. Nearer at hand was the broad stretch of railway, and half-invisible trains shunted – a steady puffing and rumbling, with every run a ringing concussion and a rhymthic series of impacts, and a passage of intermittent puffs of white steam across the further view. And to the left, between the railway and the dark mass of the low hill beyond, dominating the whole view, colossal, inky-black, and crowned with smoke and fitful flames, stood the great cylinders of the Jeddah Company Blast

Furnaces, the central edifices of the big ironworks of which Horrocks was the manager. They stood heavy and threatening, full of an incessant turmoil of flames and seething molten iron, and about the feet of them rattled the rolling-mills, and the steam-hammer beat heavily and splashed the white iron sparks hither and thither. Even as they looked, a truckful of fuel was shot into one of the giants, and the red flames gleamed out, and a confusion of smoke and black dust came boiling upwards towards the sky.

"Certainly you get some colour with your furnaces," said Raut, breaking a silence that had become apprehensive.

Horrocks grunted. He stood with his hands in his pockets, frowning down at the dim steaming railway and the busy ironworks beyond, frowning as if he were thinking out some knotty problem.

Raut glanced at him and away again. "At present your moonlight effect is hardly ripe," he continued, looking upward; "the moon is still smothered by the vestiges of daylight."

Horrocks stared at him with the expression of a man who has suddenly awakened. "Vestiges of daylight? ... Of course, of course." He too looked up at the moon, pale still in the midsummer sky. "Come along," he said suddenly, and gripping Raut's arm in his hand, made a move towards the path that dropped from them to the railway.

Raut hung back. Their eyes met and saw a thousand things in a moment that their lips came near to say. Horrocks's hand tightened and then relaxed. He let go, and before Raut was aware of it, they were arm in arm, and walking, one unwillingly enough, down the path.

"You see the fine effect of the railway signals towards Burslem," said Horrocks, suddenly breaking into loquacity, striding fast and tightening the grip of his elbow the while – "little green lights and red and white lights, all against the haze. You have an eye for effect, Raut. It's fine. And look at those furnaces of mine, how they rise upon us as we come down the hill. That to the right is my pet – seventy feet of him. I packed him myself, and he's boiled away cheerfully with iron in his guts for five long years. I've a particular fancy for *him*. That line of red there — a lovely bit of warm orange you'd call it, Raut — that's the puddlers' furnaces, and there, in the hot light, three black figures — did you see the white splash of the steam-hammer then? — that's the rolling mills. Come along! Clang, clatter, how it goes rattling across the floor! Sheet tin, Raut, — amazing stuff. Glass mirrors are not in it when that stuff comes from the mill. And, squelch! there goes the hammer again. Come along!"

He had to stop talking to catch at his breath. His arm twisted into Raut's with benumbing tightness. He had come striding down the black path towards the railway as though he was possessed. Raut had not spoken a word, had simply hung back against Horrocks's pull with all his strength.

"I say," he said now, laughing nervously, but with an undertone of snarl in his voice, "why on earth are you nipping my arm off, Horrocks, and dragging me along like this?"

At length Horrocks released him. His manner changed again. "Nipping your arm off?" he said. "Sorry. But it's you taught me the trick of walking in that friendly way."

"You haven't learnt the refinements of it yet then," said Raut, laughing artificially again. "By Jove! I'm black and blue." Horrocks offered no apology. They stood now near the bottom of the hill, close to the fence that bordered the railway. The ironworks had grown larger and spread out with their approach. They looked up to the blast furnaces now instead of down; the further view of Etruria and Hanley had dropped out of sight with their descent. Before them, by the stile, rose a notice-board, bearing, still dimly visible, the words, "*Beware of the Trains*," half hidden by splashes of coaly mud.

"Fine effects," said Horrocks, waving his arm. "Here comes a train. The puffs of smoke, the orange glare, the round eye of light in front of it, the melodious rattle. Fine effects! But these furnaces of mine used to be finer, before we shoved cones in their throats, and saved the gas."

"How?" said Raut. "Cones?"

"Cones, my man, cones. I'll show you one nearer. The flames used to flare out of the open throats, great – what is it? – pillars of cloud by day, red and black smoke, and pillars of fire by night. Now we run it off – in pipes, and burn it to heat the blast, and the top is shut by a cone. You'll be interested in that cone."

"But every now and then," said Raut, "you get a burst of fire and smoke up there."

"The cone's not fixed, it's hung by a chain from a lever, and balanced by an equipoise. You shall see it nearer. Else, of course, there'd be no way of getting fuel into the thing. Every now and then the cone dips, and out comes the flare."

"I see," said Raut. He looked over his shoulder. "The moon gets brighter," he said.

"Come along," said Horrocks abruptly, gripping his shoulder again, and moving him suddenly towards the railway crossing. And then came one of those swift incidents, vivid, but so rapid that they leave one doubtful and reeling. Half-way across, Horrocks' hand suddenly clenched upon him like a vice, and swung him backward and through a half-turn, so that he looked up the line. And there a chain of lamp-lit carriage windows telescoped swiftly as it came towards them, and the red and yellow lights of an engine grew larger and larger, rushing down upon them. As he grasped what this meant, he turned his face to Horrocks, and pushed with all his strength against the arm that held him back between the rails. The struggle did not last a moment. Just as certain as it was that Horrocks held him there, so certain was it that he had been violently lugged out of danger.

"Out of the way," said Horrocks with a gasp, as the train came rattling by, and they stood panting by the gate into the ironworks.

"I did not see it coming," said Raut, still, even in spite of his own apprehensions, trying to keep up an appearance of ordinary intercourse.

Horrocks answered with a grunt. "The cone," he said, and then, as one who recovers himself, "I thought you did not hear."

"I didn't," said Raut.

"I wouldn't have had you run over then for the world," said Horrocks.

"For a moment I lost my nerve," said Raut.

Horrocks stood for half a minute, then turned abruptly towards the ironworks again. "See how fine these great mounds of mine, these clinker-heaps, look in the night! That truck yonder, up above there! Up it goes, and out-tilts the slag. See the palpitating red stuff go sliding down the slope. As we get nearer, the heap rises up and cuts the blast furnaces. See the quiver up above the big one. Not that way! This way, between the heaps. That goes to the puddling furnaces, but I want to show you the canal first." He came and took Raut by the elbow, and so they went along side by side. Raut answered Horrocks vaguely. What, he asked himself, had really happened on the line? Was he deluding himself with his own fancies, or had Horrocks actually held him back in the way of the train? Had he just been within an ace of being murdered?

Suppose this slouching, scowling monster *did* know anything? For a minute or two then Raut was really afraid for his life, but the mood passed as he reasoned with himself. After all, Horrocks might have heard nothing. At any rate, he had pulled him out of the way in time. His odd manner might be due to the mere vague jealousy he had shown once before. He was talking now of the ash-heaps and the canal.

"Eigh?" said Horrocks.

"What?" said Raut. "Rather! The haze in the moonlight. Fine!"

"Our canal," said Horrocks, stopping suddenly. "Our canal by moonlight and firelight is immense. You've never seen it? Fancy that! You've spent too many of your evenings philandering up in Newcastle there. I tell you, for real florid quality—But you shall see. Boiling water ..."

As they came out of the labyrinth of clinker-heaps and mounds of coal and ore, the noises of the rolling-mill sprang upon them suddenly, loud, near, and distinct. Three shadowy workmen went by and touched their caps to Horrocks. Their faces were vague in the darkness. Raut felt a futile impulse to address them, and before he could frame his words they passed into the shadows. Horrocks pointed to the canal close before them now: a weird-looking place it seemed, in the blood-red reflections of the furnaces. The hot water that cooled the tuyères came into it, some fifty yards up – a tumultuous, almost boiling affluent, and the steam rose up from the water in silent white wisps and streaks, wrapping damply about them, an incessant succession of ghosts coming up from the black and red eddies, a white uprising that made the head swim. The shining black tower of the larger blast-furnace rose overhead out of the mist, and its tumultuous riot filled their ears. Raut kept away from the edge of the water, and watched Horrocks.

"Here it is red," said Horrocks, "blood-red vapour as red and hot as sin; but yonder there, where the moonlight falls on it, and it drives across the clinker-heaps, it is as white as death."

Raut turned his head for a moment, and then came back hastily to his watch on Horrocks. "Come along to the rolling-mills," said Horrocks. The threatening hold was not so evident that time, and Raut felt a little reassured. But all the same, what on earth did Horrocks mean about "white as death" and "red as sin"? Coincidence, perhaps?

They went and stood behind the puddlers for a little while, and then through the rolling-mills, where amidst an incessant din the deliberate steam-hammer beat the juice out of the succulent iron, and black, half-naked Titans rushed the plastic bars, like hot sealing-wax, between the wheels, "Come on," said Horrocks in Raut's ear; and they went and peeped through the little glass hole behind the tuyères, and saw the tumbled fire writhing in the pit of the blast-furnace. It left one eye blinded for a while. Then, with green and blue patches dancing across the dark, they went to the lift by which the trucks of ore and fuel and lime were raised to the top of the big cylinder.

And out upon the narrow rail that overhung the furnace Raut's doubts came upon him again. Was it wise to be here? If Horrocks did know--everything! Do what he would, he could not resist a violent trembling. Right under foot was a sheer depth of seventy feet. It was a dangerous place. They pushed by a truck of fuel to get to the railing that crowned the thing. The reek of the furnace, a sulphurous vapour streaked with pungent bitterness, seemed to make the distant hillside of Hanley quiver. The moon was riding out now from among a drift of clouds, half-way up the sky above the undulating wooded outlines of Newcastle. The steaming canal ran away from below them under an indistinct bridge, and vanished into the dim haze of the flat fields towards Burslem.

"That's the cone I've been telling you of," shouted Horrocks; "and, below that, sixty feet of fire and molten metal, with the air of the blast frothing through it like gas in soda-water."

Raut gripped the hand-rail tightly, and stared down at the cone. The heat was intense. The boiling of the iron and the tumult of the blast made a thunderous accompaniment to Horrocks's voice. But the thing had to be gone through now. Perhaps, after all...

"In the middle," bawled Horrocks, "temperature near a thousand degrees. If *you* were dropped into it ... flash into flame like a pinch of gunpowder in a candle. Put your hand out and feel the heat of his breath. Why, even up here I've seen the rain-water boiling off the trucks. And that cone there. It's a damned sight too hot for roasting cakes. The top side of it's three hundred degrees."

"Three hundred degrees!" said Raut.

"Three hundred centigrade, mind!" said Horrocks. "It will boil the blood out of you in no time."

"Eigh?" said Raut, and turned.

"Boil the blood out of you in ... No, you don't!"

"Let me go!" screamed Raut. "Let go my arm!"

With one hand he clutched at the hand-rail, then with both. For a moment the two men stood swaying. Then suddenly, with a violent jerk, Horrocks had twisted him from his hold. He clutched at Horrocks and missed, his foot went back into empty air; in mid-air he twisted himself, and then cheek and shoulder and knee struck the hot cone together.

He clutched the chain by which the cone hung, and the thing sank an infinitesimal amount as he struck it. A circle of glowing red appeared about him, and a tongue of flame, released from the chaos within, flickered up towards him. An intense pain assailed him at the knees, and he could smell the singeing of his hands. He raised himself to his feet, and tried to climb up the chain, and then something struck his head. Black and shining with the moonlight, the throat of the furnace rose about him.

Horrocks, he saw, stood above him by one of the trucks of fuel on the rail. The gesticulating figure was bright and white in the moonlight, and shouting, "Fizzle, you fool! Fizzle, you hunter of women! You hot-blooded hound! Boil! boil! boil!"

Suddenly he caught up a handful of coal out of the truck, and flung it deliberately, lump after lump, at Raut.

"Horrocks!" cried Raut. "Horrocks!"

He clung, crying, to the chain, pulling himself up from the burning of the cone. Each missile Horrocks flung hit him. His clothes charred and glowed, and as he struggled the cone dropped, and a rush of hot, suffocating gas whooped out and burned round him in a swift breath of flame.

His human likeness departed from him. When the momentary red had passed, Horrocks saw a charred, blackened figure, its head streaked with blood, still clutching and fumbling with the chain, and writhing in agony – a cindery animal, an inhuman, monstrous creature that began a sobbing, intermittent shriek.

Abruptly at the sight the ironmaster's anger passed. A deadly sickness came upon him. The heavy odour of burning flesh came drifting up to his nostrils. His sanity returned to him.

"God have mercy upon me!" he cried. "O God! what have I done?"

He knew the thing below him, save that it still moved and felt, was already a dead man – that the blood of the poor wretch must be boiling in his veins. An intense realisation of that agony came to his mind, and overcame every other feeling. For a moment he stood irresolute, and then, turning to the truck, he hastily tilted its contents upon the struggling thing that had once been a man. The mass fell with a thud, and went radiating over the cone. With the thud the shriek ended, and a boiling confusion of smoke, dust, and flame came rushing up towards him. As it passed, he saw the cone clear again.

Then he staggered back, and stood trembling, clinging to the rail with both hands. His lips moved, but no words came to them.

Down below was the sound of voices and running steps. The clangour of rolling in the shed ceased abruptly.

A Young Person's Guide to the Gothic

Five: ANTAGONISTS
(MOSTLY MONSTERS)

I was struggling (and probably still am) with the title for this section, which of course brings together some of the most familiar and conspicuous inhabitants of the Gothic. In the **Characters** section we looked at what literary critics like to call protagonists – the **Hero** and **Heroine**: the people who are the centre of the action in a novel. The **Antagonist** is the person – or monster, or even institution – against whom - or which - the protagonist must do battle. In longer stories the Antagonist can often simply be the **Villain** or **Villainess**, but we expect a Villain to be at least part human, to have a theoretical potential for good, so we can relate to and be appalled by their evilness. An Antagonist, on the other hand, can be just about anything, so long as he, she or it represents a threat to the protagonist. The film *Alien* is a wonderful example of modern Gothic (the spaceship is the **Castle**, Sigourney Weaver's character Ripley the Hero/Heroine); but it does not seem right to call the alien itself a Villain. The monster that hunts the ship's crew through the dank and decrepit interior of the ship has no morals, it is not behaving wickedly, it is simply doing what it does: it is the **Antagonist**.

The list of possible Antagonists is a long one. I have picked the stand-out classics for the next segments, but there are of course plenty more. What, for instance, about Zombies? Or Bandits?

Actually, Zombies and Bandits are interesting.

Zombies are currently very fashionable. There's been *The Walking Dead* on television, the 2013 film *World War Z*, and Charlie Higson's series of novels (beginning with *The Enemy*), where anyone over the age of 14 has either died, or gone mad and developed a taste for human flesh. So you might have expected them to have their own segment, but Zombies simply do not appear outside the modern Gothic: there are no extracts to use. The best I can find is this fragment from the 1929 book *The Magic Island*, which is presented by its author William Seabrook as a factual travelogue about Haiti, in the Caribbean.

> The eyes were the worst. It was not my imagination. They were in truth like the eyes of a dead man, not blind, but staring, unfocused, unseeing. The whole face, for that matter, was bad enough. It was vacant, as if there was nothing behind it. It seemed not only expressionless, but incapable of expression.

The locals, according to Seabrook, believed that voodoo magic brought corpses back to life, mostly so that they could be used as a sort of slave labour. The three that he personally encountered and described were working in a field. These living dead were known as zombies in the local language, and we have Seabrook to thank for introducing the word into English. His other claim to fame has an appropriately Gothic flavour: he wrote a supposedly factual account of his own act of cannibalism, claiming to have cooked and eaten human meat from a healthy body recently killed in an accident. And so, neatly, to our modern Zombies, with their taste for human flesh, which have even more recent origins, appearing for the first time in 1968 film *Night of the Living Dead*. Nowadays, instead of witchcraft, it is a mysterious disease or apocalyptic event that is blamed for creating hordes of rotting undead. Zombies are popular today, as **Antagonists**, because they embody – almost literally - what we, as a society, most fear: nuclear holocaust, environmental apocalypse and man-made plague.

Bandits, on the other hand, barely feature in the contemporary Gothic, but are present in a great number of the original novels (as *Banditti*). Back in the day, people were genuinely scared by the idea of robber bands, lurking in the forests of Europe and ready to prey on unwary travellers. Nowadays, not so much.

Snakes anyone? Spiders?

THE VAMPIRE

The sharp-fanged predator with the garlic phobia seems to be everybody's favourite **Antagonist**. Stories of evil beings that drink blood have been told in most cultures since very early times, but the **Vampire** as we recognise him or her today came to widespread popular notice in 18th Century Eastern Europe. People genuinely believed certain individuals returned from the grave to prey on the living, with two famous cases in the 1720s fully investigated and documented by the authorities in what is now Serbia (Peter Plogojowitz and Arnold Paole, in case you want to do some research). These stories and beliefs spread westwards into the rest of Europe, and Vampires began to make walk-on appearances in poetry. The first piece of proper Gothic prose with a Vampire taking a lead role is John Polidori's *The Vampyre*, published in 1819.

> There was no colour upon her cheek, not even upon her lip; yet there was a stillness about her face that seemed almost as attaching as the life that once dwelt there: – upon her neck and breast was blood, and upon her throat were the marks of teeth having opened the vein: – to this the men pointed, crying, simultaneously struck with horror, "A Vampyre! a Vampyre!"

The victim is Ianthe, one of two significant targets of the Villain, **Antagonist** and **Vampire** Lord Ruthven. Polidori was Lord Byron's doctor and took inspiration from his patron's own writing. His tale caught the imagination of the time, becoming the stimulus not only for Stoker's famous *Dracula* (1897), but a whole run of other Vampire stories. One of the most entertaining is *Varney the Vampire*, originally published as a serial "Penny dreadful" between 1845 and 1847. These forerunners of our contemporary "comics" first appeared in the 1830s and were cheaply produced (and sold!) pamphlets, each containing the next instalment of a sensational story. James Malcolm Rymer, author of *Varney*, co-wrote another famous serial, *The String of Pearls*, which introduced the character of murderous barber Sweeney Todd. This is the first instalment of his **Vampire** serial, both magnificently over-the-top and very familiar, thanks to similar scenes in several horror films. Some very Gothic **Weather** is in full flow and the descriptions of the **Heroine** are luxurious to the point of steamy. (There is a famous painting, *The Nightmare*, in which a sleeping woman holds exactly the same pose as the one depicted here. It was painted by Henry Fuseli in 1781: Google it to see how the Gothic isn't just confined to literature.)

The solemn tones of an old cathedral clock have announced midnight--the air is thick and heavy – a strange, death like stillness pervades all nature. A faint peal of thunder now comes from far off. Like a signal gun for the battle of the winds to begin, it appeared to awaken them from their lethargy, and one awful, warring hurricane swept over a whole city, producing more devastation in the four or five minutes it lasted, than would a half century of ordinary phenomena.

It was as if some giant had blown upon some toy town, and scattered many of the buildings before the hot blast of his terrific breath; for as suddenly as that blast of wind had come did it cease, and all was as still and calm as before.

Sleepers awakened, and thought that what they had heard must be the confused chimera of a dream. They trembled and turned to sleep again.

All is still – still as the very grave. Not a sound breaks the magic of repose. What is that – a strange, pattering noise, as of a million of fairy feet? It is hail – yes, a hail-storm has burst over the city. Leaves are dashed from the trees, mingled with small boughs; windows that lie most opposed to the direct fury of the pelting particles of ice are broken, and the rapt repose that before was so remarkable in its intensity, is exchanged for a noise which, in its accumulation, drowns every cry of surprise or consternation which here and there arose from persons who found their houses invaded by the storm.

Now and then, too, there would come a sudden gust of wind

that in its strength, as it blew laterally, would, for a moment, hold millions of the hailstones suspended in mid air, but it was only to dash them with redoubled force in some new direction, where more mischief was to be done.

Oh, how the storm raged! Hail – rain – wind. It was, in very truth, an awful night.

There is an antique chamber in an ancient house. Curious and quaint carvings adorn the walls, and the large chimney-piece is a curiosity of itself. The ceiling is low, and a large bay window, from roof to floor, looks to the west. The window is latticed, and filled with curiously painted glass and rich stained pieces, which send in a strange, yet beautiful light, when sun or moon shines into the apartment. There is but one portrait in that room, although the walls seem panelled for the express purpose of containing a series of pictures. That portrait is of a young man, with a pale face, a stately brow, and a strange expression about the eyes, which no one cared to look on twice.

There is a stately bed in that chamber, of carved walnut-wood is it made, rich in design and elaborate in execution; one of those works of art which owe their existence to the Elizabethan era. It is hung with heavy silken and damask furnishing; nodding feathers are at its corners – covered with dust are they, and they lend a funereal aspect to the room. The floor is of polished oak.

God! how the hail dashes on the old bay window! Like an occasional discharge of mimic musketry, it comes clashing, beating, and cracking upon the small panes; but they resist it – their small size saves them; the wind, the hail, the rain, expend their fury in vain.

The bed in that old chamber is occupied. A creature formed in all fashions of loveliness lies in a half sleep upon that ancient couch – a girl young and beautiful as a spring morning. Her long hair has escaped from its confinement and streams over the blackened coverings of the bedstead; she has been restless in her sleep, for the clothing of the bed is in much confusion. One arm is over her head, the other hangs nearly off the side of the bed near to which she lies. A neck and bosom that would have formed a study for the rarest sculptor that ever Providence gave genius to, were half disclosed. She moaned slightly in her sleep, and once or twice the lips moved as if in prayer – at least one might judge so, for the name of Him who suffered for all came once faintly from them.

Oh, what a world of witchery was in that mouth, slightly parted, and exhibiting within the pearly teeth that glistened even in the faint light that came from that bay window. How sweetly the long silken eyelashes lay upon the cheek. Now she moves, and one shoulder is entirely visible – whiter, fairer than the spotless clothing of the bed on which she lies, is the smooth skin of that fair creature, just budding into womanhood, and in that transition state which presents to us all the charms of the girl – almost of the child, with the more matured beauty and gentleness of advancing years.

Was that lightning? Yes—an awful, vivid, terrifying flash – then a roaring peal of thunder, as if a thousand mountains were rolling one over the other in the blue vault of Heaven! Who sleeps now in that ancient city? Not one living soul. The dread trumpet of eternity could not more effectually have awakened any one.

The hail continues. The wind continues. The uproar of the elements seems at its height. Now she awakens – that beautiful girl on the antique bed; she opens those eyes of celestial blue, and a faint cry of alarm bursts from her lips. At least it is a cry which, amid the noise and turmoil without, sounds but faint and weak. She sits upon the bed and presses her hands upon her eyes. Heavens! what a wild torrent of wind, and rain, and hail!

Another flash – a wild, blue, bewildering flash of lightning streams across that bay window, for an instant bringing out every colour in it with terrible distinctness. A shriek bursts from the lips of the young girl, and then, with eyes fixed upon that window, which, in another moment, is all darkness, and with such an expression of terror upon her face as it had never before known, she trembled, and the perspiration of intense fear stood upon her brow.

"What – what was it?" she gasped; "real, or a delusion? Oh, God, what was it? A figure tall and gaunt, endeavouring from the outside to unclasp the window. I saw it. That flash of lightning revealed it to me. It stood the whole length of the window."

There was a lull of the wind. The hail was not falling so thickly – moreover, it now fell, what there was of it, straight, and yet a strange clattering sound came upon the glass of that long window. It could not be a delusion—she is awake, and she hears it. What can produce it? Another flash of lightning—another shriek—there could be now no delusion.

A tall figure is standing on the ledge immediately outside the long window. It is its finger-nails upon the glass that produces the sound so like the hail, now that the hail has ceased. Intense fear paralysed the limbs of that beautiful girl. That one shriek is all she can utter – with hands clasped, a face of marble, a heart beating so wildly in her bosom, that each moment it seems as if it would break its confines, eyes distended and fixed upon the window, she waits, frozen with horror. The pattering and clattering of the nails continue. No word is spoken, and now she fancies she can trace the darker form of that figure against the window, and she can see the long arms moving to and fro, feeling for some mode of entrance. What strange light is that which now gradually creeps up into the air? red and terrible – brighter and brighter it grows. The lightning has set fire to a mill, and the reflection of the rapidly consuming building falls upon that long window. There can be no mistake. The figure is there, still feeling for an entrance, and clattering against the glass with its long nails, that appear as if the growth of many years had been untouched. She tries to scream again but a choking sensation comes over her, and she cannot. It is too dreadful—she tries to move—each limb seems weighed down by tons of lead—she can but in a hoarse faint whisper cry,—

"Help—help—help—help!"

And that one word she repeats like a person in a dream. The red glare of the fire continues. It throws up the tall gaunt figure in hideous relief against the long window. It shows, too, upon the one portrait that is in the chamber, and that portrait appears to fix its eyes upon the attempting intruder, while the flickering light from the fire makes it look fearfully life-like. A small pane of glass is broken, and the form from without introduces a long gaunt hand, which seems utterly destitute of flesh. The fastening is removed, and one-half of the window, which opens like folding doors, is swung wide open upon its hinges.

And yet now she could not scream—she could not move. "Help!—help!—help!" was all she could say. But, oh, that look of terror that sat upon her face, it was dreadful – a look to haunt the memory for a lifetime – a look to obtrude itself upon the happiest moments, and turn them to bitterness.

The figure turns half round, and the light falls upon the face. It is perfectly white—perfectly bloodless. The eyes look like polished tin; the lips are drawn back, and the principal feature next to those dreadful eyes is the teeth—the fearful looking teeth—projecting like those of some wild animal, hideously, glaringly white, and fang-like. It approaches the bed with a strange, gliding movement. It clashes together the long nails that literally appear to hang from the finger ends. No sound comes from its lips. Is she going mad—that young and beautiful girl exposed to so much terror? she has drawn up all her limbs; she cannot even now say help. The power of articulation is gone, but the power of movement has returned to her; she can draw herself slowly along to the other side of the bed from that towards which the hideous appearance is coming.

But her eyes are fascinated. The glance of a serpent could not have produced a greater effect upon her than did the fixed gaze of those awful, metallic-looking eyes that were bent on her face. Crouching down so that the gigantic height was lost, and the horrible, protruding, white face was the most prominent object, came on the figure. What was it?—what did it want there?—what made it look so hideous—so unlike an inhabitant of the earth, and yet to be on it?

Now she has got to the verge of the bed, and the figure pauses. It seemed as if when it paused she lost the power to proceed. The clothing of the bed was now clutched in her hands with unconscious power. She drew her breath short and thick. Her bosom heaves, and her limbs tremble, yet she cannot withdraw her eyes from that marble-looking face. He holds her with his glittering eye.

The storm has ceased – all is still. The winds are hushed; the church clock proclaims the hour of one: a hissing sound comes from the throat of the hideous being, and he raises his long, gaunt arms – the lips move. He advances. The girl places one small foot from the bed on to the floor. She is unconsciously dragging the clothing with her. The door of the room is in that direction – can she reach it? Has she power to walk?--can she withdraw her eyes from the face of the intruder, and so break the hideous charm? God of Heaven! is it real, or some dream so like reality as to nearly overturn the judgment for ever?

The figure has paused again, and half on the bed and half out of it that young girl lies trembling. Her long hair streams across the entire width of the bed. As she has slowly moved along she has left it streaming across the pillows. The pause lasted about a minute – oh, what an age of agony. That minute was, indeed, enough for madness to do its full work in.

With a sudden rush that could not be foreseen—with a strange howling cry that was enough to awaken terror in every breast, the figure seized the long tresses of her hair, and twining them round his bony hands he held her to the bed. Then she screamed—Heaven granted her then power to scream. Shriek followed shriek in rapid succession. The bed-clothes fell in a heap by the side of the bed – she was dragged by her long silken hair completely on to it again. Her beautifully rounded limbs quivered with the agony of her soul. The glassy, horrible eyes of the figure ran over that angelic form with a hideous satisfaction – horrible profanation. He drags her head to the bed's edge. He forces it back by the long hair still entwined in his grasp. With a plunge he seizes her neck in his fang-like teeth – a gush of blood, and a hideous sucking noise follows. The girl has swooned, and the vampire is at his hideous repast!

The instalment of course ends on a cliff-hanger. You would have had to buy the next one, for a penny, to discover how Varney's meal is interrupted in time to save the **Heroine** (who is called Flora, by the way). As the story develops, the author shows increasing sympathy for his **Antagonist**, who we learn is suffering from a curse and hates what he finds himself forced to do. This is a pattern that has proved particularly popular in our modern **Vampire** stories.

To mix it up a little, these next extracts, from a short story published in 1922, are about a female blood-drinker. Although not as prevalent as the male, there have been plenty of women Vampires, perhaps inspired by the shocking tales associated with the genuine historical figure of Elizabeth Bathory. Born in Transylvania in 1560, this Hungarian noblewoman, according to the unreliable evidence of the period, tortured and murdered as many as 650 victims. Later legends about her claimed she bathed in her victims' blood to delay her own aging. The first female Vampire in Gothic literature is Sheridan Le Fanu's *Carmilla*, published in 1872, the title character showing all the proper predatory instincts, but E. F. Benson's cheerful *Mrs Amworth* is a worthy successor. She is a widow, newly arrived in Maxley, an English country village.

Big and energetic, her vigorous and genial personality speedily woke Maxley up to a higher degree of sociality than it had ever known. Most of us were bachelors or spinsters or elderly folk not much inclined to exert ourselves in the expense and effort of hospitality, and hitherto the gaiety of a small tea-party, with bridge afterwards and galoshes (when it was wet) to trip home in again for a solitary dinner, was about the climax of our festivities. But Mrs. Amworth showed us a more gregarious way, and set an example of luncheon-parties and little dinners, which we began to follow.

She was always cheery and jolly; she was interested in everything, and in music, in gardening, in games of all sorts was a competent performer. Everybody (with one exception) liked her, everybody felt her to bring with her the tonic of a sunny day. That one exception was Francis Urcombe; he, though he confessed he did not like her, acknowledged that he was vastly interested in her. This always seemed strange to me, for pleasant and jovial as she was, I could see nothing in her that could call forth conjecture or intrigued surmise, so healthy and unmysterious a figure did she present. But of the genuineness of Urcombe's interest there could be no doubt; one could see him watching and scrutinising her. In matter of age, she frankly volunteered the information that she was forty-five; but her briskness, her activity, her unravaged skin, her coal-black hair, made it difficult to believe that she was not adopting an unusual device, and adding ten years on to her age instead of subtracting them.

It seems clear that Urcombe is right and everyone else wrong. A young boy falls ill, and has the tell-tale (to **Vampire**-spotters) double puncture mark on his neck. The narrator begins having nightmares.

I dreamed that I woke, and found that both my bedroom windows were shut. Half-suffocating I dreamed that I sprang out of bed, and went across to open them. The blind over the first was drawn down, and pulling it up I saw, with the indescribable horror of incipient nightmare, Mrs. Amworth's face suspended close to the pane in the darkness outside, nodding and smiling at me. Pulling down the blind again to keep that terror out, I rushed to the second window on the other side of the room, and there again was Mrs. Amworth's face. Then the panic came upon me in full blast; here was I suffocating in the airless room, and whichever window I opened Mrs. Amworth's face would float in, like those noiseless black gnats that bit before one was aware. The nightmare rose to screaming point, and with strangled yells I awoke to find my room cool and quiet with both windows open and blinds up and a half-moon high in its course, casting an oblong of tranquil light on the floor. But even when I was awake the horror persisted, and I lay tossing and turning.

Later in the tale our **Antagonist** is knocked down and killed by a car, but of course her burial is not the end of the story.

The CONSTRUCT

The first appearance of the **Construct** as a Gothic **Antagonist** remains the most famous. Frankenstein's Monster has lurched and staggered his way through many film, theatre and even book adaptations, although recent ideas of what the creature looks like owe far more to Boris Karloff in the 1931 film than the original from Mary Shelley's novel of 1818. In the book, Victor Frankenstein has discovered the secret of bringing dead flesh to life, and aims to build a beautiful human figure. To help with the intricacies of the internal plumbing, he scales things up, until his creation is eight feet tall. After two years of work the climactic night arrives.

> It was on a dreary night of November that I beheld the accomplishment of my toils. With an anxiety that almost amounted to agony, I collected the instruments of life around me, that I might infuse a spark of being into the lifeless thing that lay at my feet. It was already one in the morning; the rain pattered dismally against the panes, and my candle was nearly burnt out, when, by the glimmer of the half-extinguished light, I saw the dull yellow eye of the creature open; it breathed hard, and a convulsive motion agitated its limbs.
> How can I describe my emotions at this catastrophe, or how delineate the wretch whom with such infinite pains and care I had endeavoured to form? His limbs were in proportion, and I had selected his features as beautiful. Beautiful! Great God!

His yellow skin scarcely covered the work of muscles and arteries beneath; his hair was of a lustrous black, and flowing; his teeth of a pearly whiteness; but these luxuriances only formed a more horrid contrast with his watery eyes, that seemed almost of the same colour as the dun-white sockets in which they were set, his shrivelled complexion and straight black lips.

Unlike many later versions, this original Monster turns out to be highly intelligent, and does not at first have any evil plans or instincts. It is only after being rejected by his creator, and then experiencing negative reactions in other human encounters, that the Monster develops an urge to do "wrong", driven by a wish to avenge himself on humanity in general and Frankenstein in particular.

H. G. Wells, the grandfather of Science Fiction writers, and author of our **Lights Go Out** and **Antihero** stories, explored his take on the dangers of humans interfering with the natural world in *The Island of Doctor Moreau*, published in 1896. A shipwrecked man is picked up and brought to a small island inhabited by the title character and a collection of strange looking people.

> Before me, squatting together upon the fungoid ruins of a huge fallen tree and still unaware of my approach, were three grotesque human figures. One was evidently a female; the other two were men. They were naked, save for swathings of scarlet cloth about the middle; and their skins were of a dull pinkish-drab colour, such as I had seen in no savages before. They had fat, heavy, chinless faces, retreating foreheads, and a scant bristly hair upon their heads. I never saw such bestial-looking creatures.

It turns out that Dr Moreau has been experimenting with vivisection, cutting up animals and grafting parts together, trying to manufacture a man. The three described above are the results of his work with pigs. There are numerous others, where he has used other animals, or combinations of animals, as a starting point. The shipwrecked narrator later tries to describe them.

Most striking, perhaps, in their general appearance was the disproportion between the legs of these creatures and the length of their bodies; and yet—so relative is our idea of grace—my eye became habituated to their forms, and at last I even fell in with their persuasion that my own long thighs were ungainly. Another point was the forward carriage of the head and the clumsy and inhuman curvature of the spine. Even the Ape-man lacked that inward sinuous curve of the back which makes the human figure so graceful. Most had their shoulders hunched clumsily, and their short forearms hung weakly at their sides. Few of them were conspicuously hairy, at least until the end of my time upon the island.

The next most obvious deformity was in their faces, almost all of which were prognathous, malformed about the ears, with large and protuberant noses, very furry or very bristly hair, and often strangely-coloured or strangely-placed eyes. None could laugh, though the Ape-man had a chattering titter. Beyond these general characters their heads had little in common; each preserved the quality of its particular species: the human mark distorted but did not hide the leopard, the ox, or the sow, or other animal or animals, from which the creature had been moulded. The voices, too, varied exceedingly. The hands were always malformed; and though some surprised me by their unexpected human appearance, almost all were deficient in the number of the digits, clumsy about the finger-nails, and lacking any tactile sensibility.

The two most formidable Animal Men were my Leopard-man and a creature made of hyena and swine. Larger than these were the three bull-creatures who pulled in the boat. Then came the silvery-hairy-man, M'ling, and a satyr-like creature of ape and goat. There were three Swine-men and a Swine-woman, a mare-rhinoceros-creature, and several other females whose sources I did not ascertain. There were several wolf-creatures, a bear-bull, and a Saint-Bernard-man. I have already described the Ape-man, and there was a particularly hateful (and evil-smelling) old woman made of vixen and bear, whom I hated from the beginning. Smaller creatures were certain dappled youths and my little sloth-creature.

When Gothic authors choose a Construct as their Antagonist, we can be sure they are planning to show up the foolishness and vanity of an over-confident scientist. In the Introduction we saw how part of appeal of the Gothic lies with its tendency to undermine the value of pure science and reason, how its popularity is connected to the way it operates in a world beyond what reason can explain. How better to undermine science than have a scientist get things very badly wrong?

THE DANCING PARTNER
JEROME K. JEROME

This short story definitely fits the pattern for **Construct Antagonists**, featuring a well-intentioned inventor soon regretting his efforts to improve on imperfect humanity. It was published in 1893 and the author, Jerome K. Jerome, is best known for his humorous writing, including the famous *Three Men in a Boat*. Notice how he uses a very simple device as he opens the story to make it seem like an account of events that actually took place.

"This story," commenced MacShaugnassy, "comes from Furtwangen, a small town in the Black Forest."

There lived there a very wonderful old fellow named Nicholaus Geibel. His business was the making of mechanical toys, at which work he had acquired an almost European reputation. He made rabbits that would emerge from the heart of a cabbage, flop their ears, smooth their whiskers, and disappear again; cats that would wash their faces, and mew so naturally that dogs would mistake them for real cats and fly at them; dolls with phonographs concealed within them, that would raise their hats and say, "Good morning; how do you do?" and some that would even sing a song.

But, he was something more than a mere mechanic; he was an artist. His work was with him a hobby, almost a passion. His shop was filled with all manner of strange things that never would, or could, be sold — things he had made for the pure love of making them. He had contrived a mechanical donkey that would trot for two hours by means of stored electricity, and trot, too, much faster than the live article, and with less need for exertion on the part of the driver, a bird that would shoot up into the air, fly round and round in a circle, and drop to earth at the exact spot from where it started; a skeleton that, supported by an upright iron bar, would dance a hornpipe, a life-size lady doll that could play the fiddle, and a gentleman with a hollow inside who could smoke a pipe and drink more lager beer than any three average German students put together, which is saying much.

Indeed, it was the belief of the town that old Geibel could make a man capable of doing everything that a respectable man need want to do. One day he made a man who did too much, and it came about in this way:

Young Doctor Follen had a baby, and the baby had a birthday. Its first birthday put Doctor Follen's household into somewhat of a flurry, but on the occasion of its second birthday, Mrs. Doctor Follen gave a ball in honour of the event. Old Geibel and his daughter Olga were among the guests.

During the afternoon of the next day some three or four of Olga's bosom friends, who had also been present at the ball, dropped in to have a chat about it. They naturally fell to discussing the men, and to criticizing their dancing. Old Geibel was in the room, but he appeared to be absorbed in his newspaper, and the girls took no notice of him.

"There seem to be fewer men who can dance at every ball you go to," said one of the girls.

"Yes, and don't the ones who can give themselves airs," said another; "they make quite a favour of asking you."

"And how stupidly they talk," added a third. "They always say exactly the same things: "How charming you are looking to-night." "Do you often go to Vienna? Oh, you should, it's delightful." "What a charming dress you have on." "What a warm day it has been." "Do you like Wagner?" I do wish they'd think of something new."

"Oh, I never mind how they talk," said a forth. "If a man dances well he may be a fool for all I care."

"He generally is," slipped in a thin girl, rather spitefully.

"I go to a ball to dance," continued the previous speaker, not noticing the interruption. "All I ask is that he shall hold me firmly, take me round steadily, and not get tired before I do."

"A clockwork figure would be the thing for you," said the girl who had interrupted.

"Bravo!" cried one of the others, clapping her hands, "what a capital idea!"

"What's a capital idea?" they asked.

"Why, a clockwork dancer, or, better still, one that would go by electricity and never run down."

'The girls took up the idea with enthusiasm.

"Oh, what a lovely partner he would make," said one; "he would never kick you, or tread on your toes."

"Or tear your dress," said another.

"Or get out of step."

"Or get giddy and lean on you."

"And he would never want to mop his face with his handkerchief. I do hate to see a man do that after every dance."

"And wouldn't want to spend the whole evening in the supper-room."

"Why, with a phonograph inside him to grind out all the stock remarks, you would not be able to tell him from a real man," said the girl who had first suggested the idea.

"Oh yes, you would," said the thin girl, "he would be so much nicer."

Old Geibel had laid down his paper, and was listening with both his ears. On one of the girls glancing in his direction, however, he hurriedly hid himself again behind it.

After the girls were gone, he went into his workshop, where Olga heard him walking up and down, and every now and then chuckling to himself; and that night he talked to her a good deal about dancing and dancing men — asked what dances were most popular — what steps were gone through, with many other questions bearing on the subject.

Then for a couple of weeks he kept much to his factory, and was very thoughtful and busy, though prone at unexpected moments to break into a quiet low laugh, as if enjoying a joke that nobody else knew of.

A month later another ball took place in Furtwangen. On this occasion it was given by old Wenzel, the wealthy timber merchant, to celebrate his niece's betrothal, and Geibel and his daughter were again among the invited.

When the hour arrived to set out, Olga sought her father. Not finding him in the house, she tapped at the door of his workshop. He appeared in his shirt-sleeves, looking hot but radiant.

"Don't wait for me," he said, "you go on, I'll follow you. I've got something to finish."

As she turned to obey he called after her, "Tell them I'm going to bring a young man with me — such a nice young man, and an excellent dancer. All the girls will like him." Then he laughed and closed the door.

Her father generally kept his doings secret from everybody, but she had a pretty shrewd suspicion of what he had been planning, and so, to a certain extent, was able to prepare the guests for what was coming. Anticipation ran high, and the arrival of the famous mechanist was eagerly awaited.

At length the sound of wheels was heard outside, followed by a great commotion in the passage, and old Wenzel himself, his jolly face red with excitement and suppressed laughter, burst into the room and announced in stentorian tones:

"Herr Geibel — and a friend."

Herr Geibel and his "friend" entered, greeted with shouts of laughter and applause, and advanced to the centre of the room.

"Allow me, ladies and gentlemen," said Herr Geibel, "to introduce you to my friend, Lieutenant Fritz. Fritz, my dear fellow, bow to the ladies and gentlemen."

Geibel placed his hand encouragingly on Fritz's shoulder, and the Lieutenant bowed low, accompanying the action with a harsh clicking noise in his throat, unpleasantly suggestive of a death-rattle. But that was only a detail.

"He walks a little stiffly" (old Geibel took his arm and walked him forward a few steps. He certainly did walk stiffly), "but then, walking is not his forte. He is essentially a dancing man. I have only been able to teach him the waltz as yet, but at that he is faultless. Come, which of you ladies may I introduce him to as a partner? He keeps perfect time; he never gets tired; he won't kick you or tread on your dress; he will hold you as firmly as you like, and go as quickly or a slowly as you please; he never gets giddy; and he is full of conversation. Come, speak up for yourself, my boy."

The old gentleman twisted one of the buttons at the back of his coat, and immediately Fritz opened his mouth, and in thin tones that appeared to proceed from the back of his head, remarked suddenly, "May I have the pleasure?" and then shut his mouth again with a snap.

That Lieutenant Fritz had made a strong impression on the company was undoubted, yet none of the girls seemed inclined to dance with him. They looked askance at his waxen face, with its staring eyes and fixed smile, and shuddered. At last old Geibel came to the girl who had conceived the idea.

"It is your own suggestion, carried out to the letter," said Geibel, "an electric dancer. You owe it to the gentleman to give him a trial."

She was a bright, saucy little girl, fond of a frolic. Her host added his entreaties, and she consented.

Her Geibel fixed the figure to her. Its right arm was screwed round her waist, and held her firmly; its delicately jointed left hand was made to fasten upon her right. The old toymaker showed her how to regulate its speed, and how to stop it, and release herself.

"It will take you round in a complete circle," he explained; "be careful that no one knocks against you, and alters its course."

The music struck up. Old Geibel put the current in motion, and Annette and her strange partner began to dance.

For a while everyone stood watching them. The figure performed its purpose admirably. Keeping perfect time and step, and holding its little partner tight clasped in an unyielding embrace, it revolved steadily, pouring forth at the same time a constant flow of squeaky conversation, broken by brief intervals of grinding silence.

"How charming you are looking tonight," it remarked in its thin, far-away voice. "What a lovely day it has been. Do you like dancing? How well our steps agree. You will give me another, won't you? Oh, don't be so cruel. What a charming gown you have on. Isn't waltzing delightful? I could go on dancing for ever — with you. Have you had supper?"

As she grew more familiar with the uncanny creature, the girl's nervousness wore off, and she entered into the fun of the thing.

"Oh, he's just lovely," she cried, laughing; "I could go on dancing with him all my life."

Couple after couple now joined them, and soon all the dancers in the room were whirling round behind them. Nicholaus Geibel stood looking on, beaming with childish delight at his success.

Old Wenzel approached him, and whispered something in his ear. Geibel laughed and nodded, and the two worked their way quietly towards the door.

"This is the young people's house to-night," said Wenzel, as soon as they were outside; "you and I will have a quiet pipe and glass of hock, over in the counting-house."

Meanwhile the dancing grew more fast and furious. Little Annette loosened the screw regulating her partner's rate of progress, and the figure flew round with her swifter and swifter. Couple after couple dropped out exhausted, but they only went the faster, till at length they remained dancing alone.

Madder and madder became the waltz. The music lagged behind: the musicians, unable to keep pace, ceased, and sat staring. The younger guests applauded, but the older faces began to grow anxious.

"Hadn't you better stop, dear," said one of the women, "you'll make yourself so tired."

But Annette did not answer.

"I believe she's fainted," cried out a girl who had caught sight of her face as it was swept by.

One of the men sprang forward and clutched at the figure, but its impetus threw him down on to the floor, where its steel-cased feet laid bare his cheek. The thing evidently did not intend to part with its prize so easily.

Had any one retained a cool head, the figure, one cannot help thinking, might easily have been stopped. Two or three men acting in concert might have lifted it bodily off the floor, or have jammed it into a corner. But few human heads are capable of remaining cool under excitement. Those who are not present think how stupid must have been those who were; those who are reflect afterwards how simple it would have been to do this, that, or the other, if only they had thought of it at the time.

The women grew hysterical. The men shouted contradictory directions to one another. Two of them made a bungling rush at the figure, which had the end result of forcing it out of its orbit at the centre of the room, and sending it crashing against the walls and furniture. A stream of blood showed itself down the girl's white frock, and followed her along the floor. The affair was becoming horrible. The women rushed screaming from the room. The men followed them.

One sensible suggestion was made: "Find Geibel — fetch Geibel."

No one had noticed him leave the room, no one knew where he was. A party went in search of him. The others, too unnerved to go back into the ballroom, crowded outside the door and listened. They could hear the steady whir of the wheels upon the polished floor as the thing spun round and round; the dull thud as every now and again it dashed itself and its burden against some opposing object and ricocheted off in a new direction.

And everlastingly it talked in that thin ghostly voice, repeating over and over the same formula: "How charming you look to-night. What a lovely day it has been. Oh, don't be so cruel. I could go on dancing for ever — with you. Have you had supper?"

Of course they sought Geibel everywhere but where he was. They looked in every room in the house, then they rushed off in a body to his own place, and spent precious minutes waking up his deaf old housekeeper. At last it occurred to one of the party that Wenzel was missing also, and then the idea of the counting-house across the yard presented itself to them, and there they found him.

He rose up, very pale, and followed them; and he and old Wenzel forced their way through the crowd of guests gathered outside, and entered the room, and locked the door behind them.

From within there came the muffled sound of low voices and quick steps, followed by a confused scuffling noise, then silence, then the low voices again.

After a time the door opened, and those near it pressed forward to enter, but old Wenzel's broad head and shoulders barred the way.

I want you — and you, Bekler," he said, addressing a couple of the elder men. His voice was calm, but his face was deadly white. "The rest of you, please go — get the women away as quickly as you can."

From that day old Nicholaus Geibel confined himself to the making of mechanical rabbits, and cats that mewed and washed their faces.

The MUMMY

No weak jokes about female parents from me. **Mummies** are relative late-comers to the Gothic, and are not in the **Antagonist** first team, although they have flourished in modern films. Their popularity ties in with our enduring fascination with antique artefacts: strange objects and symbols from the past. Lara Croft and Indiana Jones are constantly plunging into Gothic **Settings** and doing battle with Gothic **Villains** and Antagonists, as they pursue their profession as archaeologists.

Our interest in ancient bandage-wrapped corpses in particular dates from the birth of "modern" Egyptology – the study of Ancient Egypt – which began following the French invasion of Egypt under Napoleon at the start of the 19th Century. Mary Shelley, in *Frankenstein*, expects us to know what her **Hero** means when he says of the Monster "A mummy again endued with animation could not be so hideous as that wretch" and later describes one of its hands as "in colour and apparent texture like that of a mummy." These are just passing references though, and the first starring role for a Mummy seems to be Cheops, from Jane C. Loudon's splendidly titled *The Mummy!*, published in 1827. The book's subtitle, *A tale of the Twenty Second Century*, gives away the fact that it is as much science fiction as Gothic (among other predictions, the author portrayed women of the future wearing trousers!). The novel's Hero Edric decides (in the 22nd Century) to attempt the re-animation of an Egyptian Mummy. Here he is, in a tomb beneath the pyramids, looking at his subject.

Awful, indeed, was the gloom that sat upon that brow, and bitter the sardonic smile that curled those haughty lips. All was perfect as though life still animated the form before them, and it had only reclined there to seek a short repose. The dark eyebrows, the thick raven hair which hung upon the forehead, and the snow-white teeth seen through the half open lips, forbade the idea of death; whilst the fiend-like expression of the features made Edric shudder, as he recollected the purpose that brought him to the tomb, and he trembled at the thought of awakening such a fearful being from the torpor of the grave to all the renewed energies of life.

The re-animation method involves electric shocks, and manages to generate some proper Gothic Weather.

Innumerable folds of red and white linen, disposed alternately, swathed the gigantic limbs of the royal mummy; and upon his breast lay a piece of metal, shining like silver, and stamped with the figure of a winged globe. Edric attempted to remove this, but recoiled with horror, when he found it bend beneath his fingers with an unnatural softness; whilst, as the flickering light of the lamp fell upon the face of the mummy, he fancied its stern features relaxed into a ghastly laugh of scornful mockery. Worked up to desperation, he applied the wires of the battery and put the apparatus in motion, whilst a demoniac laugh of derision appeared to ring in his ears, and the surrounding mummies seemed starting from their places and dancing in unearthly merriment. Thunder now roared in tremendous peals through the Pyramids, shaking their enormous masses to the foundation, and vivid flashes of light darted round in quick succession. Edric stood aghast amidst this fearful convulsion of nature. A horrid creeping seemed to run through every vein, every nerve feeling as though drawn from its extremity, and wrapped in icy dullness round his heart. Still, he stood immoveable, and gazing intently on the mummy, whose eyes had opened with the shock, and were now fixed on those of Edric, shining with supernatural lustre. In vain Edric attempted to rouse himself; – in vain to turn away from that withering glance. The mummy's eyes still pursued him with their ghastly brightness; they seemed to possess the fabled fascination of those of the rattle-snake, and though he shrank from their gaze, they still glared horribly upon him. Edric's senses swam, yet he could not move from the spot; he remained fixed, chained, and immoveable, his eyes still riveted upon those of the mummy, and every thought absorbed in horror. Another fearful peal of thunder now rolled in lengthened vibrations above his head, and the Mummy rose slowly, his eyes still fixed upon those of Edric, from his marble tomb. The thunder pealed louder and louder. Yells and groans seemed mingled with its roar, the sepulchral lamp flared with redoubled fierceness, flashing its rays around in quick succession, and with vivid brightness; whilst by its horrid and uncertain glare, Edric saw the Mummy stretch out its withered hand as though to seize him. He saw it rise gradually - he heard the dry, bony fingers rattle as it drew them forth - he felt its tremendous gripe - human nature could bear no more - his senses were rapidly deserting him; he felt, however, the fixed steadfast eyes of Cheops still glowing upon his failing orbs, as the lamp gave a sudden flash, and then all was darkness! The brazen gates now shut with a fearful clang, and Edric, uttering a shriek of horror, fell senseless upon the ground, whilst his shrill cry of anguish rang wildly through the marble vaults, till its re-echoes seemed like the yell of demons joining in fearful mockery.

In, fact, after this promising scene, the revived Cheops, although he looks pretty grim, turns out to be a wise and civilised being, and the novel retreats from the Gothic. We have to wait until 1892 before Conan Doyle introduces a properly unpleasant reanimated **Mummy**, in his short story *Lot No. 249*. This is the **Hero** Smith's first sight of the ancient **Antagonist**, before it has been brought back to life.

The features, though horribly discoloured, were perfect, and two little nut-like eyes still lurked in the depths of the black, hollow sockets. The blotched skin was drawn tightly from bone to bone, and a tangled wrap of black coarse hair fell over the ears. Two thin teeth, like those of a rat, overlay the shrivelled lower lip. In its crouching position, with bent joints and craned head, there was a suggestion of energy about the horrid thing which made Smith's gorge rise. The gaunt ribs, with their parchment-like covering, were exposed, and the sunken, leaden-hued abdomen, with the long slit where the embalmer had left his mark; but the lower limbs were wrapt round with coarse yellow bandages.

The **Mummy**, we learn, was bought at auction - hence the title of the story - by Bellingham, the **Villain** of the piece (a good example of how Villain and **Antagonist** do not have to be one and the same). Bellingham has discovered not only how to bring it back to life, but also how to command it, and uses it against his enemies. This is what happens when Smith, who has begun to suspect, decides to walk to a friend's house one evening.

Early as it was, Smith did not meet a single soul upon his way. He walked briskly along until he came to the avenue gate, which opened into the long gravel drive leading up to Farlingford. In front of him he could see the cosy red light of the windows glimmering through the foliage. He stood with his hand upon the iron latch of the swinging gate, and he glanced back at the road along which he had come. Something was coming swiftly down it.

It moved in the shadow of the hedge, silently and furtively, a dark, crouching figure, dimly visible against the black background. Even as he gazed back at it, it had lessened its distance by twenty paces, and was fast closing upon him. Out of the darkness he had a glimpse of a scraggy neck, and of two eyes that will ever haunt him in his dreams. He turned, and with a cry of terror he ran for his life up the avenue. There were the red lights, the signals of safety, almost within a stone's throw of him. He was a famous runner, but never had he run as he ran that night.

The heavy gate had swung into place behind him, but he heard it dash open again before his pursuer. As he rushed madly and wildly through the night, he could hear a swift, dry patter behind him, and could see, as he threw back a glance, that this horror was bounding like a tiger at his heels, with blazing eyes *and one stringy arm out-thrown*. Thank God, the door was ajar. He could see the thin bar of light which shot from the lamp in the hall. Nearer yet sounded the clatter from behind. He heard a hoarse gurgling at his very shoulder.

How will the pursuit end?

The WEREWOLF

Werewolves have become almost as popular as **Vampires** in contemporary Gothic, with Jacob and his pack howling their way through the *Twilight* series and Remus Lupin playing a crucial role in the Harry Potter saga. As with their blood-drinking co-**Antagonists**, there has been an increasing tendency to portray Werewolves as victims of their condition rather than simple embodiments of evil. And, also as with Vampires, stories of human beings turning into aggressive wild animals, and back again, occur in most cultures and can be traced as far back as classical Greek and Roman writers. These fables and tales explore contrasts between "civilised" human behaviour and the violence and wickedness of "animal" or "bestial" acts of immorality.

If you are familiar with Robert Louis Stevenson's celebrated non-Gothic novel of pirates and buried gold, *Treasure Island*, you'll know he is interested in characters who can be both good and bad (Long John Silver is a fine example of an **Antihero**). His *The Strange Case of Dr Jekyll and Mr Hyde* (published in 1886) takes the idea to the extreme with its famous transformation, between the good Dr Jekyll and evil Mr Hyde, although the latter is not a wolf-man, whatever some later film adaptations of the story have suggested. In this extract Dr Jekyll has just drunk a potion which he hopes will in the end free him of the wicked urges he feels inside himself; this part of the book is supposedly taken from his diary.

> The most racking pangs succeeded: a grinding in the bones, deadly nausea, and a horror of the spirit that cannot be exceeded at the hour of birth or death. Then these agonies began swiftly to subside, and I came to myself as if out of a great sickness. There was something strange in my sensations, something indescribably new and, from its very novelty, incredibly sweet. I felt younger, lighter, happier in body; within I was conscious of a heady recklessness, a current of disordered sensual images running like a mill-race in my fancy, a solution of the bonds of obligation, an unknown but not an innocent freedom of the soul. I knew myself, at the first breath of this new life, to be more wicked, tenfold more wicked, sold a slave to my original evil; and the thought, in that moment, braced and delighted me like wine. I stretched out my hands, exulting in the freshness of these sensations; and in the act, I was suddenly aware that I had lost in stature.

So Dr Jekyll actually shrinks to become Mr Hyde, but the important changes are internal, as he relishes the freedom to enjoy his own wickedness. His new body is never described in detail, and while we do learn that Mr Hyde's hands are pale, "knuckly" and covered in dark hair, that's pretty much it for the physical side. Stevenson is more interested in describing the character's lack of morals and his lust for pleasure. He even makes a point of how the man's appearance is disguised by the overall sense of his wrongness. Another character who has dealings with Mr Hyde is asked to describe him.

> "He is not easy to describe. There is something wrong with his appearance; something displeasing, something downright detestable. I never saw a man I so disliked, and yet I scarce know why. He must be deformed somewhere; he gives a strong feeling of deformity, although I couldn't specify the point. He's an extraordinary-looking man, and yet I really can name nothing out of the way. No, sir; I can make no hand of it; I can't

describe him. And it's not want of memory; for I declare I can see him this moment."

The transformation in Stevenson's classic may be mostly internal, but in Captain Marryat's *The Phantom Ship* (published much earlier in 1839 and mostly about the haunted vessel known as the Flying Dutchman) there is a self-contained story about what we might call a "proper" **Werewolf**. The narrator is one of three children, looking back on a time when he and his brother and sister (Marcella) were very young, living with their father in an isolated cottage in the forests of northern Germany. Their mother is dead and their father eventually remarries a beautiful young woman. The children begin to have suspicions about their stepmother ('mother-in-law" in Marryat's text), and by the start of this extract the elder son has already been killed, apparently by wolves, and buried next to the cottage.

One day, when my father and I were in the field, Marcella being with us, my mother-in-law came out, saying that she was going into the forest, to collect some herbs my father wanted, and that Marcella must go to the cottage and watch the dinner. Marcella went, and my mother-in-law soon disappeared in the forest, taking a direction quite contrary to that in which the cottage stood, and leaving my father and I, as it were, between her and Marcella.

About an hour afterwards we were startled by shrieks from the cottage, evidently the shrieks of little Marcella.

"Marcella has burnt herself, father," said I, throwing down my spade. My father threw down his, and we both hastened to the cottage. Before we could gain the door, out darted a large white wolf, which fled with the utmost celerity. My father had no weapon; he rushed into the cottage, and there saw poor little Marcella expiring: her body was dreadfully mangled, and the blood pouring from it had formed a large pool on the cottage floor. My father's first intention had been to seize his gun and pursue, but he was checked by this horrid spectacle; he knelt down by his dying child, and burst into tears: Marcella could just look kindly on us for a few seconds, and then her eyes were closed in death.

My father and I were still hanging over my poor sister's body, when my mother-in-law came in. At the dreadful sight she expressed much concern, but she did not appear to recoil from the sight of blood, as most women do.

"Poor child!" said she, "it must have been that great white wolf which passed me just now, and frightened me so—she's quite dead."

"I know it—I know it!" cried my father in agony.

I thought my father would never recover from the effects of this second tragedy: he mourned bitterly over the body of his sweet child, and for several days would not consign it to its grave, although frequently requested by my mother-in-law to do so. At last he yielded, and dug a grave for her close by that of my poor brother, and took every precaution that the wolves should not violate her remains.

I was now really miserable, as I lay alone in the bed which I had formerly shared with my brother and sister. I could not help thinking that my mother-in-law was implicated in both their deaths, although I could not account for the manner; but I no longer felt afraid of her: my little heart was full of hatred and revenge.

The night after my sister had been buried, as I lay awake, I perceived my mother-in-law get up and go out of the cottage. I waited some time, then dressed myself, and looked out through the door, which I half opened. The moon shone bright, and I could see the spot where my brother and my sister had been buried; and what was my horror, when I perceived my mother-in-law busily removing the stones from Marcella's grave.

She was in her white night-dress, and the moon shone full upon her. She was digging with her hands, and throwing away the stones behind her with all the ferocity of a wild beast. It was some time before I could collect my senses and decide what I should do. At last, I perceived that she had arrived at the body, and raised it up to the side of the grave. I could bear it no longer; I ran to my father and awoke him.

"Father! father!" cried I, "dress yourself, and get your gun."

"What!" cried my father, "the wolves are there, are they?"

He jumped out of bed, threw on his clothes, and in his anxiety did not appear to perceive the absence of his wife. As soon as he was ready, I opened the door, he went out, and I followed him.

Imagine his horror, when (unprepared as he was for such a sight) he beheld, as he advanced towards the grave, not a wolf, but his wife, in her night-dress, on her hands and knees, crouching by the body of my sister, and tearing off large pieces of the flesh, and devouring them with all the avidity of a wolf. She was too busy to be aware of our approach. My father dropped his gun, his hair stood on end; so did mine; he breathed heavily, and then his breath for a time stopped. I picked up the gun and put it into his hand. Suddenly he appeared as if concentrated rage had restored him to double vigour; he levelled his piece, fired, and with a loud shriek, down fell the wretch whom he had fostered in his bosom.

"God of Heaven!" cried my father, sinking down upon the earth in a swoon, as soon as he had discharged his gun.

I remained some time by his side before he recovered.

"Where am I?" said he, "what has happened?—Oh!—yes, yes! I recollect now. Heaven forgive me!"

He rose and we walked up to the grave; what again was our astonishment and horror to find that instead of the dead body of my mother-in-law, as we expected, there was lying over the remains of my poor sister, a large, white she wolf.

THE GRAY WOLF
GEORGE MACDONALD

Straight transformation – human to wolf (and back) – is the usual pattern, as we have just seen, and also find in the following short tale dated 1871. The **Antagonist** is a striking combination of frightening and pitiable, and there are hints of a love story behind the horror. The author was, in his time, a famous writer of fantasy novels, known to have influenced Tolkien and C. S. Lewis.

One evening-twilight in spring, a young English student, who had wandered northwards as far as the outlying fragments of Scotland called the Orkney and Shetland Islands, found himself on a small island of the latter group, caught in a storm of wind and hail, which had come on suddenly. It was in vain to look about for any shelter; for not only did the storm entirely obscure the landscape, but there was nothing around him save a desert moss.

At length, however, as he walked on for mere walking's sake, he found himself on the verge of a cliff, and saw, over the brow of it, a few feet below him, a ledge of rock, where he might find some shelter from the blast, which blew from behind. Letting himself down by his hands, he alighted upon something that crunched beneath his tread, and found the bones of many small animals scattered about in front of a little cave in the rock, offering the refuge he sought. He went in, and sat upon a stone. The storm increased in violence, and as the darkness grew he became uneasy, for he did not relish the thought of spending the night in the cave. He had parted from his companions on the opposite side of the island, and it added to his uneasiness that they must be full of apprehension about him. At last there came a lull in the storm, and the same instant he heard a footfall, stealthy and light as that of a wild beast, upon the bones at the mouth of the cave. He started up in some fear, though the least thought might have satisfied him that there could be no very dangerous animals upon the island. Before he had time to think, however, the face of a woman appeared in the opening. Eagerly the wanderer spoke. She started at the sound of his voice. He could not see her well, because she was turned towards the darkness of the cave.

"Will you tell me how to find my way across the moor to Shielness?" he asked.

"You cannot find it to-night," she answered, in a sweet tone, and with a smile that bewitched him, revealing the whitest of teeth.

"What am I to do, then?"

"My mother will give you shelter, but that is all she has to offer."

"And that is far more than I expected a minute ago," he replied. "I shall be most grateful."

She turned in silence and left the cave. The youth followed.

She was barefooted, and her pretty brown feet went catlike over the sharp stones, as she led the way down a rocky path to the shore. Her garments were scanty and torn, and her hair blew tangled in the wind. She seemed about five and twenty, lithe and small. Her long fingers kept clutching and pulling nervously at her skirts as she went. Her face was very gray in complexion, and very worn, but delicately formed, and smooth-skinned. Her thin nostrils were tremulous as eyelids, and her lips, whose curves were faultless, had no colour to give sign of indwelling blood. What her eyes were like he could not see, for she had never lifted the delicate films of her eyelids.

At the foot of the cliff, they came upon a little hut leaning against it, and having for its inner apartment a natural hollow within. Smoke was spreading over the face of the rock, and the grateful odour of food gave hope to the hungry student. His guide opened the door of the cottage; he followed her in, and saw a woman bending over a fire in the middle of the floor. On the fire lay a large fish broiling. The daughter spoke a few words, and the mother turned and welcomed the stranger. She had an old and very wrinkled, but honest face, and looked troubled. She dusted the only chair in the cottage, and placed it for him by the side of the fire, opposite the one window, whence he saw a little patch of yellow sand over which the spent waves spread themselves out listlessly. Under this window there was a bench, upon which the daughter threw herself in an unusual posture, resting her chin upon her hand. A moment after, the youth caught the first glimpse of her blue eyes. They were fixed upon him with a strange look of greed, amounting to craving, but, as if aware that they belied or betrayed her, she dropped them instantly. The moment she veiled them, her face, notwithstanding its colourless complexion, was almost beautiful.

When the fish was ready, the old woman wiped the deal table, steadied it upon the uneven floor, and covered it with a piece of fine table-linen. She then laid the fish on a wooden platter, and invited the guest to help himself. Seeing no other provision, he pulled from his pocket a hunting knife, and divided a portion from the fish, offering it to the mother first.

"Come, my lamb," said the old woman; and the daughter approached the table. But her nostrils and mouth quivered with disgust.

The next moment she turned and hurried from the hut.

"She doesn't like fish," said the old woman, "and I haven't anything else to give her."

"She does not seem in good health," he rejoined.

The woman answered only with a sigh, and they ate their fish with the help of a little rye bread. As they finished their supper, the youth heard the sound as of the pattering of a dog's feet upon the sand close to the door; but ere he had time to look out of the window, the door opened, and the young woman entered. She looked better, perhaps from having just washed her face. She drew a stool to the corner of the fire opposite him. But as she sat down, to his bewilderment, and even horror, the student spied a single drop of blood on her white skin within her torn dress. The woman brought out a jar of whisky, put a rusty old kettle on the fire, and took her place in front of it. As soon as the water boiled, she proceeded to make some toddy in a wooden bowl.

Meantime the youth could not take his eyes off the young woman, so that at length he found himself fascinated, or rather bewitched. She kept her eyes for the most part veiled with the loveliest eyelids fringed with darkest lashes, and he gazed entranced; for the red glow of the little oil-lamp covered all the strangeness of her complexion. But as soon as he met a stolen glance out of those eyes unveiled, his soul shuddered within him. Lovely face and craving eyes alternated fascination and repulsion.

The mother placed the bowl in his hands. He drank sparingly, and passed it to the girl. She lifted it to her lips, and as she tasted – only tasted it – looked at him. He thought the drink must have been drugged and have affected his brain. Her hair smoothed itself back, and drew her forehead backwards with it; while the lower part of her face projected towards the bowl, revealing, ere she sipped, her dazzling teeth in strange prominence. But the same moment the vision vanished; she returned the vessel to her mother, and rising, hurried out of the cottage.

Then the old woman pointed to a bed of heather in one corner with a murmured apology; and the student, wearied both with the fatigues of the day and the strangeness of the night, threw himself upon it, wrapped in his cloak. The moment he lay down, the storm began afresh, and the wind blew so keenly through the crannies of the hut, that it was only by drawing his cloak over his head that he could protect himself from its currents. Unable to sleep, he lay listening to the uproar which grew in violence, till the spray was dashing against the window. At length the door opened, and the young woman came in, made up the fire, drew the bench before it, and lay down in the same strange posture, with her chin propped on her hand and elbow, and her face turned towards the youth. He moved a little; she dropped her head, and lay on her face, with her arms crossed beneath her forehead. The mother had disappeared.

Drowsiness crept over him. A movement of the bench roused him, and he fancied he saw some four-footed creature as tall as a large dog trot quietly out of the door. He was sure he felt a rush of cold wind. Gazing fixedly through the darkness, he thought he saw the eyes of the damsel encountering his, but a glow from the falling together of the remnants of the fire revealed clearly enough that the bench was vacant. Wondering what could have made her go out in such a storm, he fell fast asleep.

In the middle of the night he felt a pain in his shoulder, came broad awake, and saw the gleaming eyes and grinning teeth of some animal close to his face. Its claws were in his shoulder, and its mouth in the act of seeking his throat. Before it had fixed its fangs, however, he had its throat in one hand, and sought his knife with the other. A terrible struggle followed; but regardless of the tearing claws, he found and opened his knife. He had made one futile stab, and was drawing it for a surer, when, with a spring of the whole body, and one wildly contorted effort, the creature twisted its neck from his hold, and with something betwixt a scream and a howl, darted from him. Again he heard the door open; again the wind blew in upon him, and it continued blowing; a sheet of spray dashed across the floor, and over his face. He sprung from his couch and bounded to the door.

It was a wild night – dark, but for the flash of whiteness from the waves as they broke within a few yards of the cottage; the wind was raving, and the rain pouring down the air. A gruesome sound as of mingled weeping and howling came from somewhere in the dark. He turned again into the hut and closed the door, but could find no way of securing it.

The lamp was nearly out, and he could not be certain whether the form of the young woman was upon the bench or not. Overcoming a strong repugnance, he approached it, and put out his hands – there was nothing there. He sat down and waited for the daylight: he dared not sleep any more.

When the day dawned at length, he went out yet again, and looked around. The morning was dim and gusty and gray. The wind had fallen, but the waves were tossing wildly. He wandered up and down the little strand, longing for more light.

At length he heard a movement in the cottage. By and by the voice of the old woman called to him from the door.

"You're up early, sir. I doubt you didn't sleep well."

"Not very well," he answered. "But where is your daughter?"

"She's not awake yet," said the mother. "I'm afraid I have but a poor breakfast for you. But you'll take a dram and a bit of fish. It's all I've got."

Unwilling to hurt her, though hardly in good appetite, he sat down at the table. While they were eating, the daughter came in, but turned her face away and went to the farther end of the hut. When she came forward after a minute or two, the youth saw that her hair was drenched, and her face whiter than before. She looked ill and faint, and when she raised her eyes, all their fierceness had vanished, and sadness had taken its place. Her neck was now covered with a cotton handkerchief. She was modestly attentive to him, and no longer shunned his gaze. He was gradually yielding to the temptation of braving another night in the hut, and seeing what would follow, when the old woman spoke.

"The weather will be broken all day, sir," she said. "You had better be going, or your friends will leave without you."

Ere he could answer, he saw such a beseeching glance on the face of the girl, that he hesitated, confused. Glancing at the mother, he saw the flash of wrath in her face. She rose and approached her daughter, with her hand lifted to strike her. The young woman stooped her head with a cry. He darted round the table to interpose between them. But the mother had caught hold of her; the handkerchief had fallen from her neck; and the youth saw five blue bruises on her lovely throat – the marks of the four fingers and the thumb of a left hand. With a cry of horror he darted from the house, but as he reached the door he turned. His hostess was lying motionless on the floor, and a huge gray wolf came bounding after him.

There was no weapon at hand; and if there had been, his inborn chivalry would never have allowed him to harm a woman even under the guise of a wolf. Instinctively, he set himself firm, leaning a little forward, with half outstretched arms, and hands curved ready to clutch again at the throat upon which he had left those pitiful marks. But the creature as she sprung eluded his grasp, and just as he expected to feel her fangs, he found a woman weeping on his bosom, with her arms around his neck. The next instant, the gray wolf broke from him, and bounded howling up the cliff. Recovering himself as he best might, the youth followed, for it was the only way to the moor above, across which he must now make his way to find his companions.

All at once he heard the sound of a crunching of bones--not as if a creature was eating them, but as if they were ground by the teeth of rage and disappointment; looking up, he saw close above him the mouth of the little cavern in which he had taken refuge the day before. Summoning all his resolution, he passed it slowly and softly. From within came the sounds of a mingled moaning and growling.

Having reached the top, he ran at full speed for some distance across the moor before venturing to look behind him. When at length he did so, he saw, against the sky, the girl standing on the edge of the cliff, wringing her hands. One solitary wail crossed the space between. She made no attempt to follow him, and he reached the opposite shore in safety.

THE INQUISITION

Enough with the monsters; it's time for a different sort of **Antagonist**.

A key theme in a number of the first Gothic novels was hostility to religion – plenty of **Villains** and **Villainesses** are priests, monks and nuns. The authors of these books were influenced by the Enlightenment thinkers of the time, who were more and more convinced the world could be rationally explained through science, and so challenged the authority of the Church and its representatives to dictate the "truth". Add to that a long tradition of exaggerated stories of extreme penances and punishments associated with religion in the Medieval period (self-flagellation, torture of non-believers), and parallel stories of corruption within church hierarchies (monks and monasteries more interested in growing rich and living comfortably than following God), and you have an irresistible stock of Gothic goings-on.

Ann Radcliffe's *The Italian* features a notorious priest-Villain in the person of Father Schedoni, who – before becoming a priest - murdered his own brother and wife. His scheming leads to the **Hero** and **Heroine** (Vivaldi and Ellena) being arrested by the **Inquisition** and in this passage Vivaldi and his Loyal Servant Paulo have just been brought into the organisation's prison in Rome.

Having entered one of the passages, Vivaldi perceived a person clothed in black, and who bore a lighted taper, crossing silently in the remote perspective; and he understood too well from his habit, that he was a member of this dreadful tribunal.

The sound of footsteps seemed to reach the stranger, for he turned, and then paused, while the officers advanced. They then made signs to each other, and exchanged a few words, which neither Vivaldi or his servant could understand, when the stranger, pointing with his taper along another avenue, passed away. Vivaldi followed him with his eyes, till a door at the extremity of the passage opened, and he saw the Inquisitor enter an apartment, whence a great light proceeded, and where several other figures, habited like himself, appeared waiting to receive him. The door immediately closed; and, whether the imagination of Vivaldi was affected, or that the sounds were real, he thought, as it closed, he distinguished half-stifled groans, as of a person in agony.

Radcliffe could rely on her readers, like Vivaldi, assuming the prison was full of innocent victims of the **Inquisition** who are being tortured into confessing to sins they have not committed.

The avenue, through which the prisoners passed, opened, at length, into an apartment gloomy like the first they had entered, but more extensive. The roof was supported by arches, and long arcades branched off from every side of the chamber, as from a central point, and were lost in the gloom, which the rays of the small lamps, suspended in each, but feebly penetrated.

They rested here, and a person soon after advanced, who appeared to be the jailor, into whose hands Vivaldi and Paulo were delivered. A few mysterious words having been exchanged, one of the officials crossed the hall, and ascended a wide staircase, while the other, with the jailor and the guard, remained below, as if awaiting his return.

A long interval elapsed, during which the stillness of the place was sometimes interrupted by a closing door, and, at others, by indistinct sounds, which yet appeared to Vivaldi like lamentations and extorted groans. Inquisitors, in their long black robes, issued, from time, to time from the passages, and crossed the hall to other avenues. They eyed the prisoners with curiosity, but without pity. Their visages, with few exceptions, seemed stamped with the characters of demons. Vivaldi could not look upon the grave cruelty, or the ferocious impatience, their countenances severally expressed, without reading in them the fate of some fellow creature, the fate, which these men seemed going, even at this moment, to confirm; and, as they passed with soundless steps, he shrunk from observation, as if their very looks possessed some supernatural power, and could have struck death. But he followed their fleeting figures, as they proceeded on their work of horror, to where the last glimmering ray faded into darkness, expecting to see other doors of other chambers open to receive them.

The author then has her **Hero** make a little speech (to himself!) that uses our understanding of the evil nature of the **Inquisition** to comment on our uniquely human ability to do wrong while believing we are right.

"Is this possible!" said Vivaldi internally, "Can this be in human nature! — Can such horrible perversion of right be permitted! Can man, who calls himself endowed with reason, and immeasurably superior to every other created being, argue himself into the commission of such horrible folly, such inveterate cruelty, as exceeds all the acts of the most irrational and ferocious brute. Brutes do not deliberately slaughter their species; it remains for man only, man, proud of his prerogative of reason, and boasting of his sense of justice, to unite the most terrible extremes of folly and wickedness!"

Scenes follow in which Vivaldi is questioned by Inquisitors who show terrifying skill in twisting his words, while stating that they alone can control the truth. The Inquisition is a dangerous **Antagonist**.

William Godwin was the father of *Frankenstein* author Mary Shelley. A famous political philosopher, he argued that government and its associated institutions stood in the way of human development. He also found time to write a number of novels with distinctly Gothic overtones. In his 1799 book *St Leon* the title character experiences a number of misfortunes, including a run-in with the Spanish Inquisition. He is arrested without being told what his crime is supposed to be.

Upon entering the prison of the Inquisition I was first conducted to a solitary cell. It is not my intention to treat of those particulars of the holy office, which are already to be found in innumerable publications. I have no pleasure in reviving the images of this sojourn of horrors.

Our **Hero** chooses not to describe the physical unpleasantness of his circumstances. Through him, the author points out that there are plenty of other descriptions of the **Inquisition's** terrible prisons in other books. St Leon then has what turns into a bit of a philosophical debate with his Inquisitor, of which the following is just a fragment. He is complaining that he has not been told of what he is accused, and by whom, so can hardly defend himself.

> The mode of your proceeding, cried I, is the mockery of a trial. From your fatal bar no man can go forth acquitted. How is a story to be refuted, when hardly and with difficulty you suffer your prisoner to collect the slightest fragments of it? If I would detect a calumny, is it not requisite that I should be acquainted with its history, and know its authors and propagators? Then I may perhaps be able to confound their forgeries, to show the groundlessness of their allegations, to expose the baseness of their purposes and the profligacy of their characters. I am informed of nothing; yet I am bid, first to be my own accuser, and then to answer the accusations of others. It is only by following a falsehood through all its doublings, that it can be effectually destroyed. You bid me unravel a web, and will not suffer me to touch it with one of my fingers. The defence of the purest innocence is often difficult, sometimes impossible, against the artfulness of a malicious tale, or the fortuitous concurrence of unfavourable appearances.

He is a bit waffly. To be honest, Godwin is too focused on making a reasoned argument to give us a proper fix of Gothic goose-bumps. His only hint of the awful methods associated with the Inquisition comes when St Leon states that the Inquisitor's speeches "were variously interspersed through the three examinations, to which I was subjected a short time after I became an inhabitant of the holy house". Godwin and his contemporary readers would have known that the "three examinations" were the three stages of torture traditionally applied to victims of the Spanish **Inquisition**, but there are no gory (or even Gothic) details to be found in the text. (OK, if you insist, those three stages are: *Garrucha* (or *Strappado*) where the victim was suspended by the wrists with their hands behind their back; *Toca*, where a cloth was placed over or into the victim's mouth, with water then poured onto it, which felt like drowning — what is now called 'waterboarding'; and *Potro*, or 'the rack', where the victim's wrists and ankles were slowly pulled in opposite directions.)

TORTURE BY HOPE
AUGUSTE VILLIERS DE L'ISLE ADAM

There is no description of physical torture of the traditional type in this short story, but more than enough suffering. (The *fra redeptor* in the first paragraph, *brother redeemer* in Latin, was the title of the **Inquisition's** torturers.) Written by French author Auguste Villiers De l'Isle Adam, it was first published in English in 1891. The Spanish Inquisition that it describes was particularly concerned to persecute Jews, regarded as heretics by the religious authorities of the time. What do you make of the title?

Many years ago, as evening was closing in, the venerable Pedro Arbuez d'Espila, sixth prior of the Dominicans of Segovia, and third Grand Inquisitor of Spain, followed by a *fra redemptor*, and preceded by two familiars of the Holy Office, the latter carrying lanterns, made their way to a subterranean dungeon. The bolt of a massive door creaked, and they entered a mephitic cell, where the dim light revealed between rings fastened to the wall a blood-stained rack, a brazier, and a jug. On a pile of straw, loaded with fetters and his neck encircled by an iron collar, sat a haggard man, of uncertain age, clothed in rags.

This prisoner was no other than Rabbi Aser Abarbanel, a Jew of Arragon, who—accused of usury and pitiless scorn for the poor—had been daily subjected to torture for more than a year. Yet "his blindness was as dense as his hide," and he had refused to abjure his faith.

Proud of a filiation dating back thousands of years, proud of his ancestors—for all Jews worthy of the name are vain of their blood—he descended Talmudically from Othoniel and consequently from Ipsiboa, the wife of the last judge of Israel, a circumstance which had sustained his courage amid incessant torture. With tears in his eyes at the thought of this resolute soul rejecting salvation, the venerable Pedro Arbuez d'Espila, approaching the shuddering rabbi, addressed him as follows:

"My son, rejoice: your trials here below are about to end. If in the presence of such obstinacy I was forced to permit, with deep regret, the use of great severity, my task of fraternal correction has its limits. You are the fig tree which, having failed so many times to bear fruit, at last withered, but God alone can judge your soul. Perhaps Infinite Mercy will shine upon you at the last moment! We must hope so. There are examples. So sleep in peace to-night. Tomorrow you will be included in the *auto da fé*: that is, you will be exposed to the *quémadero*, the symbolical flames of the Everlasting Fire: it burns, as you know, only at a distance, my son; and Death is at least two hours (often three) in coming, on account of the wet, iced bandages, with which we protect the heads and hearts of the condemned. There will be forty-three of you. Placed in the last row, you will have time to invoke God and offer to Him this baptism of fire, which is of the Holy Spirit. Hope in the Light, and rest."

With these words, having signed to his companions to unchain the prisoner, the prior tenderly embraced him. Then came the turn of the *fra redemptor*, who, in a low tone, entreated the Jew's forgiveness for what he had made him suffer for the purpose of redeeming him; then the two familiars silently kissed him. This ceremony over, the captive was left, solitary and bewildered, in the darkness.

Rabbi Aser Abarbanel, with parched lips and visage worn by suffering, at first gazed at the closed door with vacant eyes. Closed? The word unconsciously roused a vague fancy in his mind, the fancy that he had seen for an instant the light of the lanterns through a chink between the door and the wall. A morbid idea of hope, due to the weakness of his brain, stirred his whole being. He dragged himself toward the strange *appearance*.

Then, very gently and cautiously, slipping one finger into the crevice, he drew the door toward him. Marvellous! By an extraordinary accident the familiar who closed it had turned the huge key an instant before it struck the stone casing, so that the rusty bolt not having entered the hole, the door again rolled on its hinges.

The rabbi ventured to glance outside. By the aid of a sort of luminous dusk he distinguished at first a semicircle of walls indented by winding stairs; and opposite to him, at the top of five or six stone steps, a sort of black portal, opening into an immense corridor, whose first arches only were visible from below.

Stretching himself flat he crept to the threshold. Yes, it was really a corridor, but endless in length. A wan light illumined it: lamps suspended from the vaulted ceiling lightened at intervals the dull hue of the atmosphere—the distance was veiled in shadow. Not a single door appeared in the whole extent! Only on one side, the left, heavily grated loopholes, sunk in the walls, admitted a light which must be that of evening, for crimson bars at intervals rested on the flags of the pavement. What a terrible silence! Yet, yonder, at the far end of that passage there might be a doorway of escape! The Jew's vacillating hope was tenacious, for it was the last.

Without hesitating, he ventured on the flags, keeping close under the loopholes, trying to make himself part of the blackness of the long walls. He advanced slowly, dragging himself along on his breast, forcing back the cry of pain when some raw wound sent a keen pang through his whole body.

Suddenly the sound of a sandaled foot approaching reached his ears. He trembled violently, fear stifled him, his sight grew dim. Well, it was over, no doubt. He pressed himself into a niche and, half lifeless with terror, waited.

It was a familiar hurrying along. He passed swiftly by, holding in his clenched hand an instrument of torture—a frightful figure—and vanished. The suspense which the rabbi had endured seemed to have suspended the functions of life, and he lay nearly an hour unable to move. Fearing an increase of tortures if he were captured, he thought of returning to his dungeon. But the old hope whispered in his soul that divine *Perhaps*, which comforts us in our sorest trials. A miracle had happened. He could doubt no longer. He began to crawl toward the chance of escape. Exhausted by suffering and hunger, trembling with pain, he pressed onward. The sepulchral corridor seemed to lengthen mysteriously, while he, still advancing, gazed into the gloom where there *must* be some avenue of escape.

Oh! oh! He again heard footsteps, but this time they were slower, more heavy. The white and black forms of two inquisitors appeared, emerging from the obscurity beyond. They were conversing in low tones, and seemed to be discussing some important subject, for they were gesticulating vehemently.

At this spectacle Rabbi Aser Abarbanel closed his eyes: his heart beat so violently that it almost suffocated him; his rags were damp with the cold sweat of agony; he lay motionless by the wall, his mouth wide open, under the rays of a lamp, praying to the God of David.

Just opposite to him the two inquisitors paused under the light of the lamp—doubtless owing to some accident due to the course of their argument. One, while listening to his companion, gazed at the rabbi! And, beneath the look—whose absence of expression the hapless man did not at first notice—he fancied he again felt the burning pincers scorch his flesh, he was to be once more a living wound. Fainting, breathless, with fluttering eyelids, he shivered at the touch of the monk's floating robe. But—strange yet natural fact—the inquisitor's gaze was evidently that of a man deeply absorbed in his intended reply, engrossed by what he was hearing; his eyes were fixed—and seemed to look at the Jew *without seeing him.*

In fact, after the lapse of a few minutes, the two gloomy figures slowly pursued their way, still conversing in low tones, toward the place whence the prisoner had come; *he had not been seen!* Amid the horrible confusion of the rabbi's thoughts, the idea darted through his brain: "Can I be already dead that they did not see me?" A hideous impression roused him from his lethargy: in looking at the wall against which his face was pressed, he imagined he beheld two fierce eyes watching him! He flung his head back in a sudden frenzy of fright, his hair fairly bristling! Yet, no! No. His hand groped over the stones: it was the *reflection* of the inquisitor's eyes, still retained in his own, which had been refracted from two spots on the wall.

Forward! He must hasten toward that goal which he fancied (absurdly, no doubt) to be deliverance, toward the darkness from which he was now barely thirty paces distant. He pressed forward faster on his knees, his hands, at full length, dragging himself painfully along, and soon entered the dark portion of this terrible corridor.

Suddenly the poor wretch felt a gust of cold air on the hands resting upon the flags; it came from under the little door to which the two walls led.

Oh, Heaven, if that door should open outward. Every nerve in the miserable fugitive's body thrilled with hope. He examined it from top to bottom, though scarcely able to distinguish its outlines in the surrounding darkness. He passed his hand over it: no bolt, no lock! A latch! He started up, the latch yielded to the pressure of his thumb: the door silently swung open before him.

"Halleluia!" murmured the rabbi in a transport of gratitude as, standing on the threshold, he beheld the scene before him.

The door had opened into the gardens, above which arched a starlit sky, into spring, liberty, life! It revealed the neighbouring fields, stretching toward the sierras, whose sinuous blue lines were relieved against the horizon. Yonder lay freedom! Oh, to escape! He would journey all night through the lemon groves, whose fragrance reached him. Once in the mountains and he was safe! He inhaled the delicious air; the breeze revived him, his lungs expanded! He felt in his swelling heart the "Lazarus, Come forth!" And to thank once more the God who had bestowed this mercy upon him, he extended his arms, raising his eyes toward Heaven. It was an ecstasy of joy!

Then he fancied he saw the shadow of his arms approach him—fancied that he felt these shadowy arms enclose, embrace him—and that he was pressed tenderly to some one's breast. A tall figure actually did stand directly before him. He lowered his eyes—and remained motionless, gasping for breath, dazed, with fixed eyes, fairly drivelling with terror.

Horror! He was in the clasp of the Grand Inquisitor himself, the venerable Pedro Arbuez d'Espila, who gazed at him with tearful eyes, like a good shepherd who had found his stray lamb.

The dark-robed priest pressed the hapless Jew to his heart with so fervent an outburst of love, that the edges of the monastic haircloth rubbed the Dominican's breast. And while Aser Abarbanel with protruding eyes gasped in agony in the ascetic's embrace, vaguely comprehending *that all the phases of this fatal evening were only a prearranged torture, that of hope,* the Grand Inquisitor, with an accent of touching reproach and a look of consternation, murmured in his ear, his breath parched and burning from long fasting:

"What, my son! On the eve, perchance, of salvation—you wished to leave us?"

AN AFTERWORD

Here is a last thought, which rather relies on you having read the Introduction, and remembering a bit about it, in particular the idea that Gothic stories are popular because they help us deal with our fears, and are most popular, with a given society, when that society is changing and has most to fear.

You may have noticed that a significant number of the original Gothic novels were written by young authors. Matthew Lewis was under twenty when he completed *The Monk*, Shelley was still at school when he wrote *Zastrozzi* and William Beckford was twenty-one when he took a matter of days to finish *Vathek*.

The Gothic, in the same way that it helps a society deal with worries about change, can also help us, as young people, deal with the uncertainties of growing up. Not forgetting of course that we have plenty of fun along the way: maybe not quite reaching for the sublime, but certainly enjoying the terror!